Where We Come From,
WHERE WE GO
Tales From The Seven Sisters

Uddipana Goswami

Illustrated by
Pankaj Thapa

TRANQUEBAR PRESS
An imprint of westland ltd
61, II Floor, Silverline Building, Alapakkam Main Road, Maduravoyal, Chennai 600095
93, I Floor, Sham Lal Road, Daryaganj, New Delhi 110002

First published in TRANQUEBAR PRESS by westland ltd 2015

Copyright © Uddipana Goswami 2015

10 9 8 7 6 5 4 3 2 1

ISBN: 978-93-84030-92-6

Typeset by PrePSol Enterprises Pvt. Ltd.

TRANQUEBAR PRESS
WHERE WE COME FROM, WHERE WE GO

Uddipana Goswami is editor of the *Northeast Review* and teaches English at a college in Guwahati. She is the author of an academic study *Conflict and Reconciliation: The Politics of Ethnicity in Assam* (Routledge 2013), a short story collection *No Ghosts In This City* (Zubaan 2014), two poetry collections *We Called the River Red: Poetry from a Violent Homeland* (Authorspress 2010) and *Green Tin Trunk* (Authorspress 2014), besides an edited volume, *Indira Goswami: Passion and the Pain* (Spectrum 2012).

Pankaj Thapa is an Associate Professor and Head of the Department of English at the Sikkim Government College since 1984.

Educated at the Irish Missionary-run St. Edmund's School and College in Shillong, his passion for sketching can be traced back to his history text-books in school.

He did his Masters in English Literature from the North-Eastern Hill University and dabbled in journalism for a while before taking up teaching as a career in scenic Sikkim.

As an avid fan of comics and graphic novels, he began doodling at an early age and sketching has been a hobby/stress-buster for him. At a time when TV and the internet weren't around, Pankaj Thapa grew up on a diet of comics, and has a graphic novel of his own called *The Boy Who Had A Dream* (Finhorn Press, Scotland), a nomadic folktale from Tibet, which he illustrated for his friend and ex-colleague, Ven. Ringu Tulku Rimpoche.

He has been a member of Sahitya Akademi, New Delhi and a judge for the Sikkim Sahitya Parishad, and the Sikkim Academy of Fine Arts in Gangtok . He has also illustrated *Around The Hearth, Khasi Folk Tales* by Kynpham Singh Nongkynrih and *Legends of the Lepchas* by Yishey Doma.

Presently he is illustrating a children's book for Scholastic Publications, titled *The Stubborn Tooth,* by Reshma Thapa.

He has a daily comic strip in a local newspaper, *The Sikkim Express,* where he exercises his funny bone. Samples of his sketchy humour are scattered on *www* for the curious.

He lives in Gangtok, Sikkim with his wife and son, and enjoys teaching at all levels. During his spare time he likes organizing literary and musical meets for friends and family.

For

My brother, Anabil, and sister-in-law, Indrani
Because you are always there

Contents

Introduction

This book is one of my many efforts at understanding the place I call home, and the place I call home is the Northeast. This place has always fascinated me. After all, it is a place where very hill and every brook, every tree and every bird that ever sat on it has a tale to tell. Or at least, we the people who live here do, about them.

There are any number of these tales told and retold among the many communities living in this wonderfully multiethnic region. I have picked only thirty of them to tell, again. Almost entirely, they are narratives about the causes and origins and effects and endings of things, peoples, cultures, and values. Just a few of them are about all that is in between.

Broadly, then, the tales in this collection touch upon the following questions that eternally engage our interest and curiosity: where have we come from, what do we have and where do we go in the end? How did we come to be who we are and where we are? When did we first utter express our inner selves? How did we learn to do that? What do we derive meaning from and why? Do we ever, to end with, go from here; if so, where?

These are the questions we keep asking ourselves because we hope that they hold clues to our identities. But our identities are always in flux, we change from minute to minute. We adapt, and we adopt new selves, become new persons, new peoples. And along with us, our narratives keep changing. Our tales acquire new directions and dimensions, characters and characteristics. We mould them and are moulded by them in turn.

That is why, perhaps, folktales always have so many different versions. Sometimes dramatic, sometimes subtle, there are, nonetheless, variations in the same tale told by different tellers. The names of the characters, their fates and foibles, the meanings and moralities that they are agents of may all change. It is almost as if with each retelling of a tale, a new world, a new *weltanschauung* can be—and is—generated.

And yet, despite these changes, despite the differences, our primal narrative, the original tale remains the same. We are all the same people, we come from the same place. We sometimes disperse here and there, we often forget, we often fight. But in the end, we always come back to our native narrative, we always return home.

While threading these tales together, I was also trying to find my way home.

Arunachal Pradesh

A brief note:

Frontierized and often forgotten under colonial rule, Arunachal Pradesh was known as the North East Frontier Agency (NEFA) even as far into the post-colonial period as 1972 when it became a Union Territory. It attained full statehood only in 1987, but the process of 'nationalizing' its largely disputed territory and predominantly non-Aryan people started with the imposition of the Sanskritized name, however apt. And perhaps the nationalizing policies of the Indian State in Arunachal Pradesh have been a success, because the state has largely been free from militancy and insurgency.

The comparatively quiescent people of Arunachal Pradesh fall broadly into three cultural groups. The first of these are the Monpas and Sherdukpens of Tawang and West Kameng districts, the Membas and Khambas of the high mountain regions along the northern borders and the Khamptis and Singphos in the eastern areas, all of whom are mostly Buddhists. Secondly, there are the Adis, Akas, Apatanis, Bangnis, Nishis, Mishmis, Mijis, Thongsas and others who worship Donyi-Polo and Abo-Tani. And lastly, the Noctes and Wanchos, of Tirap district adjoining Nagaland, some of whom have taken up the practice of an elementary form of Vaishnavism.

'Adi' literally means 'hill person'. Till some decades back, they were known as Abor, a nomenclature used mostly by the Assamese and largely considered derogatory. The name Adi is, therefore, preferred. They are found mostly in East, West, and Upper Siang districts, Upper Subansiri and Dibang Valley districts of Arunachal Pradesh. Their people are also scattered in some contiguous parts of Assam, besides certain areas of neighbouring China (Tibet) and Bhutan. Their language is Tibeto-Burman in origin. There are, of course, many dialectical variations among the different Adi tribes and all of them use the Latin script. Though Buddhism and Christianity have also been making inroads, the Adis traditionally practise animism, and their main god is Donyi–Polo. Adi myths are incorporated mainly in the *aabang*, which are stylised narratives about the origin and creation of beings, things and traditions, performed by specialists known variously as *Miri, Bari, Nyibo* or *Menjik*.

The Mishmis (known also as Dengs in Tibet) mainly live in Lohit, Upper Dibang Valley and Lower Dibang Valley districts and are divided into three groups—Idus or Chulikatas, Digarus or Taroan and Mijus or Kaman. Of them, it has been surmised that the Idu Mishmis were the first to migrate into the Northeast from Burma. Their language belongs to the Tibeto-Burman family. Mishmis are well known as traders who, in the early days, would travel to the plains of Assam dealing in medicinal plants and musk. They are largely agriculturists. Some Idu Mishmis are expert weavers and craftspeople. Animists originally, Idu Mishmis stand out because of their typical hairstyle and the unique woven motifs on their dresses.

Mostly found in the Lower Subansiri district, the Nyishis were earlier known as the Daflas. They are also sometimes called 'Nyashang', meaning 'people of the land'. Traditionally, they are experts at hunting and fishing, although they also cultivate on the hill slopes. Their men stand out among those of other tribes in their customary headgear—they sport long hair which they tie in a knot (padum) at the forehead with the help of a woven cane cap with a hornbill beak (bopia). This practice, of course, has now been largely discontinued. Being mostly animists, they believe that after death the spirits of the dead travel to the 'village of the ancestors'.

The Singphos are related to the Kachins of Burma and Jingpo in China. In Arunachal Pradesh, they live in Lohit and Changlang districts mostly. Some of them live in adjoining parts of Assam. They are usually agriculturists and expert blacksmiths, besides being adept at weaving. They variously follow Buddhism and a form of animism. Tea is very important in the Singpho's life—it was from the Singphos, in fact, that the British learnt to drink tea. Like the Nyishis, the Singpho men in traditional attire also tie their long hair in a knot on their crown, as do many women. They believe that spirits reside in all animate and inanimate objects, and all living creatures have souls.

Akin to the Konyak and Nocte Naga people, the Wanchos inhabit mostly the western part of Tirap district which is adjacent to the state of Nagaland. Customarily, they were head-hunters, a practice long abandoned now. Unlike among the neighbouring Naga tribes, among the Wanchos, Christianity was late in coming and some Wanchos still practise animism. Some have even embraced Hinduism. The traditional Wancho society is highly organized and a council of elders known as the Wangham or Wangsa govern society. Tattooing is a common social custom among them. In the olden days, both men and women used to adorn themselves with tattoos. Weaving and wood carving are special skills among the Wancho people.

1. Adi

Invisible to evil

The God of the Adis is Sedi, who is the creator of the Sky and the Earth. The Abang (lengthy narratives) of the Adis say, '*Keyum Kero Melo Bomong Kola Bo Ko Dine Mambie Duyi Lento.*' In other words, Sedi also begot Bomong and Bo. Bomong is the Sun and Bo is the Moon. Sedi set them in the Sky and these heavenly bodies were now decreed to give light to all living objects on Earth. It is because Bomong and Bo live in the Sky that the creatures of the Earth can live and breathe.

Now Sedi also gave birth to Pedong Nane. But Pedong Nane felt all alone. Seeing her plight, Sedi said, 'I shall create a companion for you. The two of you will live together and continue the work of creation for me.'

And Sedi created Yidum Bote as her partner and mate. Pedong Nane and Yidum Bote got married. When they mated, they gave birth to all the living beings on earth.

At first Pedong Nane gave birth to Pedong Doding Dimu Taya. They were the spirits of the hills.

She also gave birth to Pedong Dolang Ladang Layo. They were the spirits of the water.

This was followed by the birth of Pedong Doiri Minur. That was the blacksmith.

From Pedong Nane's womb were also born the Monkey, who was called Pedong Dorot Rotmang Masi Sibe.

Yet another offspring of Pedong Nane and Yidum Bote came to be named Pedong Domi Mili Minam. This was the spirit of disease.

All the siblings were then given their own land to live on by their mother and sent out into the world.

In the end, Pedong Nane and Yidum Bote mated again to procreate human beings. She gave birth to two human siblings—both male—and they were named Pedong Doro Robo and Pedong Doni or Tani. Doni was the youngest son of Pedong Nane and Yidum Bote.

Doni was the weakest of all their children and that was the reason why he had to be showered with more attention than his elder siblings. This made Robo feel that their parents loved Doni more than they did him.

'My younger brother is more favoured by our parents. I am their elder son but they do not love me as much. Mother and Father are both partial towards Doni, such is my luck,' Robo used to think.

Now Robo was a tall and stout lad. He was very strongly built physically but lacked intelligence. Doni, on the other hand, though physically weaker, was mentally very sharp. He was a good learner and through his quick wit and intelligence, he mastered all the arts and crafts. He also excelled in the use of weapons. Robo became extremely jealous of him. As the brothers grew up together, there was always a deep-seated ill-feeling harboured by the elder brother against the younger.

As time went by, both human children reached a certain age when they were thought to be mature enough to take responsibility of the land and property of their parents.

'It is time for you children to take up the responsibility of all that we possess,' Pedong Nane and Yidum Bote told them one day.

But that posed a problem. A dispute arose between the two brothers on the question of how the land and property should be shared between them. Neither of them was willing to settle for the share allotted to each. As the dispute escalated, it reached a stage where it could not be settled amicably any more.

In the end, they decided, 'We have to settle this dispute one way or the other. The best way to do that would be through an archery competition between the two of us. Whoever wins the competition will be entitled to all the fertile land and movable valuables.' The assets included artefacts like the *arem*, a brass plate, and the *tadok*, beads. Both brothers started preparing for the competition in earnest—there was a lot at stake.

As already stated, however, Doni was much better than his brother in all activities, and this included the sport of archery. Naturally, therefore, the accomplished younger brother was the one who came out victorious in the competition. As a result, he became the owner of all the fertile land and his parents' valuables. The competition out of the way, Doni eventually settled down to enjoy his victory.

In stark contrast to his good fate, however, the unfortunate elder brother, Robo, was driven away to live in the barren hills and rocky mountains. As a result, the resentment that he had nurtured against his younger brother all his life began to grow and fester with greater intensity.

'My brother has always had the best of everything,' he complained. 'I have always had to settle for the worst. Such is my fate.'

While the fires of jealousy continued to consume Robo, Doni, in the meantime, had made himself busy in managing his asscts. Gifted as he was with superior intelligence, he did not remain satisfied with merely enjoying the fruits of his skilful victory.

'What I got from my parents is my inheritance. But I also have to prove my own worth,' he resolved.

He, therefore, entered the tutelage of Doying Bote who is the god of wisdom and human welfare. Under the able guidance of this deity, he multiplied his land and property manifold. Soon, Doni became a very rich man and started to live a happy and comfortable life.

Doni's affluence and prosperity now started to make all the rest of his siblings jealous of him as well. These included all the spirits that Pedong Nane and Yidum Bote had begotten before they had borne the two brothers. All of them now came together in council.

'This Doni has become too prosperous. He has always been favoured by everybody, including our parents. We cannot let his good fortune continue forever,' they said to each other.

And in their blind jealousy, they started to instigate the elder human brother against the younger. Consumed by envy and covetousness, they started telling Robo that Doni had done nothing but cheat him of his rightful share of the land and riches of their parents.

It is true, of course, that Robo had been jealous of his younger brother. He had not, however, thought vengeful thoughts against him so far. But with the other children of his parents now egging him on, the simple-minded Robo started to believe that he had indeed been cheated by his brother.

'I have always been blaming my destiny for my plight. But maybe there is some truth in what my siblings say. Maybe Doni did cheat me out of all things that were rightfully mine,' he began to think.

The more he thought, the more convinced he became that Doni was the cause of his downfall. 'Yes, Doni has cheated me,' he told himself. 'It is because of Doni that I am where I am today. And look at him, how he sits so comfortably amidst all the pomp and splendour that should have been mine and mine alone.'

That Doni had won everything in a fair competition, with his superior skills, was not something Robo or any of the other siblings were willing to acknowledge. Under their influence, Robo started hating Doni all the more and began devising a plan to get back all the land and riches from the younger brother.

'Let's go to war,' the siblings finally told Robo. 'You should fight for your right. You should get back what is yours.' And it was decided that the elder siblings would side with Robo when he went to battle against Doni.

As Doni put up a valiant fight, Ladang Layo, the spirit of the water, and Mili Minam, the spirit of diseases, came to Robo's aid. Both of them surrounded Doni on all sides as they rushed to attack him. A tumultuous battle ensued. Doni was all alone and had to defend himself against his elder brother and all the other siblings who were aiding and abetting Robo.

It was an unfair battle to say the least, but Doni would not give up. He was resolute as he stood alone in battle. But with so many adversaries at his heels, surrounding him on all sides and fighting him with their innate skills, desperation was slowly creeping in on Doni despite the innumerable skills he had acquired and the indomitable courage he inherently possessed. Seeing this, his parents and Doying Bote took pity on him.

'That poor child is all alone, fighting his stronger elder siblings. We must rush to help him,' they said.

The deity of fortune, Doying Yingue Ute Boro, also decided to come to his aid. After all, fortune does always favour the brave. With reinforcements thus pouring in, Doni finally managed to outwit his adversaries in battle.

But Doni's mother was shrewd and she knew that this was not the end. 'They will continue badgering Doni this way if I don't do something about it,' she realized.

So she gave him a shield that would ensure that his enemies could not catch up to her younger son. It was made of a leaf that made him invisible with his brother and the rest of his army. With the help of that shield, the first Adi man on earth set up his own habitation, independent and outside the reach of his other human foes.

The Adi forefather then built a shelter called a *moshup* which Doying Bote blessed. In this moshup or *dere*, Doni lived and prospered once again under Doying Bote's protection, as well as the protection given to him by the other deities, Ute Popo and Gumin Soyin. Evil spirits, they say, can never enter this shelter and do humans any harm.

2. *Idu-Mishmi*

Begotten by the gods

*I*n the beginning, only gods and women lived on earth. The Idu Mishmi believe that men were created much later than women, and only after the gods sowed the seeds of humankind in the womb of the first mortal woman.

Although there are different traditions that have divergent views on who or of what nature these gods were, the one we speak of here first says that in the days of yore, there were only evil gods who lived on earth. The first mortal to inhabit the earth after them was the Woman.

These evil gods were vindictive and licentious. They were extremely troublesome and made life impossible for all the other creatures who also lived on the same earth. As time went by, things came to such a pass that the god Nyu-Anjuru began to rue the day that he had created the world. 'What has become of my creation? I did not create gods to indulge in such ungodly behaviour! What will happen to the rest of my creation?'

He could not tolerate the evil that he saw being perpetrated by the gods and at the same time, he was unable to see any way out. In the end, he decided to destroy his own creation— the whole of it—by setting the earth and all living beings on it on fire.

'The fire,' he said, 'will rid the Earth of these profligates. I shall burn it all down and create anew.'

In this, he called upon the god of the wind, Inni Anjemo, to help him. The latter opened his wings and fanned the fire which spread throughout the world. It engulfed the entire earth for several days, continuously burning and razing everything in its way to ashes. At the end of the great fire, when everything else had been eliminated, Nyu-Anjuru saw that there yet remained alive on earth, a few women.

'This is quite propitious,' thought Nyu-Anjuru, for although he had initially willed his entire creation to burn down, he had not expected to encounter the utter emptiness and sense of barrenness he now saw all around him.

'This Earth used to be a vibrant place, full of life. Now it is all gone!' he bemoaned when he found that without the living beings and everything else that had supported life on earth so far, the earth was nothing but a bare expanse of nothingness. He realized he would have to remedy that, and in the course of his new creative venture, he decided the women who had survived the great fire would be his partners.

'The women shall bear me my offspring. And my offspring shall be the new life on Earth,' he pronounced.

Nyu-Anjuru was one but he had the choice of many women. He chose a few of them for his purpose of creating new life on Earth. These women bore him a great many children who went out into the world and fulfilled his desire to populate it once again.

At first, he kept Arru Maseng as his wife. After their marriage, Arru Maseng bore him a child. They named him Emmo. To Nyu-Anjuru's disappointment, however, Emmo turned out to be a dullard. 'Not only is this boy a blockhead himself, but anybody who comes in contact with him also becomes dull and half-witted eventually,' noticed Nyu-Anjuru.

After Emmo, Arru Maseng bore Nyu-Anjuru another child. Emmo's younger brother was named Amroho, and even he could not bring peace to his parents. As the years went by and Amroho grew up, he showed a strange propensity for wild behaviour. Finally, he went to live in the forest. But whenever he was angered by anything, he would search out human habitations and burn them down.

Nyu-Anjuru now turned his attention to another woman, Inni Asige. After he took her for his wife, Inni Asige bore him eight sons.

Of these eight, the eldest was called Adde. He was the spirit of ailments, the demon of fever and jaundice. Nyu-Anjuru and Inni Asige's second son was called Enna. He was the god of the leeches. The third son of the god and his human consort was named Anna. Anna was the demon of pain and suffering. Their fifth son was called Arramo. He turned out to be the god of the winds. His main job was to hurl thunderbolts upon the earth and to guide the winds on their way from hither to thither. The next of their numerous sons was known as Siddi. This one was a remarkably terrifying demon and his very appearance could frighten human beings to death, such was his visage. Only the youngest of all of the sons of Nyu-Anjuru and Inni Asige was somewhat less ferocious than his elder brothers, and his name was Ayajon.

'These sons too are a disappointment to me. It is true that the youngest one is somewhat better than the elder ones, but I am unhappy still. Inni Asige cannot bear me the offspring I desire,' Nyu-Anjuru felt.

So he decided to take himself another wife. His third wife was named Uini Arru.

Uini Arru mated with Nyu-Anjuru to bear three sons in the course of time. These three sons were named Trummi, Gallan and Aja. Gallan, was a loner and he liked solitude above all else. When he grew up, he went away to the forest and took to living there on his own.

His brother Aja, though, was different from him and their third sibling, Trummi, in every way. 'What a majestic countenance this Aja has,' said everybody who saw the boy. He was also blessed with a tall figure and full cheeks. The Idu-Mishmis believe the *sahib* is the progeny of this magnificent son of Nyu-Anjuru and Uini Arru.

Even Uini Arru, however, could not captivate Nyu-Anjuru's affections forever. Very soon, the god became fascinated with Inni-o-mago. She was a girl from the plains and Nyu-Anjuru did not waste much time before making her his next wife.

After they got married, Inni-o-mago gave birth to a boy child. This child left his parents' home while he was still a little boy and he went away to live in the south-eastern region. He lived and prospered there.

'He shall be the progenitor of the Khampti people,' it was decreed. From Inni-o-mago's firstborn son, then, sprang the entire population of the Khampti.

The second child of Inni-o-mago and Nyu-Anjuru, another boy, was known as Mesa or Cuili. This boy eventually gave birth to the Assamese people of the plains below.

The plains were always a fascinating place and when Nyu-Anjuru felt the need for another wife to keep him company, he decided to go find another from the plains. In due course, he became besotted by yet another girl from the flatlands below. Her name was Ladu.

Ladu bore the god two sons. Of them, the second son was named Idu. The Idu Mishmis of Arunachal Pradesh claim to have descended from this offspring of the human mother and heavenly father.

⌃

Incidentally, the Idu-Mishmis have another narrative of how they came to be. In this particular narrative, they are not the children of Ladu and the god Nyu-Anjuru. Of course, they do, however, believe—even in this version of the creation myth—that when the earth first came into being, there was no man who lived upon it.

In the beginning they say, there was only the Woman. The other inhabitants of the earth included the gods of the sun and the moon, as well as the deities of the wind and fire.

In those early days, the notion of shame and the concept of covering the physical form with clothes had not yet come into prevalence. The Woman and the gods, therefore, lived completely naked. They did not know the use of clothes or the craft of weaving them, nor did they feel the need for the same. They lived as they were born, and roamed the whole wide world free from any inhibitions of any sort.

Those were also the days that the gods had no knowledge of sex. They did not know how to procreate, nor did they feel any urge to consummate their sexual urges and carnal desires. This was for the simple reason, of course, that they did not feel any of these urges or desires. These had not yet manifested themselves in the divine creatures.

It was the Woman who first felt the need for sex. As she wandered all over the world, somewhere, at some point in her travels over the hills and valleys, the sex instinct made itself felt inside her. It set her wondering, 'What is this fire burning in me?' And suddenly, she was feeling the need to mate and procreate.

The problem, however, was that she did not know how to. This was the first time carnal desire had been awakened inside her, but she had not been given the accompanying knowledge to sate that desire. As the fire continued to consume her, she kept thinking of how to quench it. 'It will not leave me in peace. How do I douse this intense desire?'

Finally, she followed her instincts and sat down on the top of a hill with her legs wide apart. 'Something is bound to happen,' she thought. And waited.

Now the wind god Amaya Khinyu happened to live on the hill that the Woman had settled down on. Like all other gods and indeed, like all beings of Creation, he also had no idea about sex, lust or mating. When he saw the Woman on top of his hill, though, he felt a strong sense of curiosity. 'Who is this Woman? Why is she sitting upon my hill in this manner?' Such and other questions started building within him, and his rapidly growing curiosity pulled him towards her. Finally, he made his way between her legs and into her womb.

The result was that, with the wind in her womb, the Woman's belly started bloating. It began to grow larger and larger with each passing day, till one fine day, she gave birth to a male child. This child, when he became a fully grown man, became the progenitor of the Idu-Mishmis.

3. Nyishi

The end of avarice

Among the Nyishis, there was once a man named Tai Bida. One day, Tai Bida decided to go into the forest to hunt. Little did he know when he set forth into the heart of the forest that his life would change forever on that very same day. For there, in the middle of the forest, stood a she-*mithun*.

'This is wonderful,' thought Tai Bida. 'If I can capture this she-mithun and take her home with me, I will be a rich man. Everybody in the village and in my clan will respect me.'

These thoughts occurred to Tai Bida because mithuns are very resourceful animals, and among the Nyishis, to own a mithun is a sign of great eminence. So he caught hold of the mithun and took her home with him. Soon the mithun got domesticated and became very much a part of Tai Bida's household.

What the lucky man did not know just yet, however, was that the mithun was actually a goddess in disguise. Goddess Bur was the deity of the water, and she had decided that day to bless Tai Bida with her presence and to bring him good fortune.

'I shall make this man rich and prosperous,' she decided, as she settled down in Tai Bida's house.

Very soon, the she-mithun blessed Tai Bida with her offspring. His social standing rose with every offspring that the mithun produced. Simultaneously also, his worldly wealth multiplied. Tai Bida was becoming a rich man by all accounts.

He could buy and sell mithuns now, and he could also buy new wives in exchange for these mithuns.

'I am all alone in this world. I need a companion. Maybe it's time now to get myself a wife,' Tai Bida realized one fine day. And so he paid a few mithuns as bride-price to get himself a wife of his choosing.

Now mithuns are the favoured bride-price among the Nyishis and so long as Tai Bida could afford to pay three mithuns or more as bride-price, he could take as many wives as he wanted. Soon after marrying his first wife, therefore, he decided to get himself another, and then another, and then one more. After all, polygamy is very much a part of Nyishi culture.

The many wives of Tai Bida, over the years, gave birth to many children and his household was thus transformed from a quiet hovel to an affluent homestead echoing with the laughter and cries of small children and the pattering of busy feet at all times of the day.

To manage his household and to look after his children as well as to serve himself and his many wives, Tai Bida could also now afford to keep slaves. These slaves were many in number and they too could be paid for with mithuns. Thus, the she-mithun's blessings brought a lot of material wealth to Tai Bida, who was now a happy and fulfilled man.

We should have been able to end our story on this happy note—in the opulence found by a mortal man through the blessings of a divine creature. But such a happy ending was not to be. The mortal man turned out to be his own enemy and destroyed his own happiness eventually.

When the goddess had decided to take the form of a mithun and help Tai Bida achieve all this affluence, she had not foreseen the kind of change it would bring about in the heart and soul of the man. For he soon became avaricious and godless. All the wealth that the goddess had brought him turned him into a haughty man who started to value only his worldly possessions. Over the years, the goddess, in the form of the she-mithun who remained tied to the mithun shed in Tai Bida's house, had seen the changes creeping in on the mortal she had chosen to favour. She watched as he began to remain less and less satisfied with his lot and started to yearn for more and more. His good fortune had come to him unbidden, but now he thought that he could earn more riches and more renown if he propitiated the gods with sacrifices. Since he had a lot of mithuns and mithuns are precious animals, he sacrificed them off and on to pray to the gods to give him more.

In his increasing lust for more wealth and more power, Tai Bida soon lost respect for all the values held dear by his people. Even the mithuns that were the cause of his rise to eminence became just another means of satiating his avarice. In the end, he turned his attention to the she-mithun herself, the one who had heralded his good fortune in the first place. He thought that if he sacrificed her, like he did her offspring, he would gain all the wealth in the world.

He said to himself, 'She was the cause of my good fortune. If I sacrifice her, it will be the ultimate appeasement I can offer the gods. Maybe then they will shower on me everything else that I do not have, everything else that will make me happy!'

Being a goddess in disguise, the she-mithun divined Tai Bida's intentions as soon as the thought even occurred to him. On the night before she was to be sacrificed, she appeared to him in his dream. She came to him in the guise of an old woman, and reproached him.

'Have you lost all respect for everything? Do you value nothing? Even me, who came to your house and brought you your good fortune?' she asked him. As she continued to speak to him, tears flowed from her eyes, and she wailed, 'One day, you had nothing. Then I appeared before you in the middle of the forest and let you lead me back to your own house. I made this house a home, gave you the people in your life, made you rich and gave you a high status in society. Is this how you intend to pay me back for my kindness to you? By slaughtering me?'

As the woman kept wailing thus in his dreams all night long, the mithuns that were tied outside the house also continued to raise a hue and cry till the break of dawn. They were lamenting the misfortune that had befallen the mother of the herd.

When Tai Bida woke up in the morning, he immediately remembered his strange dream. At first, it made no sense to him, but when he thought more deeply about it, he realized the true import of the old woman's lament. And he ran to the shed outside to check on his mithuns. When he reached there, however, he saw that it was totally empty. The ropes that had tied the mithuns to their respective places in the shed were all there, but the mithuns had all been untied from them, and they were all missing.

'Who has done this?' he demanded of everybody in his house. His entire household woke up at his shouts and came running to his side, but all his wives, children and slaves denied having anything to do with the missing mithuns.

'This is a very strange happening!' they all said.

'What could be the meaning of this?' they all enquired.

After some deliberation, it was decided that they should go in search of the missing mithuns. Tai Bida led the team of searchers and they set forth from their village. The further they went looking for the lost herd, the more convinced they became that all the mithuns had left as one, and they had all followed the mother of the herd. They could not, however, catch up with the runaway animals. Many a hill, valley, mountain and river came in their way, but they crossed them all to continue searching for the lost herd. On and on went Tai Bida and his search party, for days and nights and weeks on end, till one day, they came upon a river.

They had to cross this river in order to go ahead on their way. No sooner had they reached the other bank, though, than suddenly, they saw the entire herd of mithuns in front of their eyes. Tai Bida was overjoyed to have found his missing possessions, but to his dismay, he was not to have them back, ever again.

There in front of them all was a deep lake. It was called Gekal Sinyi. One after the other, led by the mother of the herd, the mithuns were making their way towards the lake. And even as the search party watched helplessly, they started jumping into the waters of the lake. And as they jumped, they disappeared. The goddess of the waters, Bur, had returned to her abode. With her, she had taken all her young ones.

Dejectedly then, Tai Bida and his followers returned to the village. Once there, everybody left him. After all, without the mithuns, Tai Bida was just another ordinary man. And without the blessings of the Goddess Bur, his worldly wealth also left his possession. From a rich and eminent man, Tai Bida very quickly slid into poverty and disrepute.

Once again, this could have been where the story ended. But Tai Bida started tempting fate yet again. He would often lament, 'Ah me! What all did I have in my possession and how ruthlessly was it all snatched away from me!'

And he started fretting and worrying. 'What if this is the end? What if there is no hope left in my life? What if I am to lose everything? My life, my world, my family, all of it?' he would often question.

In the end, when his anxiety reached a peak, he decided to go pray to god. He stood on a big rock and called upon him to give him some answers.

'Oh lord,' he called out from where he stood on the rock. 'Tell me what lies in store for me? Tell me how much more I am supposed to lose. Give me a sign if I am to be left with nothing.'

His apprehensions were eating into him. So he pleaded with god, 'Send me a Budum snake, make it appear before me if what I fear is right.'

No sooner had he uttered this prayer than the earth shook and the ground parted. Before him, appeared a Budum snake, and it danced in front of him.

Tai Bida was thus convinced that he was in for some grave misfortune, graver than anything that had befallen him so far. He rushed home to check on his near and dear ones, but he was too late. When he reached home, he saw that his wives and children had all been attacked by some deadly disease. There was no medicine that he could find anywhere that could cure his family. One by one, they all died right in front of his eyes. And then, Tai Bida also caught a deadly disease and before long, death claimed him as well.

4. Singpho

Dying to celebrate

No Singpho person ever died. That was the way the creator had made them.

The creator had also placed the two worlds close to each other, the world of the celestial bodies, and the human world. The inhabitants of the celestial bodies, that is to say the creatures that inhabited the Sun and the Moon, could therefore easily communicate with human beings. And they did so during festivities and celebrations of all kinds.

'The people who live on earth are our neighbours. We must have a cordial relationship with them,

and make them a part of our social and community life,' they would say to each other.

And as they socialized with the inhabitants of the earth more and more, they came to form a very close friendship with the Singpho people in particular. Such was the bond between the inhabitants of the Sun and the Moon on the one hand and the Singpho people on the other, that no ceremony, religious or social, was ever deemed complete if the Singphos were not present.

One such festival was Manglup. The Manglup ceremony was performed when any inhabitant of the Sun or the Moon died. It was a beautiful ceremony which celebrated the passing of an individual. The Singphos just loved to be a part of the Manglup festivities.

The ritual consisted of the entire gathering encircling the corpse of the deceased. They would then celebrate the passing of the soul by singing and dancing around the dead body. It was a rite that called for much pomp and splendour, and was celebrated with much ceremonial grandeur.

Every time the Singphos participated in this ceremony, they would come back wishing they themselves had such a grand tradition of their own.

'If only we had such festivities,' they would talk among themselves. 'How enjoyable the Manglup is, how our friends on the Sun and the Moon enjoy themselves during the festival. Why can't we have such a ceremony ourselves? Why can't our entire community come together to celebrate in this way? If we could, we would also have been able to return the hospitality of our friends to the Sun and the Moon. We could invite them to our community and provide them with as much pomp and pageantry as they provide us with when we are invited to their midst. Why do we always have to be the guests and not the hosts for a change?'

The answer to these questions, of course, was known to all. They could not host or celebrate anything like the Manglup festival because Manglup was associated with death, and death never occurred among the Singphos.

It is true that they could have celebrated any other occasion with as much ritual and grandeur. Life offers so many occasions to commemorate and such commemoration can be associated with as much fun and merriment as people want to introduce into their collective life. But such a thought did not occur to the Singphos. So taken were they by the Manglup festivities in particular that they wanted to observe the same rituals and go through the same ceremonial fanfare that the inhabitants of the Sun and the Moon did to herald death.

'But we never die!' they wailed. 'If nobody among us dies, how can we celebrate death? From where do we find a corpse whose death we can solemnize?' In this way, they would often sit together and wrack their brains over the dilemma.

The more they thought, the more desperate they became to have a Manglup of their own. Their desperation reached such a level that they were willing to go to any lengths.

In the end, they took a decision. 'If we cannot produce a corpse, we will just have to invent one,' they concluded. And a Manglup was staged. The Singphos who never died started preparing for a ceremony that revolves around death.

A Sikhai, which is a kind of lizard, had died not very far from the village. They decided that its corpse would serve their purpose as any other. After all, they only needed to pretend that somebody had died so that they could invite the inhabitants of the Sun and the Moon to come down to sing and dance with them. So they placed the Sikhai's dead body in a coffin and made some of the other arrangements for the Manglup as they had seen their neighbours do so many times. The invitations were sent out next and then, they waited eagerly for the guests to arrive.

Now the inhabitants of the Sun and the Moon knew that death never occurred among the Singphos. So they started wondering, 'How do they propose to observe Manglup if they do not die? And even if somebody did die, how would they know how to observe the rites? They have only seen us performing when they visited us as our guests. They have no idea how to make arrangements for the rituals and ceremonies involved. It is not all about the songs and the dances. Don't they know that?'

A huge amount of curiosity was building up. They finally decided that the best way to satisfy this curiosity would be to accept the invitation and go see for themselves how the Singphos were planning to observe the festival.

When they reached the Singpho village, they were pleasantly surprised to see that their hosts had indeed done a good job of arranging for the ceremony. At least, it seemed so to them on the surface. So they decided that the next thing to do would be to examine the corpse.

'We would like you to uncover the coffin, dear friends,' they said. 'We want to see who died.'

But the Singphos were reluctant to comply. This got the inhabitants of the Sun and the Moon extremely inquisitive, and a bit suspicious too. They insisted, 'We have to see the corpse. Or how will we know whose death we are observing?'

Once again, the Singphos declined their request. The guests were now quite chagrined and demanded that they be allowed to see the dead body.

Unable to resist any further, the Singphos finally gave in and opened the casket. As soon as they did that, the inhabitant of the Sun and the Moon, of course, realized that they had been tricked. They could not believe that their friends had lied to them in such a big way and manipulated them into taking part in a terrible charade.

'Is this how you treat your friends? Is this how you entertain your guests? By deceiving them?' they demanded.

Seeing their friends thus peeved, the Singphos realized that nothing they did or said now would appease them. Still, they tried to explain to them why they had staged the ceremony and faked death: 'We also wanted to celebrate death like you do. But death is unknown to us. How were we to celebrate Manglup without it? And we only wanted to return your hospitality. You have always been our gracious hosts. For once, we wanted to have you as our guests and give you the same grand reception that you always give us in your world.'

This did not quite melt the hearts of the inhabitants of the Sun and the Moon, but at least, they could not doubt the sincerity of the words. So even if they could not quite bring themselves to revert to their old friendship or to take part in any more celebrations with the Singphos, the neighbours decided to teach them the rites and rituals associated with Manglup. That way, at least, the humans would celebrate the ceremony as it was meant to be.

The Singphos were happy to learn everything that they did not know about Manglup rituals and were grateful to their old friends for teaching it all to them. The rituals, however, were only about commemorating a central event, and the central event was death which never came to the Singpho people. Without death, then, the rituals they now learnt would be meaningless. So when the inhabitants of the Sun and the Moon were leaving, they pronounced, 'From now on, death will be a part of your lives on earth.'

And so the Singphos started dying. And whenever any Singpho died, the entire community would gather around the deceased and observe the Manglup ceremony. And they would all sing and dance.

5. Wancho

Fireflies and the darkness of death

When there was no earth, there was the sky, vast and limitless. The god of this sky was Rang.

Rang created the earth from a star that he projected into the sky. This star took many years to transform into the earth, but when it did, it was inhabited by human beings as well as by all kinds of flora and fauna.

Now Rang has a knife, and that knife is lightning. When he dances in the sky and waves his knife in the air, we say that lightning flashes in the sky.

Watching these lightning flashes, human beings learnt how to shoot. Just as lightning shoots through the atmosphere to hit its mark on earth, so also men learnt to set their targets and shoot through their guns. They got these guns from Rang himself who was the sole custodian of these weapons and kept them with him in the skies.

After all, Rang was a great hunter, and he would often fire thunderbolts through his guns. It was only sometimes that he missed his mark. When he did, the thunderbolt would fall to the earth and enter the ground and go deep inside. There it would lie buried for four years. At the end of the fourth year, it would grow out of the earth as a tree.

Sometimes, however, Rang's bullets would hit the trees and not enter the ground. These trees then become the carrier of diseases, especially leprosy. When human beings touched the leaves of a tree struck by Rang's bullets, they would become lepers. Unlike other diseases, leprosy is the product of Rang's bullet fired from the sky.

All other diseases emanated from the earth itself. When the earth blew out its foul breath, much like we blow out air from our mouths sometimes, human beings contracted various diseases.

In the beginning it was very easy for human beings to catch a number of such diseases that the earth expelled from its insides in the form of poisoned air. This was because, in those ancient times, human beings had really very flimsy skins. It was very easy for diseases to enter the human body through these sheer membranes and to infect them.

But diseases or not, human beings in those days had two very peculiar attributes which marked them apart from human beings today. For one, they could change form. For instance, a human being could thus become a caterpillar one day, or a butterfly the next, if he so desired. Actually, they were not very different from caterpillars and butterflies in this respect—after all, caterpillars and butterflies also change form.

The thin skins humans beings had then, were meant to facilitate such transfiguration. And because they would change forms so easily, they could also just as easily evade death. Human beings, thus, were immortal. Ironically, though, these very characteristic traits of human beings ended up being their bane, and they became mortal and unable to change shape. This did not, of course, happen overnight, but was a result of the humans' growing hubris and their contempt and utter disregard for the welfare of the other creatures on earth.

Because humans were immortal, they began to grow exponentially in numbers. The earth, therefore, became overpopulated with people. And these people soon began to pose a threat to the other creatures who shared their habitat. They began to kill birds and animals indiscriminately for food. When they did not kill, they changed form and snatched away the other creatures' food. This made all the birds and animals on earth detest human beings and also quite wary of them. But human beings did not change their ways. And that is why they had to be cursed with mortality and their powers of transformation taken away.

It happened like this:

One day, a crane was out hunting for food when a man caught sight of it.

'Ah ha!' he thought. 'Today is my lucky day. I do not have to put in any extra effort to hunt or fish. This bird here will catch my food for me today.'

And he stood by watching as the crane swooped down into the waters and dexterously caught a fish in its beak. Then it flew towards the shore, happily contemplating feeding on its catch. It folded its wings and stood on the river bank and was just about to place the fish it had caught on the ground before it when the man rushed in and snatched its food away from its beak. Without any thought for the poor bird that had worked so hard to catch its prey, the man started devouring the fish with relish.

'It is a very tasty fish indeed. And to think I chanced upon it so effortlessly!' he thought gleefully as he ate.

The poor crane could do very little but watch the man eat the fish it caught. And as it watched, it started growing very angry. 'These humans have no consideration for anybody else. They only want everything for themselves. How could this selfish man snatch away my food? Now I have to go hungry for the day.'

As it ranted, the crane also realized that human beings had grown so arrogant because they had been given immortality. 'No matter what they do, they know that there can be no reckoning, no end for them. This has made them disregard even basic civility. If only they knew the fear of death, they would learn to value things, perhaps.'

So saying, it cursed the man that he would soon die. When the man heard the crane curse, he only laughed.

'Ha ha!' he guffawed. 'You foolish crane, don't you know human beings do not die? What are you cursing me for? Come here, I will show you what it means to put a curse on me.'

And he ran at the crane, caught hold of it and hit it on the head. So hard did he hit the poor crane that it lost all the feathers from the top of its head. That is why, till today, the crane is bald.

After this incident, human beings only grew in their insolence and disregarded the well-being of their fellow creatures all the more. Finally, a crow sealed their fate.

Another man on another day deprived a crow of its meal. The crow had collected a mouthful of meat from somewhere and was about to savour it when a man appeared from nowhere. Just as the dreadful man with the crane had deprived the poor bird of its fish, this other terrible man also took away the meat from the crow's beak and started gobbling it up.

'Oh, these humans!' the crow lamented. 'They are the bane of our existence. If they live on, we will all surely die. What are we to do?'

The god Tatchak Namlong heard the crow's lament. And he understood that human beings were indeed growing to be a terrible menace on earth.

'If they continue this way, the rest of the creation will continue to suffer. This is not as it should be. For one species, all the others should not be made to suffer. Their immortality will lead to the death of all other creatures,' he realized.

Therefore, he declared, 'Human beings will henceforth begin to die.'

And that was how mortality first manifested itself among human beings, and one by one, humans began to die.

Now, the first man who died went to where all dead souls were intended to go. But being the only one dead, he started feeling very unhappy all alone. 'I wonder how my family is doing, my brothers and sisters, parents, aunts and uncles, my wife and children, everybody,' he thought. 'My friends must be missing me, as I miss them. There is nothing here for me. Why did I have to come here? What do I do all on my own?'

The more he missed his old life, the more he longed to go back to it. Finally, one day, he made up his mind to fulfil his wish to return to earth. His only concern now was how to undertake his return journey. He was a dead soul and the souls of the dead can only roam around in places bereft of light. They thrive in the dark. The earth, though, was filled with light. How then was he to pass from darkness to light?

'What is it that can lead me out of this darkness? What is it that can bring me a little light?' he kept wondering, till one day, he caught a firefly and its feeble glow suddenly turned out to be the answer to his prayers.

This firefly acted as his torch to light the way ahead of him. It led him up a tall dark mountain till they reached the very top of it. From the peak, the man saw his village and all his friends and family in it. He was so overjoyed at the sight that he danced all the way down from the top. But when he reached there, everybody was crying at his demise.

This alarmed the firefly because it was afraid that all the tears that were flowing from the villagers' eyes would quench its light.

And it fled from there. Once again plunged into darkness, the dead man also had to return to wherever it is that dead souls go.

Till today, it is believed that fireflies do not go to the place of the dead—tears at the funeral scare them away. And the souls of the newly dead always dance around for a while before going out into the darkness beyond to join others who had died before them.

Assam

A brief note:

The Seven Sisters, as we know them today, only took shape after the formation of the youngest Indian states of Mizoram and Arunachal Pradesh in 1987. Prior to that, most of what is today known as the Northeast—barring the erstwhile princely states of Manipur and Tripura—were once part of Assam. The idea of 'Bar Axam' or 'Greater Assam' has its roots in this geo-political history. This idea (or ideal) has sometimes acted as a binding agent among the many sisters, but more often than not, it has also caused a lot of bad blood to flow down the rivers that descend from the surrounding hilly states into the plains of Assam. Mizoram, for instance, broke away from the state after a prolonged insurgent movement.

Indeed, militant nativism has often led to violent ethnic conflicts and insurgencies in Assam, and these conflicts still rage within the state, between its many ethnic communities. The resultant gory reality often eclipses its boundless beauty and poly-cultural richness. Officially, after all, as many as 115 communities of different racial groups live in Assam, which has historically been the meeting ground of the Aryan and non-Aryan civilizations, of the people migrating from the east (mainly, China and Southeast Asia) and those migrating from the west (especially, the Indian mainland).

The Ahoms were fairly late migrants into Assam, coming in hordes from across the Patkai Mountain since the 13th century AD. Of Tai origin, the Ahoms subjugated many of the autochthonous inhabitants of the new land they had come to and assimilated with them. Later, they adopted Hinduism and also introduced the same among their subjects. In many instances, the earlier inhabitants also submerged their identities in that of the Ahoms. Indeed, the Axamiya identity as a whole and as it stands today, has grown out of such and other similar assimilative processes. The Ahoms are also said to have originally given Assam its name. The period of Ahom rule over the land stretched for nearly 600 years before the British finally entered Assam, colonized it and gave it its present Anglicized name.

The Bodo people constitute the largest plains tribe of Assam, and since 2003, they have had their own autonomous arrangement—the Bodoland Autonomous Territorial Districts (BTAD)—within the state of Assam. The grant of territorial autonomy to the Bodos was preceded by a nearly two-decade-long, often extremely violent, struggle for statehood that started in 1987. The Bodos are a part of the huge Kachari community, the earliest migrants into Assam, who entered the land from both the eastern and western borders. Since the 18th century, however, they have largely been clustered in the northern bank of the Brahmaputra valley. Traditionally, they are practitioners of the Bathou religion, but a form of Hinduism called Brahmaism is also practised by some of them. Christianity was also introduced among them by the missionaries.

The Dimasas also belong to the larger Kachari community, which consists of 18 ethnic sub-groups. However, since the term Kachari is considered derogatory, the appellation has now been abandoned. Like the Bodos', their language is also of Tibeto-Burman origin. Many Dimasas have adopted Hinduism but their indigenous beliefs and practices are also very much alive. They are mostly clustered in and around the present Dima Hasao district, formerly known as the North Cachar Hills district. The name 'Cachar' no doubt derives from the Kachari kingdom of medieval Assam, to which the Dimasas as well as the Bodos trace their origin. Following the Bodo Movement for statehood, the Dimasas have also been raising the demand for a separate state. Like most ethnic communities of Assam, they also raised insurgent armies since the 1990s, which subsequently broke into various factions and sub-groups. Currently, they have their own autonomous council.

Adjacent to Dima Hasao is the home of the Karbis. Formerly known as the Mikirs, the Karbis are mostly concentrated in the hill district of Karbi Anglong which has an autonomous council since 1951. Insurgency in demand of statehood has been a part and parcel of Karbi life since the late 1980s. Of Tibeto-Burman origin, the Karbis are surmised to have entered Assam in ancient times through Central Asia. At various times in history, they have been subjects of the Kachari, Jaintia and Ahom kingdoms and it is said that they were driven into the hills and forests of Karbi Anglong during the infamous Burmese invasion of Assam. The Karbis who stayed behind and continue to live in the plains are known as Dumrali. The village headman of a Karbi village wields immense power over the community. The community still has a king whom they respect and a parliament that selects the king.

The Rabhas are also a Kachari tribe of Tibeto-Burman origin. They have close affinity with the Koch community of Assam and West Bengal. Some of them are also found in neighbouring Meghalaya in the Garo Hills. Although they have their own dialects—like Rongdani and Maituri—a majority of the Rabhas in Assam speak Axamiya. Some also speak Bengali and/or Garo. Mostly Hindus, some animistic beliefs have, however, survived among them. A small proportion of the Rabhas have also embraced Christianity. Since 2000, the Rabhas have had their own autonomous arrangement—the Rabha Hasong Autonomous Council—but the political and militant struggles for more substantive powers of self-determination are still on among the community.

6. Ahom

Life inside a gourd

*P*ha is the Supreme Being. Before the process of creation began, Pha had no form, just light. From this light the first shapes emerged, even Pha's own contours, and the water and the earth and everything in it, and the sun and the moon and the stars and all the other heavenly bodies.

Many communities in the world believe that their present civilization was born after the destruction of an older one. The Ahoms also attribute their origin to the aftermath of one such act of destruction. They say that once, the sun became intensely hot. It sent down its fierce rays upon the earth and scorched almost all living beings on it to death. The earth itself cracked up in places and from these cracks, there poured out a huge deluge of boiling water. So great was the volume of this water that it inundated the entire earth. The humans, animals or plants and organisms that the sun's fierce rays did not burn to ashes were swept away by the boiling waters it caused to flow over the surface of the earth.

Only one man survived, and a cow. The old man was known as Thaolipling. He and the cow hid themselves in a boat made of stone which protected them from the heat and the flood. This boat floated on the boiling water and finally reached Ipa. Now Ipa was a high mountain range far away to the northeast, and Thaolipling was a wise old man. When he saw that the stone boat had set them down on the summit of Mount Ipa, the old man thought to himself, 'This is as good a place as any to ensconce ourselves till the waters subside. If we are to survive the flood, we have to stay on high ground. Hereabouts, it doesn't get any higher than this.'

His wisdom thus saved two lives, but all the rest perished. When the great flood receded, the old man could see the devastation it had left behind below his perch on the mountain. The dead bodies of human beings, animals and other living things were strewn all over. Even as he helplessly watched the remnants of life on earth lying here and there, he could see that they were all starting to fester and rot. An evil smell started emanating from these festering carcasses and it started creeping upwards. The smell travelled even beyond the old man's mountain and reached the abode of the gods.

The gods were disgusted with the smell. 'What an obnoxious odour this is!' they roared. 'We cannot have this stench prevailing on earth and plaguing our senses this way. We have to get rid of it somehow.'

After some discussion, they decided to send down to earth a huge fire to burn the rotting remains of life there. The fire was so furious that it burnt everything in its way. The immense amount of heat that it gave off soon became too much to bear for the old man. As the fire approached nearer, Thaolipling began to worry, 'This blaze has razed everything in its way. It is a good thing for the earth, because it will clean her of the impurities that now plague her. All these dead bodies need to be removed, but I am not dead yet. What about me? And this cow? We are alive yet, and this fire will surely kill us as well, for it knows not how to discriminate between the living and the dead. It knows only to annihilate everything in its path.'

In the end, the old man decided that his life was more precious than that of the cow and he must save his skin somehow, even if it was at the cost of his companion: 'My dear friend, we have been through many calamities together and survived. But now it is time for both of us to perish, or for one to survive. And if I am to survive, you must die.'

The shrewd old man once again survived another act of god through his resourcefulness. He slew the cow and climbed inside its carcass. The thick hide of the cow, he knew, would protect him from the blaze.

While he thus hid himself, he found inside the cow's body a pumpkin seed. He picked up this seed and held it in his hand till he could climb out once again. As he bid his time, he could feel the heat gradually subsiding. He realized that the fire was losing its intensity. 'It is only a matter of time now before it dies out completely. I must be ready to climb out when it does,' Thaolipling mulled to himself.

When he finally thought it safe to climb out, he found the earth cleansed of all the dead bodies and rotting flesh. It looked pristine, and also, a little barren. He then remembered the pumpkin seed he held in his hand and decided, 'The earth must have living beings on it again. I have seen this earth populated by all manner of living creatures. This barrenness saddens me. I must do something about it.'

And he planted the pumpkin seed in the undisturbed ground.

He watched as the seed germinated and tended to it as it eventually grew into a big tree. This tree, to his surprise, threw out four branches. Each of these four branches pointed to one of the four points of the compass.

The old man, Thaolipling, watched as the northern branch of the tree he had planted withered and died from sheer cold. Then he looked towards the southern branch and saw that it had fallen into the fire—the remnants of which were still burning here and there. He directed his sight now to the western branch, but even as he watched the remnants of the last of the waters of the great flood came and washed it away. Only the eastern branch remained.

Thaolipling watched with joy as this branch grew and flourished. It gave him great satisfaction to see, one day, that this branch had also started flowering. 'If it is flowering it will surely bear fruit,' he said to himself and in due course of time, when the flower had withered away, the eastern branch produced a giant gourd.

What was amazing about this gourd was not just that it was huge in size. The really remarkable thing about it was that its insides were filled chock-a-block with human beings of all shapes and sizes, every kind of animal, birds, fishes and plants, creepers and trees that could populate the earth once more.

But, of course, no matter how big a gourd grows, it cannot comfortably house so many creatures inside it. So its inhabitants soon became restless. Because they were packed so closely together inside the gourd, they started squirming to get out. Only, there *was* no way out for them. What a clamour they created when they realized they were all trapped inside! 'We are all going to perish here', they cried. 'Somebody help us out!'

As their clamour rose, their struggles increased. So loud did their cries ring out that they soon reached the ears of Lengdon, the almighty god. 'What is all this commotion?' he enquired.

Nobody in heaven knew. So Lengdon decided to send a messenger down to earth to find out. He sent Panthoi.

When Panthoi descended to earth, he was led to the tree by the cries of the living creatures trapped inside the gourd. He heard their laments and their desperate pleas for help and reported these to Lengdon when he returned once more to heaven.

'I must do something about this then,' determined Lengdon. 'Those poor creatures must be released and allowed to roam free on earth. They will populate the earth once more.'

So saying, he directed his eldest son, Aiphalan, to go down to the gourd-bearing tree and put the living things out of their misery. 'Go there, my son,' he directed, 'and free those creatures. They cannot find a way out of the gourd and only you can make a way for them. Use your lightning bolts and carve them an escape route.'

But when Aiphalan came to earth and prepared to execute his father's command, a big problem arose. To break open the gourd and set them free, Aiphalan would have to direct his lightning bolt at some point on the surface of the gourd. This would mean that whatever creatures were taking shelter in that part of the gourd would be annihilated by the lightning. So when he raised his lightning shaft for the first time, he heard the human beings scream out, 'Do not kill us, Aiphalan! We want to live. If you break open another part of the gourd, we can survive and proliferate. We will then settle down in different parts of the world and cultivate.'

Hearing their entreaties, Aiphalan decided to spare them. This time, he directed his lightning shaft at yet another part of the gourd. But in this part, the cattle were waiting to clamber out. 'Do not kill us, Aiphalan. If you let us live, we will go with the humans and help them in their cultivation. They will need us for ploughing their fields. You cannot kill us!' they pleaded.

Aiphalan spared them as well, but every time he tried to strike his lightning at some part of the giant gourd, some other creature would cry out and beseech him not to annihilate them. 'How can I do my father's bidding if all creatures cry to be spared? There is no way but to use my lightning to carve an escape route. How do I solve this dilemma unless somebody is willing to bear the brunt of the bolt?' he despaired.

In the end, Thaolipling came to his rescue, and hence, to the rescue of all the living beings inside the gourd. He was sitting at the point in the gourd where the flower had dried off. It was as good an entry point into the gourd as any, but to open the entrance, he would have to be removed. So he thought about it for a while. Then he told the god Aiphalan, 'I am an old man. I have lived my life well, and I have survived enough calamities in my life. I have escaped death many times, but now I think that if I can embrace death so that other living creatures can survive, my life will have ended well. As it is, life on earth as I knew it has been destroyed. If this is to be a new beginning, maybe I should allow the old life to end with me.'

So he decided to sacrifice himself for the sake of renewed life on earth. 'But,' he added, 'I have one condition. Human beings must remember with gratitude what I have done for them. They must worship me for my sacrifice forever afterwards. And they must offer me feasts.'

'We agree, we agree!' cried out the humans eagerly from the belly of the gourd. And to this day, they worship the man who saved them.

So there was nothing left for Aiphalan to do but to direct his fiery missile towards where the old man, Thaolipling, sat. As soon as the lightning struck the mouth of the gourd, the old man died but the gourd split open. Out spilled all the human beings, animals, trees and everything else that was soon to populate earth.

Having been cooped up inside a gourd for so long, however, none of the living beings knew what they were supposed to do now that they were out in the open. So it fell upon Aiphalan to teach them everything.

He taught the men different occupations and told them to go forth and prosper. He showed the birds how to build their nests and bade them live on the branches of trees, to chirp, to fly and be happy. He also showed all the other animals how to fend for themselves and survive in the wild.

7. Bodo

This bird brings death

All the shallow lands, the rivers and the streams, the ponds and the wells fill up with water in springtime. For it is in the spring that the rains are bounteous. They pour down on the parched earth and give new life to all the flora and fauna of the land. The fish, particularly, multiply abundantly in the rain water that gathers together, flowing down from all directions, and falling eventually into the fields and wetlands.

As the fish swarm everywhere, the hearts of the humans are filled with joy, for now they can catch the abundant fish and have a good meal to fill their bellies. They go out in ones and twos, or in big groups, singing and making merry, to catch the fish with nets and with various other fishing implements made of bamboo and cane. The whole year round, they craft these implements with their own hands and weave the nets waiting for the rainy season, expecting another good harvest of fish, and a good feast every now and then, as long as the gods rain down their munificence upon the earth.

The people who go out to fish in the wetlands and watery fields sing songs and trade stories as they spread their nets or lay their traps. The fish that fall into these traps or are entangled in the nets are then collected in bamboo or cane creels. When enough fish have been caught, the village folk make their way back homewards, anticipating a good meal which they will eat heartily.

But all is not song and dance about the fishing season. And at the end of each fishing trip, there might not be a full meal waiting. Because fishing is fraught with peril, and peril of a kind that human beings cannot easily overcome. After all, it is not only humans who await so eagerly the rainy season and all the fish it brings—there are evil spirits as well who love eating fish. Only, they are not as adept as humans in catching them. So when the human beings have caught their fish and put them in their creels, these malevolent spirits creep up to the fisher folk and gobble up the heads of all the fish they have caught. Sometimes, some of them also harm the humans who are out fishing, and that is a terrible thing.

In order that their efforts not go in vain, humans have, over the years, devised ways and means to outwit the spirits. It is common knowledge that evil spirits are afraid of iron. Therefore, these wily humans put pieces of iron inside their creels when they go fishing. That way, both the fish and the fisher folk remain safe. Iron, therefore, is a very valuable metal for human beings.

But one young man once destroyed a few pieces of iron meant for protection and that led to his gory end. An evil spirit sever his head, just as spirits are wont to sever the heads of fishes. It happened like this:

Two brothers lived together in a certain village. The elder brother was an accomplished hunter and would often go out into the forest to hunt. Sometimes, he would be gone for days on end and would come back with good game that the entire family would feast on for a long while.

One day, he was preparing to go out on one of his hunting expeditions when his younger brother came up to him and said, '*Ada*, I want to come hunting with you. How is it that you never allow me to accompany you on these hunting trips?'

The elder brother replied, 'You are young and simple. There are a lot of dangers in the forest. I am old enough and skilled enough to face these perils. But you have not been trained yet. How can I take you with me and put you in harm's way?'

But the younger brother was adamant. 'I am not so young, and I am fully aware of the dangers. I can do anything that you can. You have to let me come with you,' he persisted.

He was so insistent that in the end, the elder brother agreed to take him along. The next morning, at the break of dawn, the two of them set forth for the forest in search of game to hunt. They roamed about in the forest all day long but had very little luck. All the game escaped them.

As night drew nearer, they realized that if they did not find anything soon enough, they would have to spend the night in the forest itself. The elder brother wanted to avoid this as the younger one was with him. But it was not his lucky day. In the end they were forced to sleep in the forest. 'If we have to spend the night here, we have to be careful. Let us cook whatever little we have caught. Make a fire. Meanwhile, I will make our sleeping arrangements.'

After eating their meagre meal, the two brothers lay down to sleep. The elder brother had made the arrangements so that they would both be safe during the night. He was especially mindful that the younger one would not be exposed to any harmful creatures while they slept. He had already placed pieces of iron in the pouches that both of them carried. After that, he had placed a long log on the ground. He said to his brother, 'You sleep by the log, and I will sleep on your other side. That way you will be in the middle, and safe.'

The younger brother did as he was told and they were both soon fast asleep.

The forest is the hunting ground not just of human beings, but also of the malevolent spirits. Only, the spirits hunt by night. The elder brother who would often come to the forest and knew its secrets was well aware of the fact. But the younger one was not. So when the evil spirits came out to hunt in the middle of the night and started shouting and shrieking, he woke up.

'Who is making all this infernal noise?' he muttered. 'I can't sleep with all this noise about me.'

In the meantime, the iron pieces in the brothers' bags had begun to do their job, which was to ward off the spirits. When they heard the evil beings shrieking and roaming around in the vicinity of where the brothers slept, they started to shout and scream back, threatening the spirits to stay away from the humans they protected. This frightened the spirits and they dared not approach the brothers.

But when the younger brother woke up, he followed the source of the commotion and found that much of the screeching was being done by the iron pieces in his bag. He thought they were making all that noise for no reason at all. He did not know that they were actually protecting him.

Groggy from sleep and angry at being woken up after a long day trekking through the forest, the younger brother then proceeded to pick out the iron pieces from his bag. He then flung them into the fire that the elder brother had kept burning to keep the wild animals away. As soon as the fire consumed the iron, the commotion died down. The younger brother was very happy. 'How strange of my brother to make me carry all these iron pieces in my bag! They are not just heavy but also make so much noise. Good thing I got rid of them. Now I can sleep in peace.'

Little did he know though that his peace was going to be very short-lived. For no sooner had he lain down again on the ground than the evil spirits came rushing at him and severed his head from his body. Then, leaving both head and body lying on the ground, they departed.

When the elder brother woke up the next morning, he could not believe his eyes. 'How could this happen? I did everything that could be done to protect my brother and yet, the spirits came and cut his head off! Oh my dear brother, what did you do to bring this upon yourself?'

When he looked around and saw the iron pieces in the fire, however, he could easily surmise what might have happened. He then approached his dead brother and started shedding tears over the pieces of his body left behind by the spirits.

Suddenly, to his greatest amazement, the head started talking to him. '*Ada*', it said to him, 'don't leave me here, please. If you do, the wild animals will eat me up. I want to go home. Please take me home with you and let me see my sister-in-law once again.'

The younger brother had been quite attached to his sister-in-law, and knowing this, the elder brother decided to comply with the request of the talking head. He picked up the head and wrapped it in a piece of cloth. Then, he flung the head across his back and with a heavy heart, started on his long trek back home.

But as he walked on, he started feeling a strange sensation on his back. Suddenly, the head bit him. And then, it bit him again. No matter how hard he tried, the elder brother could not stop the younger brother's severed head from biting his back. Very soon, his back was filled with bite marks and he was bleeding very badly. Finally, he decided to dump the head and go fetch his wife instead. 'I have to keep my brother's last wish. But I cannot very well carry his head this way all the way home. This evil head will be the death of me if I carry it any further.'

So saying, the loving elder brother placed the head in the hollow of a tree and went on alone towards their village to fetch his wife. When he reached there, he narrated the entire story to his family and told his wife, 'Hurry up, let's go into the forest to the place where I left his head. He wanted to see you one last time, and we must respect his last wish.'

The poor sister-in-law was much grieved because she too had loved the young man as if he were her little brother. But on her husband's bidding, she immediately set forth with him to see the severed head.

When the two of them reached the spot, however, they saw that the hollow of the tree where the elder brother had placed the head was now empty. 'What could have happened?' the elder brother started contemplating.

'I am sure this is where I had left it. Where is it gone? Oh, my brother, why did I leave you here?' he lamented now.

Just then, however, a bird perched on one of the branches of the tree under which they stood, started crying out, 'Oh, my brother, take me home, I want to see my sister-in-law! Oh, my brother, take me home, I want to see my sister-in-law!'

Both husband and wife knew then that the dead brother had turned into this bird, and after shedding many tears and grieving over his loss, they slowly made their way home.

It is believed that this bird continues to cry this way even today. And when it does, some evil and a certain death follows.

8. Dimasa

Food fit for demons

Before the world was created, and all the living beings in it, there was only water, water everywhere. And in the midst of all the water, there was an island. On this island dwelt Banglaraja, the god who was to become the creator, and his wife, the goddess Arikidima.

The urge to procreate manifested itself in Banglaraja one fine day. 'This is a barren world,' he contemplated. 'I need to create a universe with living beings, with trees and birds and bees and animals.'

And he decreed, 'They shall all be my progeny and shall inhabit the new world that I and Arikidima will now create.'

So he mated with Arikidima, and in due course of time, his consort became pregnant. Eventually, when her due date approached, the goddess went to the edge of the water and laid seven eggs. She then settled down to hatch the eggs one by one.

The first egg that hatched gave birth to the first god, Brai Sibrai, whom the Hindus know as Siva. He was wondrous to look at, with his matted hair and somber air. When Arikima saw him, she was filled with pride.

Her pride only grew as she watched the five of the remaining eggs burst open one by one and out of each stepped a splendid god. Thus Brai Sibrai now had five more gods as his younger siblings: Waraja, Duraja, Naikoraja, Bongyong Braiyung, and last of all, Mongrangraja or Hamiyadao.

Arikidima then waited for the last egg to hatch, but even though she waited for a long, long time, the last egg did not break. 'What is this?' she wondered. 'All the other eggs have produced these fine sons of mine. And yet, the last one does not open. How much longer can I wait by this desolate shore?'

Finally, thinking it futile to wait any longer, she slowly made her way back home.

As time passed, the six brothers grew up, each with his individual traits. Brai Sibrai, for instance, developed a serious bent of mind. But his youngest brother, Hamiyadao, turned out to be a restless young man, recalcitrant and headstrong.

As it happens with all siblings who grow up together with widely divergent natures, a strong rivalry started brewing between the six sons of Arikidima and Banglaraja too. They started questioning as to who was the most superior of the six.

'I am superior to you,' each one said.

'You are inferior to me,' they all sneered at each other.

But, of course, there was no settling the dispute as none of them would bow down. Finally, they went to their mother.

'Our mother, who gave us life, you tell us who among us is the most accomplished, the greatest of the lot,' they pleaded.

But Arikidima was a mother like any other mother, and she could not take sides. Like all mothers, however, she was also very astute and knew who could settle the dispute once and for all. She told them, 'My sons, it is not for me to decide who among you is the best and who is the worst. For me, you are all the same. But I can gather that your differences have reached the very peak. There must be a settlement, and that is for sure. So I delegate the task of deciding on this issue to your eldest brother, Brai Sibrai.'

Unable to disregard his mothers' wishes, Brai Sibrai called a meeting of all six brothers on the water's edge, where they were all born. After they had all gathered, he tried to reason with them, 'My dear brothers, we are all offspring of the same father, born of the same mother, on the same day. We were separated in birth only by a few moments. We entered this world almost at the same time. And we grew up together, on the same island, under the same circumstances. So why this quarrel? How can we settle this dispute of who is superior or inferior based on the circumstances of our birth or the way we've lived our lives?'

But, of course, reasoning was not to be enough for the siblings at this point. Sensing the futility of such an endeavour, Bria Sibrai finally said, 'Let us then have a test. We shall put our individual skills and acumen to test. Whoever wins the test will be accepted as being superior to the others.'

And he asked his brothers, 'Are you agreeable to this?'

The brothers all being agreeable, Brai Sibrai now announced: 'Let us each one pick up a clod of earth from this water's shore. We can then throw it with all our might. Whoever can fling the clod of earth farthest into the water will win the contest, and all the rest of us will have to accept his superiority.'

When they had all picked up their own clods and the contest was about to begin, Brai Sibrai said, 'See that banyan tree there, beyond the waters? Whoever can send his clod flying nearest to that tree will be the winner.'

Now Hamiyadao, always the troublemaker, had been behind most of the discontent that had been brewing for so long between the brothers. He considered himself to be the most superior of all and wanted to prove himself as such. Therefore, when Brai Sibrai now called out, 'One, two, three,' he did not even wait for his eldest brother to finish counting. He let go of his missile before anybody else could. However, it travelled a very short distance and fell 'plop!' into the water limply. Seeing his dismal performance, all his brothers burst out laughing.

'Serves you right,' they said, 'for being in such a tearing hurry. You could at least have waited for Brai Sibrai to finish counting till three!'

This embarrassed Hamiyadao no end, and in his shame and mortification, he went and hid himself behind some stones.

It was now the turn of the other brothers to display their prowess. None of them could, however, send their clods of earth beyond the water. Finally, Brai Sibrai stood up and took his place. He would have to throw now. Just like his brothers had done before him, he bent down to pick up some earth from the water's edge. But being smart as well as strong, he used his quick wit and also dug up a beetle along with the earth. This beetle he tied to the clod in his hands and then, 'One, two, three!' he flung it across the waters. Halfway across, the clod was losing momentum and falling when the beetle started flapping its wings. And it was the beetle that carried the clod across the rest of the distance and deposited it under the banyan tree across the waters.

The brothers, of course, did not know about Brai Sibrai's little trick. They willingly accepted his superiority. 'He has done what none of us could,' they admitted.

But Hamiyadao did not give up so easily. He started grumbling. 'No, no, this will not do. We have to have a rematch. Brai Sibrai's clod of earth looked much too light—who knows if that made it fly farther? It also looked too dark to me. There is no telling whether he had flung a stone instead of a clod of earth. I cannot accept his victory.'

This set the other brothers thinking and soon enough, they also joined in the chorus for a new test, a fresh evaluation of skills. Brai Sibrai had no choice but to yield.

After thinking for a while, he went and fetched six javelins for the six contenders. He said, 'This should be our final test. Each one of us will throw a javelin. Please examine them well before we proceed.'

So saying, he turned towards his youngest brother and handed him his javelin. 'Since you started this, you should be the first one to prove yourself. Throw it. Let us see how far it goes.'

But once again, Hamiyadao could hardly send his javelin flying beyond a few paces from where they stood. And none of the other brothers could also fare any better than the first time.

So once again, it was Brai Sibrai's turn to prove himself. This time, he picked up a thin *karsala* snake, quickly, so that his brothers did not even see him do it. Just as swiftly, he tied it around his javelin and let it fly. Once again, the javelin started losing momentum halfway across and falling when the snake started stretching its body. And it was the snake that carried the javelin across the rest of the distance and deposited it under the banyan tree across the waters.

Finally, the brothers had to concede defeat. They admitted that Brai Sabrai was indeed better than them. This was how the contest between them was settled.

As they turned homewards, they suddenly heard strange noises coming out of the last unhatched egg that Arikidima had laid on the shore, the one that had not hatched for all this time. Alarmed, they said to each other, 'Something weird is happening here. What are all these thumping, tearing and jumping noises all about? We must tell our mother about this. She will be the best person to decide what needs to be done.'

So they all ran back to their mother. But Hamiyadao was not like the rest of his brothers, and he did not have the patience to hang around waiting for Arikidima to be informed. Who knew how long she would take to come down, or if she even would come down to the shore at all? He desperately wanted to know what was inside that egg and why—whatever it was—was raising all that commotion. 'I have to take matters into my own hands,' he decided and picked up a pebble. He struck the egg with the pebble and made a crack in the shell.

No sooner had he done that when out poured a number of strange beings. They were all misshapen and unsightly, and Hamiyadao immediately knew that they were *jakhas* and *rakhaxs*— demons of all shapes and sizes.

As soon as they stepped out of the egg, they laid their eyes on Hamiyadao and rushed at him. 'We will devour you now!' they shrieked.

'Oh Mother, oh Mother, what have I done!' cried Hamiyadao and fled from there. He kept running till he reached the place where Arikidama stood. He rushed into her arms and begged her to protect him.

When Arikidama saw the demons rushing towards her, she raised her hand and shouted at them, 'Stop right there! Why are you charging at your brother that way? What do you want?'

In reality, the demons were all hungry. They had not had anything to eat for a long time now. They had to be fed. They clamoured and cried, 'We are hungry. Give us meat. We want raw meat. Or the heart of a child. Or let us eat ourselves. We are famished, Mother!'

Now, even though they were all evil beings, Arikidama was still their mother. And as a mother, she could not ignore their pleas. She had to feed her young ones. She was at her wit's end, however, as to how to do that. She knew Brai Sibrai was a god of unparalleled grandeur, and humans would worship him and make sacrifices to him and give him all kinds of offerings. Who would do the same for the demons?

She thought and she thought till in the end, she had an idea. She realized that humans would also make offerings out of fear, in hopes of appeasing evil spirits and all kinds of diseases. Therefore, she created a number of ailments like fever, headache, cramps in the belly and so on and so forth and made her demon children responsible for them.

Then she said to them, 'I gave birth to you. Now it is my duty to see that you are well provided for. However, you will not be welcomed into any human home, nor will you be offered food with gladness. Therefore, you must force people to make offerings to you. In other words, you will have to find your own food.

'Listen carefully, for now I shall tell you how you will go about doing it. You will have to dwell in dark and inauspicious places, like the eaves of houses, tall trees, ditches and streams. If anybody should give you offence, posses the human being who is responsible. Out of fear, they will then offer you ducks and fowls. Only when they have fed you to your heart's content should you leave them and return to your dwelling. As your mother, this is all the advice I have to give you so that you can survive in this world.'

Convinced now that they would be able to satiate their hunger, the demons finally left for the various abodes assigned to them by their mother. Till this day, they live in all inauspicious and ill-omened places. They cause sickness and bad health among humans, who then have to appease them with food fit for the demons.

9. *Karbi*

Scattering of seeds

$\mathcal{I}$n the beginning, there were the gods. There were no human beings, nor an earth for them to call home. Two of the gods, Hemphu and Mukrang, started talking among themselves one fine day. They said to each other, 'We are all alone in eternity. It does get lonely at times, no?'

Finally, they decided to create the world and all the creatures to inhabit it. But they determined to proceed with caution, 'Let us take it slow and easy. We will start creating things one by one. We will see how it goes.'

So they marked out a few boundaries to demarcate their

creative domains and then set out on the task of creation, bringing to life one kind of living thing after another. They planted four big pillars in the four directions to fix these boundaries. Next, they borrowed six of their mother's hairs to fix the pillars in place so that the pillars would not move or fall down.

The next step was to grow things. They went looking for seeds which would produce the earth, but could find none. 'What are we going to do now?' they lamented. 'Here we have set ourselves the task of creation and we can't even create the first thing on our list! This is more difficult than we thought. Perhaps it is not something we two can do on our own. Perhaps we should seek help from the other gods.'

In despair then, they went to each of the hundred other gods and their hundred wives. They were only too willing to help. They all thought creating a new world was a great idea. So all two hundred of them, along with Hemphu and Mukrang and their two wives, put their heads together and tried to find a solution to the problem. Finally, they all came to the decision that one of the wives should be sent to the god Hajong. She would then beg him for some earth.

The task fell upon the god Bamon's wife who set out in search of Hajong. When she found him, she stated her mission, and pleaded, 'Please help us out. We have to have these seeds to produce the earth and only you have a stock of them.'

Hajong, however, refused to give her any earth. He already had a world unto himself and did not want any competition or duplication. 'I am sorry,' he said. 'But I can't help you here.'

He sent her away and gave her nothing.

As she was returning home dejected, Bamon's wife suddenly saw some wormcast on the roadside. She picked it up and hid it in her bosom. 'Surely this will come in handy somehow!' she reasoned to herself as she picked it up.

When she reached home, she laid it out for all to see. They were all happy that they at least had some earth now. But another problem faced them even at this juncture. 'So we have some earth here. But on its own it is useless. Worms have to work on it to create more out of it. It will only multiply with the worms' help. Else, it is only a clod of earth,' they said.

So they sent for Helong Recho, the king of the earthworms. He willingly complied and agreed to meet them.

When Helong Recho reached the hundred and four gods and goddesses, he was asked to enter the small mound and work it up. As he did so, the earth began to expand till it became a huge heap. This huge heap kept expanding as the king of the earthworms continued to work on it. Little by little, as the gods and their wives looked on, the earth that is our home started taking shape.

At this early stage though, the earth was very soft and moist. It was so wet and soggy that no one could walk upon it. None of the gods dared to place their feet upon the earth as it took shape at that initial stage.

'We cannot leave it in this condition,' they all agreed. 'What good would our creation do to us if we can't even step on it?'

To solve the problem then, Kaprang, the blacksmith, was called in to make the earth firmer so that the gods could walk upon it. When he heard about the situation, he came willingly to the gods' aid. He took out his bellows and produced such a strong wind that the soft mud was soon dry and it solidified into earth.

Once that was achieved, the gods said to each other, 'We should have living things growing on this earth.' So they decided it was time to grow plants on the earth.

But even after searching far and wide for the seeds of plants, they failed to get any. After racking their brains over their situation, they finally determined to send the goddess Rekbepi in the western direction. The place she was sent to in the west was by the great pillar that marked the place of the setting sun. As she prepared to leave, the gods and goddesses all instructed her, 'The Sun will help us here. Ask him for the seed. He will certainly give it to us.'

But Rekbepi did not want to go on her journey alone. So she asked Rek-kropi to go with her to the western boundary and the two together went to plead with the Sun. The Sun was quite co-operative and so the two goddesses obtained the seeds. They were very happy to have accomplished the task assigned to them by their fellow gods and, packing all the seeds in their bamboo baskets, they started on their journey back. When they reached the banks of the Kolong river (in present-day Nagaon), however, the *sinam*, or head-strap, which held the baskets on their heads broke, and the winds scattered the seeds all over the surface of the earth. This is how different plants, herbs and trees started growing in different parts of the world.

After the seeds of plants and all other green leafy living things had been sown thus, the gods decided it was time for the creation of animals. This, the gods decided to do themselves. Hemphu and Mukrang led the group and they were helped a lot in their endeavour by Pithe and Pothe ('great mother' and 'great father'). The four together created the elephant first of all. 'This creature will be a servant to humans,' they decreed.

Then they forged the tiger and they said to him, 'You will devour the wicked. That shall be your task.' Ever since, anybody who is killed by a tiger is thought to have committed some grave crime.

Now, having created the elephant and other animals to serve humans, they had necessarily to create the humans. So a great council was held. All two hundred and four gods and goddesses sat together and deliberated and ultimately decided to create a being called *arleng* (man). The first man to have ever been created was named Bamonpo.

So that Bamonpo would not be all alone, he was given two wives and a family. Of these two wives, one was Karbi and the other, Axamiya. For a long time, the first man had no issue. In desperation, his Axamiya wife finally bade him consult her elder brother. 'They say my brother understands all the secrets of nature. Maybe he can help us. There's no harm in trying.'

So Bamonpo paid his brother-in-law a visit. After he had stated the purpose of his visit, the brother-in-law instructed him, 'Go to my garden. There you will find an orange tree bearing fruit. Pick one for each of your wives, take them home and ask each of them to eat their fruit. Your problems will soon be sorted out.'

Bamonpo did as instructed and with his two oranges, he started on his homeward journey. It was a long journey and the day was hot. So on the way, he decided to cool himself off by taking a bath in a river. He placed the two oranges on the river bank and stepped into the water. But while he was bathing, a crow swooped down and carried away one of the oranges.

When Bamonpo returned from his bath, he saw he had lost the orange, and with a heavy heart, returned home to his wives. Since he had only one orange, he gave it to his Axamiya wife, whose brother had given him the fruit. She ate it and in due course, had a son named Saputi. This boy, however, grew up to be weak and puny. Around the same time that Saputi was born, the Karbi wife had also delivered a son whom she named Ram. She had picked up a piece of the orange peel that Bamonpo's Axamiya wife had discarded, and Ram was the result of that. Unlike his brother, Ram turned out to be strong and valiant. There was no demon or man on the face of the earth who would get into a fight with Ram and win. His exploits made him invincible, but that did not bring him much happiness, because Ram was lonely. He had not been able to find a wife for himself.

One day, he was out hunting. Before long, he felt thirsty. He climbed a tree to look for water and spotted a pool, at which he quenched his thirst. As he did so, he noticed something large and white nestling among the green grass by the pool. 'What is that?' he wondered. 'Maybe I should take a closer look.'

When he approached it, he saw that it was an egg. He delicately picked it up and put it in a basket and brought it home with him. And then, he forgot all about it.

Not long afterwards, though, he remembered and went to see what state it was in. To his utter surprise, he saw that the egg had broken. As he stepped forward to take a closer look, he saw a beautiful woman coming out of the shell. She was so beautiful that Ram was smitten. But then, so were the demons who tried to seize her and carry her off. The bold young man fought off all the demons, overpowered them and married the beautiful girl.

They lived together for long and bore many children. These children and their offspring together created a mighty race of men. Ram's name and fame spread all over the world. He and his descendants soon conquered most of the world and became its masters.

Power, however, is a heady thing. So much power made Ram's descendants intoxicated and, soon, they wanted to extend their mastery to the skies above. They began building a tall tower to reach the heavens. They decided to climb the tower and lay siege to the kingdoms of the gods and the demons.

'We have to do something to stop them,' the gods and the demons all cried in unison. 'These humans have mastered the earth. What if they have turned powerful enough to master the heavens as well? We cannot wait to have them reach our realm to find out.'

So saying, they smote the tower down, confounded their speech and scattered them to the four corners of the earth. So long as they were disunited, they would not be able to launch a combined attack on heaven. Thus, owing to the fear of the gods and the demons, clusters of human beings are found in different parts of the world. And they all speak different tongues.

10. Rabha

Music of the gods

Having created the earth and all the plants and trees and animals and birds in it, the creator decided it was time to educate the human beings he had placed amidst all this bounty. The best way to do it, he thought, was through song and dance.

There were three very renowned musicians in heaven at the time: Nolua, Cholua and Gondhosri. Although it would be a great loss for the heavenly beings, the creator thought that the humans on earth needed these three artistes more. So he summoned them to him one day and imparted to them all the teachings that he wished to pass on to the inhabitants of earth.

Once that was done, he said to them, 'You are all masters of the arts. Through these arts you must approach the people of the earth and win their confidence. Then you should live amidst them to impart to them my teachings as I have taught you now. So descend now to earth, but remember, you also have to be masters of your senses and emotions. Do not fall into any temptation while on earth. Or else, you will never be able to find your way back into heaven. You will be doomed to live among the mortals.'

Bowing to the creator's wish, the three musicians descended to earth. The place where they alighted, however, was desolate and uninhabited. So they started in search of a place where human beings lived. Their journey took them across many a hill, mountain top, and over rivers and dales but they did not meet any people. Tired and disheartened, they finally saw a stream beside a hill. It was a very warm day and so, they decided to rest there. But no sooner had they settled down than they realized they were not alone. They could hear human voices!

As they followed the sound of these voices, they came upon three girls bathing a little distance away. Unaware that they were being watched by three celestial beings, the girls had disrobed and walked into the stream. They were tired after the day's household chores and were therefore unwinding by frolicking about in the water. Their beauty, and the fun and laughter that they were sharing, mesmerized the three musicians.

'Surely there must be a human habitation nearby. These women are undoubtedly human, but ah, how beautiful they are! We had no idea that human beings could be so alluring, so fine-looking,' they said to each other. And as they continued watching the girls from where they hid behind a bush some distance away, the three heavenly musicians forgot about god's injunction. They gave in to temptation, they were smitten. And they started lusting after the mortal women.

In the meantime, the girls had finished bathing and were getting ready to return to their village. Suddenly, one of the musicians stepped out from behind the bush and asked them, just to be sure, 'Are you humans or divine creatures?'

The girls were startled and shocked into silence for quite some time. When they found their voices however, one of them replied, 'We are human beings. We live in that village over there. Who are you?'

Sensing that they had frightened the girls by their sudden appearance, the heavenly musicians now tried to allay their fears. 'We are also human', they said. 'Actually, we are travelling minstrels. We roam around from village to village teaching song, dance and music to people. We have reached here after a very long journey indeed, and we are very tired. Can we stay in your village for the night? We can teach your people our arts.'

The girls were quite excited when they heard this. They said, 'Our family will only be too happy to welcome you into our home. Why don't you come back to the village with us?'

So the three minstrels started walking towards the girls' village, deep in conversation with them. But the creator had already sensed the lust in their hearts, and he knew they had to be punished for having lost control over their emotions. Before they reached the village, therefore, a sudden force swooped down from heaven and swept the artistes away. They let out a loud cry each and flew away in three different directions. The girls looked on in great bewilderment and soon lost sight of them.

Frightened at what they had witnessed and much confused, the girls ran back to their village as fast as their legs would carry them. When they reached there, all the villagers gathered around them and wanted to know what had caused them so much terror. The terrible cries of the three minstrels still ringing in their ears, the girls then narrated to the villagers what had passed. The villagers went in search of the men—for they had claimed to be mortal—but could find not one of them.

Meanwhile, the creator had designed fitting punishments for each of the artistes. He turned Nolua into Nol (a species of bamboo) and bade him grow abundantly on the hill called Radang. Cholua, in his turn, was blown away to the hill called Kalapahar and transformed into Bazong (another species of bamboo). The last one of them, Gondhosri, was turned into a tree, also known as Gondhosri, on the hill called Nirgini-Sirgini.

Though many heard about the strange disappearance of the three musicians, no mortal man was aware of who they really had been and what fate had befallen them. Then one day, two brothers, Rondan and Chondan, both sons of Harikhetri, went on a hunting trip. Their search for game led them to Radang hill. There they roamed about looking for animals to hunt but no matter where or how hard they looked, they could find none. They were exhausted from walking about in the jungle the whole day and had determined to return when suddenly, they heard a melodious sound coming out from a clump of Nol bamboo nearby. '*Pe…pe…pe…,*' the sound flowed.

The brothers were intrigued and rushed nearer to the source of the sound. But when they approached, they were startled to hear the bamboo talking. It was addressing them saying, 'Fear me not, I am not Nol. I am Nolua really, a heavenly minstrel sent to this earth to teach humans the word of god through song and music. I sinned, though, and went against the wishes of the creator. That is why I am cursed and have to live the rest of my life as a clump of bamboo.

'However, I have to atone for my sins and follow god's will. I shall teach you therefore what I was sent to teach all humanity.'

So saying, Nolua taught the two brothers the art of making the flute and also the notes to tune them. This flute came to be known as Karanol. It was an amazing instrument and remarkable, with a length of six to seven feet and no holes.

The brothers were very thankful for the knowledge they had been imparted and they marked the bamboo that had spoken to them and taught them everything about the Karanol. Then they proceeded on their hunting expedition again.

Eventually, they reached Kalapahar. In that hill as well, they could find no animals to hunt. Once again, as on Radang hill, they heard a melodious sound emanating from a clump of Bazong bamboo. *'Dheti… hihiti.. .hit…hihi…hihiti…hit.'*

Once again, the brothers rushed nearer to the source of the sound in amazement. As on the earlier instance, when they approached, they heard the bamboo talking. It was addressing them saying, 'Fear me not, I am not Bazong. I am Cholua really, a heavenly minstrel sent to this earth to teach humans the word of god through song and music. I sinned, though, and went against the wishes of the creator. That is why I am cursed and have to live the rest of my life as a clump of bamboo.

'However, I have to atone for my sins and follow god's will. I shall teach you therefore what I was sent to teach all humanity.'

He then taught the brothers how to make the Badungduppa flute. He also taught them how to play it and gave them the notes they could play on it. The brothers were very thankful for the knowledge they had been imparted and they marked the bamboo that had spoken to them and taught them everything about the Badungduppa. Then they proceeded on their hunting expedition again.

After walking for a while longer, they reached Nirgini-Sirgini hill. Once again, as on Radang and Kalapahar hills, they heard a melodious sound, this time from a Gondhosri tree. *'Girim… girim… tan… girim… girim!'* the sound drummed.

Once again, the brothers rushed nearer to the source of the sound in amazement. As on the earlier instance, when they approached, they heard the tree talking. It was addressing them, saying, 'Fear me not, I am not a tree. I am a heavenly minstrel named Gondhosri sent to this earth to teach humans the word of god through song and music. I sinned, though, and went against the wishes of the creator. That is why I am cursed and have to live the rest of my life as a clump of bamboo.

'However, I have to atone for my sins and follow god's will. I shall teach you therefore what I was sent to teach all humanity.'

He then taught the brothers how to make the Kham. It is a kind of drum, six to seven feet long. He also taught them how to play it and showed them the beats they could play on it. The brothers were very thankful for the knowledge they had been imparted and they marked the tree that had spoken to them and taught them everything about the Kham.

This time they decided to return to their village. They realized they would not find any game on that particular hunting trip. When they reached their village, they narrated their experiences of the day. All the villagers were awed, and wanted to see for themselves the wondrous bamboo and the talking tree. So they asked Rondan and Chondan to lead them to the places where the three minstrels now lived. The two brothers complied and when the people reached the specific places, they cut down the Nol bamboo, the Bazong bamboo and the Gondhosri tree. Then, as instructed, they shaped the musical instruments and acquired the skills to play those instruments. Thus, god's words finally did come down to earth through music and songs.

Manipur

A brief note:

One of the few places in the Northeast to have come under the influence of Hinduism and/or Sanskritization in the pre-colonial era, Manipur was earlier known by various names: Meitrabak, Kangleipak or Meiteileipak. A princely state under the British, the controversial manner of its accession to the Indian Union left much scope for resentment among the people of the state and has resulted in a number of armed insurgencies that continue to rage even today. The ethnic diversity of Manipur is also a contributing factor in these armed militant movements—almost every ethnic group or sub-group in Manipur has militant armies and many factions claiming to represent them.

Of all the communities in Manipur, the Meiteis are the most dominant. They are mostly Hindus but the indigenous Sanamahi religion is equally revered. The Muslim Pangals are also Meiteis while the Bhamons are the non-Meiteis. These three groups share the valley area of the state. Christianity has a significant presence in both the valley and the hills of Manipur. The hills comprise 90 per cent of the land area of Manipur and they are occupied by the Naga, Kuki and other hill communities. The ethnic variety of the state is such that there are as many as 29 different dialects spoken there.

The Kukis have a significant presence in Manipur, but are spread out in many other parts of the Northeast including Assam, Nagaland, Tripura and Mizoram. They are also found in neighbouring Bangladesh and Burma. Like most of the other ethnic groups in the Northeast, the self-definition of the Kukis has also changed much over the many decades since joining the Indian Union, largely in response to prevailing political exigencies. There are many clans and sub-clans, tribes and sub-tribes included under the Kuki rubric, but their languages and dialects are all Tibeto-Burman in origin. The Kuki village community is highly organized and exerts control over the individual through the Semang (cabinet) and the Inpi (assembly).

The Maos are a Naga tribe inhabiting Manipur, mostly in the northern part of the state in Senapati district. They variously call themselves Memei or Ememei in their own language which is part of the greater Kuki-Chin-Naga language group of the Tibeto-Burman family. A Naga traditional belief holds that at one point in history, many Naga groups settled at a place called Makhel. These included the Mao, Poumai, Maram, Thangal, Angami, Chakhesang, Rengma, Lotha, Sema and the Zeliangrong. When various factors eventually forced them to disperse, they held an assembly at the foot of a wild pear tree and made a pact to come together one day. This pear tree, called the Chiitebu Kajii, is still held sacred, and Makhel and its surrounding areas continue to hold a central position in Mao culture.

The Meitei comprise nearly 60 per cent of the total population of Manipur although they occupy only about 10 per cent of the total land area—which comprises the valley. They have a glorious history which has been recorded in the *Puyas* or *Puwaris* (literally, stories about our forefathers) written under royal patronage by Maichous (Meitei scholars). Some of these are the *Ninghthou Kangbalon, Cheitharol Kumbaba, Ningthourol Lambuba, Poireiton Khunthokpa* and *Panthoibi Khongkul.* They are written in the ancient Meitei script which has now been revived after being replaced by the Bengali script in the 18th century.

Since the coming of Vaishnavite Hinduism into Manipur from neighbouring Bengal, a gradual process of Aryanization or Sanskritization of the culture and religion had set in. Revival of the indigenous belief systems, however, started with the growth of nativist sentiments in the recent decades.

A Naga tribe predominantly living in Manipur, the Tangkhuls are found mostly in the Ukhrul district of the state. They also have their ethnic kin living across the international border in Burma. The Tangkhuls of the hills and the Meiteis of the valley have shared a long history of co-operation as well as conflict over the centuries. The same fluctuations are noticeable even today. The many commonalities between the communities have not disappeared despite the fact that a section of the Tangkhuls has emotionally and politically aligned itself with the cause of the greater Naga movement for an independent country. Christianity is the most prominent religion among the Tangkhuls. The many Tangkhul tribes speak a variety of dialects, but they use the Hunphun (Ukhrul) dialect as a common language for communicating among themselves.

The Zeme, Liangmai and Rongmei Naga tribes are together known as the *Zeliangrong*. It is a fairly recent ethnonym, having been coined in 1947 at Imphal. It is actually an acronym of the prefixes of three words: 'Ze' from Zeme, 'Liang' from the Liangmai and 'Rong' from the Rongmei. The Zeliangrongs live mostly in and around the places where the territories of Assam, Nagaland and Manipur meet. In Manipur, they live in the hills— in the Tamenglong, Senapati and Churachanpur districts—as well as in the valley in the Jiribam subdivision of Imphal district. Like many other Naga groups, the Zeliangrongs also believe that they first settled in Makhel and dispersed thereafter. They speak dialects that are an offshoot of the language now spoken mostly by the Liangmais.

11. Kuki

Living, dying, loving

Nambong and Khupting were very much in love with each other. With every passing day, their love only grew stronger.

Kind-hearted Nambong had been orphaned at an early age, and he had always had to fend for himself. But he was strong, brave and hardworking and he managed very well for himself. He lived all alone in a small hut. He hoped that one day Khupting would come live with him and relieve him of his loneliness.

But Khupting's parents were vehemently opposed to their relationship. They looked down upon Nambong. They considered him to be inferior to them. Khupting's mother, especially, treated him very cruelly and insulted him on several occasions. She left no stone unturned to find ways to separate the two lovers.

However, it was not Khupting's parents who finally succeeded in separating the two lovers—it was cruel destiny.

Khupting suddenly fell extremely ill one day and she continued to be sick for a long time thereafter. Nobody, but nobody, could cure her of her strange ailment. Day by day, she grew weaker. With every passing week, she became more and more emaciated. In the end, she took to her bed.

When Nambong heard about Khupting's condition, he naturally wanted to see her and be by her side. The cruel parents, however, would not allow him inside the house. 'You cannot come anywhere near our daughter,' they told him when he came to request them to let him see her but once, and turned him away.

Disheartened, Nambong wandered about, pining away for his love, wishing he could do something to bring solace to her. He took to stealing up to Khupting's parents' house every morning before going out to work and peeping in from outside to see how she was doing. And when he saw her sorry state, he could do nothing but shed tears and cry over his cruel fate.

Now, every day when Nambong would thus stop by to secretly see how his beloved was doing, he would see her mother sitting in the house and crying. Every day, he would also hear her saying, 'If only somebody could cure my daughter! I would have rewarded them very handsomely. And if it were a man who could cure her, I would marry her off to him. If it were a woman, I would give her benefactress anything she wanted and remain forever bonded and grateful to her.'

After hearing her saying this over and over again, one morning, Nambong gathered the courage to show himself before Khupting's mother and take up her challenge. 'There will be no better chance to win Khupting's hand and her parents' approval at the same time', he thought. 'I should try and cure her myself.'

He stepped out of his hiding place and entered Khupting's house. Then, he addressed her mother and asked, 'Aunty, what is it you were just saying?'

Khupting's mother was startled to say the least. Then, when she thought Nambol might actually have heard what she had been saying, she decided to lie. She was afraid that if Nambong succeeded in curing her daughter, she would have to make good her promise. 'I wasn't saying anything,' she replied, 'I was just murmuring to myself.'

Dejectedly, Nambong had to leave the house. But he came back again the next day and waited for Khupting's mother to repeat her words. When she did, he showed himself to her as before and asked again, 'Aunty, what is it you were just saying?'

Once again, as she had done the day before, Khupting's mother lied. 'I wasn't saying anything,' she replied, 'I was just murmuring to myself and talking to the pots and pans and the fire and all.'

This happened every time for the next few days that Nambong asked her the same question. Try as he might, Nambol could not make the woman repeat her challenge in front of him, so that he might take her up on it and win his lover's hand in marriage. Every day, she had some deceptive words ready for him.

In the end, Nambong realized that he would never be allowed to see his ailing beloved, let alone try to cure her of her ailment. He therefore decided to make a statue of her and find solace in her image. Accordingly, he sculpted an image of Khupting out of honeycomb and placed it in his house. Now, whenever he felt like, he would speak to the statue. Soon, he also started carrying it around with him wherever he went.

Every disease has its own time-span. When its time is up, the person who had housed the disease for so long either grows healthy again, or her own time on earth expires. For Khupting, her disease took with it her life. She died after suffering from her strange ailment for a long long time.

Those who die pass on from one world to the other. But for those who continue to live in the world that the departed soul has left behind, life often becomes unbearable. When Nambong heard about Khupting's death, he was devastated to say the least. He was inconsolable with grief and continued to lament Khupting's death for a long time thereafter. He even stopped talking to other people. He picked up the statue of his lover that he had built from honeycomb and took it to the river one day. There, he sat on the bank and cried and cried over his loss. He remained in this state for the whole day till evening fell. Then, he left the statue on the river bank and made his way home.

Often thereafter, whenever he felt lonely, he would go back down to the river and sit by the statue. There, he would weep tears of grief and remember the happy times he had had with Khupting. This went on for a while till one fine day, he went to the river bank as usual but could not find the statue anywhere there.

For the entire day, he kept looking for the statue, searching hither and thither. He ran upstream and downstream, he looked in the thickets and the river bed, but the statue was nowhere to be found. 'Oh, my fate,' he lamented. 'The statue was all that I had left of Khupting and now, even that has been taken away from me!' And he started shouting up and down the river, 'Who has taken my statue? Who has taken my statue?'

Of course, there was no response from anyone, because there *was* no one around. Doubly dejected now, he was finally forced to go back home.

Now it so happened that after Khupting's death, her family finally realized their mistake at not letting her be with Nambong. They understood now, although very late, that Nambong had indeed loved their daughter deeply and truly. So they decided to be good to the young man now and make him a part of their family. Khupting had a sister named Selneng, and the parents now offered Selneng's hand in marriage to Nambong.

Nambong, however, would have nothing to do with Selneng. He had pledged his heart to Khupting, and even death could not change that. He did, of course, agree to go and see Khupting's family now and then, because that was one way, however tenuous, of still being in touch with his departed beloved. Being a kind-hearted young man, he also forgave Khupting's parents for all the ill treatment they had meted out to him while their daughter was alive and as the man who had loved their daughter, he tried to do his duty by them sincerely.

Once, Khupting's family wanted somebody to cut down the branches of a huge tree that stood beside their house. These branches had grown way too big and were threatening to crush the house if they ever broke or fell down. Khuting's father decided that Nambong was the best person for the job. But he did not dare ask him directly as he remembered with shame how his family members had all ill–treated the young man once. So he asked Khupting's mother to do it. She also refused. 'How can I ask him to do it?' she questioned her husband. 'We all treated him so shabbily not very long ago. We were so cruel to him while our daughter was alive. I dare not,' she declared.

But her husband was insistent. 'You have to do it,' he told her. 'Do it by any means possible.'

In desperation, the woman picked up a bundle of bamboo and went to the courtyard. There, she started cutting the bamboo poles into stripes, all the while waiting for Nambong to come by. When he did, he sat beside her and talked to her as he had become accustomed to of late.

'This is my chance,' she thought. 'I must engage him in conversation and when the time is right, ask him to do the job.'

So she started talking to him about this and that, but when the time came for Nambong to leave, she realized that she could not ask him to cut the branches of a tree for them. So she decided to let Selneng do the job.

Selneng also refused to ask Nambong directly to cut the branches of the tree. But when left with no choice, she decided to ask him indirectly, just like her mother before her. She therefore sat at the loom weaving and waiting for Nambong to come by. She said to herself, 'I must engage him in conversation and when the time is right, ask him to do the job.'

Soon enough, Nambong came by and when he saw her at the loom, he went and sat beside her and talked to her as he had become accustomed to of late.

'This is my chance,' thought Selneng. 'I am sure that by the time I have finished weaving all my threads, I would have convinced him to cut the branches of the tree for us.'

But again, like her mother before her, she could not bring herself to make the request. She finished weaving eventually and Nambong also stood up to go back home.

Selneng was distressed that she could not do her parents' bidding, but Nambong also was no fool. He had realized by now that Khupting's family wanted something from him and that had to be to cut the branches of the big tree beside the house. So he picked up his flute one day and climbed the tree. Then, he started cutting the big branches one by one.

As he did so, he kept saying to himself, 'When I cut each branch, it has to mean something. If the branches of this tree that I cut fall to the east, it must mean that there is someone in the east who loves me. If the branches of this tree that I cut fall to the west, it must mean that there is someone in the west who loves me.' And so he continued cutting branch after branch till his job was done. And then he went back home.

Khupting's family was of course overjoyed that Nambong had done the job without their having to ask him, and they tried to appease him all the more. But Nambong now realized that they only wanted to be on good terms with him because he was strong and useful around the house. Try as they might, Khupting's family could not make Nambong forget his dead lover.

Meanwhile, ever since Khupting's funeral, Nambong used to visit her burial place every day and place a bunch of beautiful flowers on it. He would collect these flowers himself and sit beside her resting place and pray for her there. This went on for a while when one day, all of a sudden, he found that the flowers he had placed there the previous day had vanished.

'Someone is stealing Khupting's flowers!' he thought in dismay. But he continued with his ritual anyway. And every day thereafter, he found the flowers missing in the same manner. After this had happened for quite some time, he thought he should find out who was behind it. So he cried out loud from where he stood beside Khupting's resting place, 'Who has taken away the flowers? Who has stolen my lover's flowers? Are you a human being or a devil? Tell me, tell me!'

There was, however, never any reply. In the end, he decided to find out for himself. So one day, with that purpose in mind, he placed the flowers as usual and prayed for Khupting as usual and then pretended to walk away as usual. In reality, however, he hid himself behind a clump of bushes and waited to see who would steal the flowers.

The whole day, nothing happened, and nothing happened for most of the night as well. Then, in the middle of the night, he finally saw a strange animal with a long tail making its way towards Khupting's burial place. He watched as the animal collected the flowers but when it turned to leave, Nambong suddenly jumped out of the bushes and caught hold of it.

'Who are you?' he demanded to know. 'Where have you come from? How dare you take away my lover's flowers?'

To his utter surprise, the animal replied, 'I am here only because Khupting has sent me to collect all these flowers which you intended for her anyway.'

This filled Nambong's heart with joy. 'What!' he exclaimed. 'She still remembers me? Does she miss me as much as I miss her? Please tell her I miss her so so much! But wait,' he suddenly thought of something. 'Can you take me to her instead? Maybe I can go and see her myself and tell her all these things myself?'

'No, no,' the animal replied. 'You cannot go to her. She is dead and in another world. You are still living. If you go to her, it will cause you much trouble.'

'I don't care,' cried the young man, who was suddenly seeing a glimmer of hope. 'I want to see Khupting again, no matter what price I have to pay for it!'

When the animal refused again, Nambong kept insisting till in the end, it took pity on him and relented. 'Catch hold of my tail then, and do not let go till we reach our destination. I shall have to fly you to where Khupting now stays. If you let go of my tail, you will fall down and surely die.'

'Thank you,' said the grateful lover. 'I shall do as you say. I shall do anything to just see her again.'

And so the two set out to where Khupting now stayed in heaven.

It was an incredibly beautiful moment when the two lovers were united once again. Their happiness at seeing each other once again knew no bounds and they were lost in each other for a long time thereafter, with not a thought about what would happen next. But there had to come a time when realization of their changed circumstances would set in, and when that time came, Khupting said to Nambong, 'As you can see, life out here is not at all like life on earth. This is the land of the dead. We who live here are the dead. But you are not dead yet. And if you stay with me, you might face many problems in adjusting with everything here. Much as I would love to hold on to you and never let you go, I know that you have to return and live on earth as a human being.'

Having found his lost lover after so long, however, Nambong was not ready to listen to reason. 'I do not want to go back to earth,' he replied adamantly. 'I love you very much, you know that. And I never ever want to go back to living without you. So I am going to stay back here with you.'

His insistence weakened Khupting's resolve and she finally had to allow him to stay on with her in the abode of the dead.

But as she had foretold, Nambong soon started facing many problems in adjusting to his new surroundings. Everything was so different in the abode of the dead that he was taken by surprise. One day, for instance, all the people in heaven went fishing. Khupting took Nambong along with her. When they reached the place where the fishes were to be caught, Nambong found that there were no fishes at all, just bamboo leaves. And the people of heaven were all catching these leaves and rejoicing. When they got back, they all fried the leaves and held a great feast and enjoyed themselves thoroughly. Only Nambong stood by, watching in amazement.

More amazement was in store for him the day the dead people went game-hunting. Nambong also joined them, expecting that this time, at least, he would be able to feast on real animal flesh— maybe the meat of some big animals like deer, tiger, elephant, or whatever—that they would catch in the forest. In the forest, however, he found only small insects, caterpillars, flies, and so on. In despair, he was returning home empty handed, when some caterpillars and flies fell on his way and bothered him. He slapped them dead and continued on his way back.

When he returned, the people of heaven asked inquisitively, 'Did you kill any animal today?'

'No, none,' he replied. 'All I saw were small insects, caterpillars and flies. They were bothering me, so I killed some of them on my way back.'

'Where are they? We want to see them,' they all exclaimed, and he was forced to lead them to the place where he had killed the caterpillars and flies. When they reached there, the people of heaven rejoiced and congratulated him on a fruitful hunting trip. For them, those small insects and bugs were like big animals. So they carried the dead caterpillars and flies back to their homes and once again, held a great feast and enjoyed themselves thoroughly. Once again, only Nambong stood by, watching in amazement.

There were many other such instances when Nambong felt totally out of place in the abode of the dead. Then came a great occasion for the people of heaven. It was a time when they watched a special game. It was a terrible game, full of gruesome fights and blood-shedding. It involved decapitation and killing and burning and other horrors which the living cannot even imagine, let alone watch being played out before their very eyes. And yet, for the people of heaven, it was just a game.

Khupting realized that it would be too much for Nambong. So she requested him not to attend the event. She warned him, 'You are a human being, you are still alive. This game is for the dead. The living cannot stomach the kind of horrors we the dead can. Therefore, I urge you not to go watch the game. Stay at home, do not venture out today. The shock might kill you.'

But just as he had been on several occasions earlier, Nambong was once again adamant. 'I will come with you,' he insisted. 'I will go wherever you go and I can tolerate anything that you can.'

So in the end, both of them went to see the ghastly game. But Khupting's warning had not been just empty words. It was indeed a game of horrors far more gruesome than any living creature can ever stand. Nambong fell down in a faint when he saw it. Finally, when he did regain consciousness, he realized that Khupting had been right all along, that the abode of the dead was not for him. When Khupting saw that he had regained consciousness, she said to him, 'I tried to warn you, didn't I? This game is only for the dead.'

'Yes, you are right,' he replied. 'You have been right all along. You are dead, and I am alive, and nothing can change that now. I should have allowed destiny to take its course, but now I do understand and maybe it is time for me to be heading back home, to earth.'

The two lovers shed many tears at their impending separation, but both knew that there were certain rules of the universe which everybody has to adhere to, no matter what. Otherwise, the consequences could be dire.

Finally, Nambong asked Khupting, 'What do I have to do to get back to earth?'

'Yes, you have to go back to earth, no matter what. But if you wish to come back to me sooner rather than later, ask the people to sacrifice a *chalong* flower for you. However, once you are back there again, if you want to stay on earth for as long as you have to, then ask them to sacrifice a pig for you.' So saying, she tearfully bid him goodbye.

Nambong then made his way back to earth, equally heartbroken. But he found that he did not want to live on without Khupting anymore. So instead of asking the people of the earth to sacrifice a pig for him, he asked them to sacrifice a chalong flower. When they did so, he died immediately and was sent straight to heaven. Both lovers were now united forever and forever afterwards, they lived together happily.

The Kuki people believe till today that Nambong and Khupting are together in heaven. When they see a full moon hidden by a cloud, they think it is a sign that Nambong is cutting the branches of a tree for Khupting in heaven.

12. Mao

How to outwit a tiger

Dzuliamosuro, the mystical woman, lived on earth at a time when the sky was green and the earth itself was flat. She was the sole inhabitant of the earth and she roamed about on her own, hither and thither, for she had no one to keep her company.

One day, tired from all her wanderings, she sat down beneath a big banyan tree to rest. She settled herself down comfortably, stretching her legs in front of her, while resting her back against the gnarled trunk of the ancient tree.

As she sat thus, a big mass of cloud named Ranaru happened

to pass by and notice her. 'Who is that?' the cloud thought. 'I have never seen anything like that before.'

Ranaru couldn't resist taking a closer look at her and when it did come closer, it couldn't stop the urge to engulf her. Droplets of water from the cloud poured all over Dzuliamosuro's body. Some of these droplets also trickled down and slowly found their way into her vagina and entered her body. As a result, Dzuliamosuro soon found herself with child.

In due course, the divine woman bore three children. She named the eldest offspring Ora, which means god. The middle one she named Okhe. Okhe was the tiger. The youngest child came to be known as Omaii. He was Dzuliamosuro's human child.

The three siblings grew up together in their mother's household, for Dzuliamosuro now found herself constrained to settle down at the place where she had borne the three children. This place came to be known as Makhraifu. In the present times, Makhraifu is known as Makhel which lies in Memai land. The Memais are none other than the Maos, and they are one of the seven fraternal Naga communities— Angami, Chakhesang, Memai (Mao), Pouchury, Poumai, Rengma and Zeliangrong—that are collectively called Tenyimia, or the Tenyi-Nagas. The Tenyi-Naga communities believe that they all dispersed to their present settlements from Makhraifu. The story of Dzuliamosuro and her three children is also the story of how the Tenyi-Nagas came to be living in Makhraifu exclusively.

Now it so happened that life was passing by quite happily for the small family of three brothers and the mother for many years after they settled down at Makhraifu. As the years passed however, things began to change. The brothers were all of different species, and their natural instincts, aptitudes and food habits were all different from each other. Although they initially tried to adjust, the older they grew, the more distant they became from each other. Omaii, especially, started feeling the need for separation from his brothers. 'This is too chaotic,' he thought to himself. 'We just cannot live together any more, although we are brothers and born of the same mother.'

Gradually, Dzuliamosuro also grew old and feeble and she required constant care and attention. Omaii found that he could not give her all the care she needed when Ora and Okhe were around. But then, they were all sons of the same mother and so, the three brothers took turns taking care of their mother.

Since Ora was the eldest, he stayed home with her first. But very soon, he lost patience and started leaving her hungry and called upon her a fever. For being a spirit, he had the power to summon the diseases when he wanted to.

When it was Okhe's turn to look after his mother, he dutifully stayed at home. But rather than feed her and nurse her, he found himself inspecting every part of her body, wondering which part would be the most delicious to eat when she finally died.

In the end, when Omaii had to stay with their mother, he was the only one who gave her all the attention she needed. He fed her well, massaged her ailing body, and gave her all the love and caring that a son should give to his mother. Dzuliamosuro was therefore, very thankful to have him around her in her old age and failing health. She knew that she would have to die soon, but she desperately hoped that when she did, it would be while Omaii was at home, and not in the presence of either Ora or Okhe.

As time passed, and Dzuliamosuro only grew weaker and older with each passing day, Ora started getting more and more frustrated with taking care of her. 'What a tedious task,' he said to himself. 'I cannot do this much longer. I have to find some way to get rid of the old woman. Maybe a bowl of chilli soup will do the trick.'

The evil eldest son was planning to murder his mother by feeding her a bowl of chilli soup! But when he prepared the concoction, and fed it to his mother, he found to his utter surprise that it had the exact opposite effect to what he had intended. Instead of killing Dzuliamosuro, the soup only energized her and she could now sit up and open her eyes. She could also speak and was, all in all, much livelier than she had been before consuming the hot chilli soup.

In his amazement, he went up to Omaii and asked him, 'Will you humans eat only matured red chillies or even the green chillies if it came to that?'

Not suspecting anything, Omaii replied, 'Why, both, of course!'

When he heard this, Ora declared, 'Very well then, humans will henceforth die both young and old. Age shall not be the only determining factor for dying.' Thus it is that to this day, human beings die irrespective of their age.

Dzuliamosuro, of course, did not recover from her ailment fully—no one can, after all, recover from old age. But she abhorred the idea of being eaten by her own son when she died. So when Omaii was home looking after her, she would often repeat, 'When I am dead, do not show my corpse to Okhe.'

As her time drew nearer, she left specific instructions with Omaii. 'Do not let Okhe see my dead body,' she reiterated. Then she added, 'Hide it from him and bury me deep under the ground. You should bury me beneath the hearth of the house and erect the furnace over my grave. Cook your food on it, and I shall always be with you. Son, you must make sure to carry out these instructions so that Okhe does not find my dead body, or else, he will eat my corpse. I cannot bear the thought of that!'

Ironically, on the day that she finally realized she was going to die, it was Okhe's turn to be with her. In order to avoid dying in the presence of her tiger son, Dzuliamosuro asked Omaii to be take care of her that day instead. But Okhe thought something might be afoot and refused to give up his turn by his mother's deathbed. 'No, Mother,' he growled, 'it is my turn to take care of you today. Let me do it. Let Omaii take a day off.'

Omaii, of course, realized his mother must have a reason behind her unusual request. So he cunningly offered Okhe a chicken in lieu of which he was to allow Omaiii to stay home that day. Okhe agreed and ate the chicken. Then, satisfied, he went off to the jungle where he roamed about all day.

Sometime during the day, Dzuliamosuro died. Omaii was heartbroken, but he remembered his mother's last wishes. So he meticulously carried out her instructions and buried her beneath the house. By the time it was evening and time for Okhe to return from his wanderings in the jungle, Dzuliamosuro lay beneath the hearth of the house and Omaii had set up the fireplace upon her grave. Next, he dug up the earth around the house and planted thorns in the ground to deter his brother from searching for their mother's remains.

When Okhe eventually returned, he could find his mother nowhere around. 'Where is she?' he demanded of Omaii. 'Tell me now! What have you done with her?'

'Brother, she died today,' replied the sorrowful Omaii. 'And according to her last wishes, I have buried her.'

'Where, where, where?' he cried. 'Tell me where you have buried her. Or I will dig everywhere till I find her remains.'

Omaii, of course, refused to tell him, and in a fit of anger, Okhe started digging the ground around the house. He could see that the earth there was soft and thought his younger brother must have buried their mother somewhere in the grounds around their mother's house. Omaii had foreseen such a reaction from his elder brother and had planted the thorns in anticipation. They now did their job and pricked Okhe whose paws started bleeding. Finally, he had to stop digging any further.

'I ask you again, brother,' he said. 'Tell me where our mother is buried.'

Omaii now reprimanded Okhe very sternly, 'What kind of a son are you, my brother? You want to eat the corpse of your mother? Is that what any decent creature would do? Don't you have any shame?'

His younger brother's rebuke stopped Okhe in his tracks and he finally gave up searching for his mother's grave.

One unpleasant situation averted, Omaii however, was soon forced to face another. Not long after their mother's death, all three brothers now started bickering over who would inherit their mother's house. Each one tried to force the other out. They tried all the tricks in the book but none of them would leave. In the end, Omaii called for a council.

'Listen, brothers,' he said. 'It does not seem like any of us is willing to move out of our mother's home. And our mother also did not make it clear as to who would inherit her house after she died. So it is a tough decision for all of us. We have tried to push and shove each other out, but to no avail. Therefore, there is only one way out of the situation. I suggest we hold a competition. Whoever wins, will inherit the house. The other two will leave without protest. Does that sound fair to you two?'

Both elder brothers thought for a while. In the end, they agreed, 'Yes, it does sound fair enough.'

As the proposer of the competition, the job of setting the task for the competition also fell upon Omaii. He suggested that the three brothers should instal a *prodzu,* which is a ball made up of plants and placed on a pole. This pole signifies ownership. When the prodzu was made, it was installed at a distance on the upper ridge of the land. 'Whoever touches the prodzu first shall inherit our mother's home,' declared Omaii.

The race began. But Ora was a god and he did not feel the need to run like his brothers. So he let out his spirit and the spirit touched the prodzu before either of his two brothers. By the time Okhe and Omaii could reach the pole, it was too late.

Omaii was highly dissatisfied with the outcome of the competition and complained that it was not fair that Ora should have let his spirit out that way. 'Let's do it again,' he suggested.

Ora and Okhe agreed. Actually, Ora had started feeling pity for Omaii, the youngest brother. So before they could compete again, he took Omaii aside and spoke to him. 'Listen, brother,' he said. 'You will never win with me and Okhe. We are both faster than you. But I have decided that I do not really want our mother's house anymore. It has no value for me. It is between you and Okhe now.'

Before Omaii could say anything, Ora continued, 'There is only one way you can defeat our brother Okhe. And that is by cunning.' He handed Omaii a catapult and said, 'Use this in the next round, and you can stay in our mother's house.'

When the race began again, Omaii knew just what he had to do with the catapult his eldest brother had given him. As the other two took off from the starting point, he launched himself from the catapult and shot across to the prodzu before the others. 'I win, I win!' he cried.

Neither of the other two brothers raised any objection, and it was agreed that Omaii was to inherit their mother's house.

Before they parted ways, however, the brothers decided that they had to do something to remember their bond as offspring of the same womb. So, at a place called Chazelophi, they carved a stone each as a sign of their co-habitation. These stones stand even today as megaliths.

Then, they decided to hold a feast to mark their parting of ways. As they sat down to feast, Omaii said to Ora, 'Brother, you go down south where the fields are. Make that your home from this day forward.'

And to Okhe he said, 'You, my brother, go up northwards to where the woods are. Make that your home from this day forward. You can live beside the Litsukri tree there.'

This decided, the brothers continued with their meal. Their conversations and plans for the future also did not cease.

As they ate, Ora said to Omaii, 'In winter time, when you see clouds forming at Chibu, stay indoors. Do not venture out, for during those cold sunless days my spirit will be roaming the land. Be they young or be they strong, anybody who encounters my spirit then will surely meet their end.'

In response, Omaii said to Ora, 'Thank you, Brother, for the warning. But let me tell you this: do not come and pay a visit during the summer months. I beseech you, if you do so, your loving brother will not be able to cultivate the land and no food will grow upon the earth. I shall surely die of starvation then.'

He then turned towards Okhe and warned him in his turn, 'Brother, take care not to set foot where man and his domestic animals inhabit. Do not even think of stretching you limbs thus far from the jungle. Because if you become reckless and start harming man, know that my spear will find its way into your very heart.'

To this, Okhe responded with a warning of his own, 'Omaii, my brother, I hear what you say. But do remember that if you ever commit incest or adultery or cause man and woman to divorce, you will surely become my food.'

Each brother thought that they had demarcated their territories quite well and laid down the boundaries between themselves for all time to come. So they ate merrily and soon the meal was over.

Ora immediately left for the fields, but to Omaii's utter surprise, Okhe refused to leave for the jungle. He stuck on, and try as Omaii would, he could not convince Okhe to go to his rightful abode. Finally, Omaii decided it was time to use cunning once again to get the better of his elder brother whom he could not, in any case, overcome with his physical prowess nor force to leave.

During the course of conversation, Omaii one day asked Okhe, 'Brother, what is the thing you fear the most?'

Not suspecting anything, Okhe replied, 'I am so powerful, I fear nothing.' After a little thought, though, he added softly, 'Well, nothing except the sounds *prai-prai, kro-kro* and *buu-buu.*'

Omaii now had the knowledge of Okhe's weaknesses. All he needed now was the implements that would stoke his fear and force him to leave.

One day, Omaii was weaving a mat for drying paddy, which is known as *ozha,* and Okhe was sleeping on it. Omaii saw his opportunity then. He tied his elder brother to the half-woven mat as the tiger slept. To his tail, he tied an *obvu,* which is something like a basket, and he dropped some stones into the *obvu.* Then he picked up a horn-trumpet and started to blow into the sleeping Okhe's ears.

Startled out of his sleep, Okhe could not quite understand what the commotion was all about. In a sudden burst of fear, he jumped up and started to run for his life. The mat swung from side to side as he ran and the stones inside the *obvu* started hitting the walls of the basket. A whole lot of commotion was created as a result and Okhe could hear nothing but the sounds he feared the most: *prai-prai, kro-kro* and *buu-buu.* He kept on and on running till he dropped the ozha at a place called Mizza. Eventually, the obvu also fell off at a place called Pibvu near Mille. The Mao Nagas believe that the *obvu* which was dropped at Pibvu later turned into a stone.

The frightened tiger, however, did not stop running till he reached the thick jungles in the north. Finally, he had reached the place that was destined to be his abode forever afterwards.

Omaii thus became the sole owner of his mother's home. And till this day, the youngest male-child in a Mao family inherits the parents' home. In due course of time, Omaii took a wife who gave birth to a son and he was named Aleo. Aleo grew up and when the time was right, he took a wife named Charani. She bore him three sons. The eldest of these three sons was named Alpha, who became the progenitor of the plains people. The second son of Aleo was named Tutto, and he became the progenitor of the Meiteis of the valley. The youngest son was named Khephio, and he became the progenitor of the Memai (Mao) people and the Tenyi tribes.

13. Meitei

The tale of two sons

𝕸anipur is a land of many gods and goddesses, but the Supreme Being is Tengbanba Mapu who is the source of everything else—all manifestations begin and, in the end return, to Tengbanba Mapu. Thus, Atingkok, the infinite expanse, and Amamba, the infinite darkness, both emanated from Tengbanba Mapu, and these were the earliest manifestations. Before that, there was a vast nothingness. This nothingness was known as Ting-Ka-Kok, which translates as total emptiness.

The act of creation began with the origination of the various deities from Tengbanba Mapu. Of them, the supreme deity is known as Atiya Kuru Shidaba or Lainingthou Salailel Shidaba. Atiya means the vast and empty sky. The word Kuru refers to the round or circular hemisphere while Sidaba is never-ending or the one in whom no birth and death can ever be present. His consort, or female principle, is Ima Leimaran, also known as Leimarel Lcishi Leipunbi. In subsequent times, Atiya Kuru Shidaba came to be worshipped as Shiva by the Meetei Hindus. But according to indigenous Meetei beliefs, Atiya Kuru Shidaba is actually another manifestation of Tengbanba Mapu, who descended on earth for the purpose of creating the world of living beings.

When Atiya Kuru Shidaba was delegated the task, he went up to Atingkok to seek guidance about how to create this new world. 'You are the infinite. Only you can guide me in this daunting task that I set upon now,' he supplicated.

Atingkok only opened his mouth wide and said to Atiya Kuru Shidaba, 'Look within and you shall understand.'

The latter did as he was bid, and much to his surprise, he saw the stars and the sun, the moon and the galaxies, and water, air and fire and many other things besides. He knew then that it was these various elements that would constitute the new universe. Armed with the knowledge, Atiya Kuru Shidaba descended on earth along with Ima Leimaran and together, they set in motion the process of creation of living beings.

That was the time when the land of Manipur was surrounded by seven hillocks and there was water, water everywhere. Over all this water and all these hills, seven suns burned bright, day and night. First, Atiya Kuru Shidaba drained out all the water by digging a hole with a trident. Then they could finally set foot on dry ground. 'Now it is time', Atiya Kuru Shidaba and Ima Leimaran decided, 'to procreate and people the earth'. But once again, they knew not how.

As they were pondering over the problem, a voice from heaven announced: 'Dig some clay from the ground. Shape it into a pitcher and for seven days thereafter, offer your prayers before it. You will see that your wish is fulfilled.'

The couple did as they were told and truly indeed, after seven days of prayer, a male child with hair the colour of gold appeared before them. He was three days old, and was really Atingkok in disguise. Atingkok had descended as a child to help Atiya Kuru Shidaba in creating the world of living beings. This child with the golden hair was named Konsen Tuleihenba. He is also sometimes known as Aseeba, but most popularly, he is revered as Sanamahi. Literally, the name Sanamahi means the liquid of life spreading in all directions like the rays of the sun. Sanamahi, therefore, is also in some senses, the sun god.

Sanamahi grew up and assisted his father in shaping the new universe. He was adept in the use of his bow and arrows, and first and foremost, he shot down the six extra suns. Then he initiated the process of creating the various creatures living on land, in water and air. These various orders of living beings were fine creations, but they did not bring a sense of fulfilment to the creator. In the end, it was decided that human beings should now be created, and they would have to be shaped in the image of Atiya Kuru Shidaba for them to be satisfactory.

When the human race was created, it turned out to be so appealing that Ima Leimaran Shidabi now wanted to have one of her own. 'Me-Khalouba is a wondrous creation,' she said to herself. Me-Khalouba was the first man on earth. 'I should have a son just like him,' she determined. In due course of time then, she was blessed with a child, and his name came to be Konchin Tukthaba. Eventually, he was given the name of Pakhangba.

As Pakhangba was growing up, Sanamahi was busy helping his father in the process of creation. It was not an easy task, and one that was fraught with numerous obstacles. Nine male deities and seven female deities were therefore assigned to assist father and son, Atiya Kuru Shidaba and Sanamahi, in their venture.

When the task was completed, Atiya Kuru Shidaba and Ima Leimaran Shidabi decided to leave the earth and ascend to heaven whence they had come. A contest now arose between the two sons as to who would inherit their father's throne. Pakhangba, the younger son, was the weaker of the two brothers. But he was also his mother's favourite. In the competition that now arose, Sanamahi therefore found himself outwitted by his own mother, although he did not quite know it yet.

In order to resolve the tussle for the throne between the two brothers, Atiya Kuru Shidaba decided to test them both. He therefore took the form of a dead cow and floated down the river. 'Let me see if either of my own two sons recognizes me. Whichever one does will be the wiser and the more trustworthy,' he decided. When Sanamahi saw the dead cow thus floating by, he said to himself, 'This cow is dead and stinking. What purpose will it serve if I retrieve it from the water now anyway. I shall therefore let it drift away on its own.' And he did nothing.

The younger son's reaction, however, was entirely different, and because it was so, he came to be known as Pakhangba—literally, one who knows his father. For he did realize it was his father, putting his two sons to test and he immediately jumped into the river and pulled the dead cow to the shore. Once on dry land, he performed all the funeral rites associated with the dead and laid the cow to rest. His father was much impressed. However, he wanted to set them another task before making the final decision.

'Listen, my sons,' he said one day after calling them to his side. 'He who must be king must be a man of wisdom, intuition as well as fortitude. You, my younger son, have proved you have the wisdom and intuition. But show me now which one of you has all these qualities, and I shall pronounce him king. Circle the universe seven times, each one of you, and he who shall come back to me first shall inherit my throne.'

Sanamahi, confident of his physical prowess, immediately set off on his journey around the universe. But Pakhangba was perturbed. He knew there was no way he could beat his elder brother in this race. In this state of worry, he went to his mother and told her about the task their father had set him and his brother. Ima Leimaran Shidabi was a shrewd woman. She listened to the entire tale patiently, thinking all the while. In the end, she said, 'Son, you are right. You cannot defeat your elder brother in this task, not with your physical ability. But be guided by me, do as I ask you to, and you shall triumph. Before I return with your father to our heavenly abode, I shall see you upon the throne.'

Overjoyed, Pakhangba asked his mother, 'What is it you would have me do, Mother? Say the word, and I shall do it.'

'Your father is the creator of all things animate and inanimate that inhabit this earth. The entire universe was created in his image—it is from him that the universe begins, within him lies its force and meaning. Circle him, therefore, my son. Go around him seven times and you would have travelled around the universe as many times as your father has asked you to.'

Overjoyed at the simple solution and in awe of his mother's sagacity, Pakhangba hurried to his father's side. 'Allow me, Father, to circle the universe in its entirety,' he bowed, and went around his pedestal seven times. And in this way, he was done satisfying his father and fulfilling his wish long before his elder brother returned from his strenuous and time-consuming journey around the universe—seven times.

The obedient elder son was greatly disturbed when he saw that the weakling of a younger brother he had was now on their father's throne. He made enquiries and was informed of the trick that was played by Pakhangba. Enraged, he rushed towards his brother and challenged him to a fight, but his mother had already installed seven female deities around her favourite son to protect him. She was well aware of what Sanamahi might do when he came to know the true story. These seven deities now rushed forward and encircled Pakhangba, shielding him from his brother's wrath.

'This is the basest of all deceptions that you have played upon me, brother!' he cried, frustrated. 'But I know you do not have the sharpness of mind required to plan such an elaborate scam. I presume therefore, that you must have had an advisor, somebody who guided you with their most vile intelligence to trick me out of my rightful inheritance.

'I promise you now, brother, that if that person be a male, I shall kill him with my own two hands. If it be a woman, I shall marry her, here and now. So say it, brother, say the name! Tell me by whose grace you are seated on that throne now!' he demanded.

When he heard his elder brother say this, Pakhangba could not suppress a smile. Haughtily he said, 'It was indeed a woman, brother. Now go marry her if you can. Our own mother guided me, she was the one who protects me still.'

When Sanamahi heard this, he was hurt to the core. 'Betrayed by my own mother!' he exclaimed. 'What a fate!' And he immediately rushed out of the court and exiled himself to the sun.

'This is where I shall live now, alone and unwanted. And this is where I shall launch now, my attack on the earth I once helped create!' So saying, Sanamahi, the creator's right hand man, now turned destroyer. He started annihilating the specimens on earth one by one.

Now everybody knew that Sanamahi had been responsible for creating these specimens on earth and they also knew that by the same token, he could very well destroy them. Thus, there was widespread panic on earth. Fearful about their existence, all mortals made their way to Atiya Kuru Shidaba's side. They appealed to him to stop Sanamahi, to save them, to do something. Atiya Kuru Shidaba was moved by their prayers and so he summoned Sanamahi to his side. Ever the dutiful son, Sanamahi appeared before his father and enquired as to why he had been thus summoned.

'My son, what is done is done. I cannot undo the fact that I have placed your younger brother on the throne,' Atiya Kuru Shidaba said. 'I can very well understand how this might disturb you. But it is not as though I have no love or consideration for you. Let me make it up to you.'

'How can you do that, Father?' Sanamahi enquired. 'Despite all my hard work and assistance in creating this beautiful land, you did make my younger brother ruler of it all, did you not?'

'Yes, my son, I did,' replied the father. 'And for that reason, Pakhangba will forever afterwards be worshipped as the ruling king of the land. You, on the other hand, are responsible for bringing all humans to life on earth. Therefore, they—and not just the royalty—shall all worship you as a household deity for all time to come. Every Meetei household shall venerate you, and you shall protect them in return.'

This satisfied Sanamahi and he was happy to become the household god of every Meetei family in the land. The Sannamahi Laishon—or the worship of the Sun—became part and parcel of every Meetei person's life and it consisted of verbal chanting and singing done on a regular basis.

Meanwhile, Pakhangba assumed the role of the king and protector, and took for his symbol a dragon god. Pakhangba Laining, or meditation, gradually developed as an art of looking into the self by the self for the self. Only the kings, nobles and scholars (*maichous*) were allowed to practise this art which requires no verbal chanting but deep concentration and meditation.

Their two sons and the whole of creation thus taken care of, Atiya Kuru Shidaba and Ima Leimaran ascended to heaven. In subsequent times, however, Ima Leimaran was reincarnated seven times, and in each incarnation, she carried out seven different tasks. One of these incarnations was that of Panthoibi or Leima Leinaotabi. As Panthoibi, she created the first earthen pot. Since the beginning of the process of creation when Atiya Kuru Shidaba and Ima Leimaran were directed to shape an earthen pitcher and pray to it, to Ima Leimaran's reincarnation as Panthoibi, pottery plays a very important part in the creation myth of the Meeteis. Often, the earthen pot becomes the metaphor for the womb, and as such, pottery still holds a very important position in Meetei life.

14. Tangkhul

Death and the discipline of the universe

$\mathcal{K}$asa Akhava created the world. All animate and inanimate objects in this universe came into being because he willed it so. He also determined the rules of the universe—the ones according to which it continues to be governed. In the beginning, however, there were a few glitches, a few anomalies to correct. For this, sometimes, new rules had to be made and established systems overturned. The universe, after all, is a dynamic place, and the created world could always use some fine-tuning, some refinement and a little amendment from time to time. This is the story of why death started occurring among human beings, who or what caused it and how they had to pay a price for setting in motion this inevitable occurrence in human life, indeed, of all life on earth.

In the early days of the creation of the universe, when the day and the night had been created to mark the passage of time, what was not foreseen was the trouble human beings might have in telling day from night without some help from some quarter. So the cock was made to crow at the break of dawn to announce to human beings that the night had ended, the day had begun and they should all go about their daily business. The exact duration of the day and the night was also thus determined by the cock's crowing.

When this system was initiated, the universe ran quite smoothly and peacefully for quite some time thereafter. Human beings were happy and contented, now that they knew when to rest and when to work, when to sleep and when to wake. But then, humans are not the only inhabitants of the universe. There are other creatures, birds and animals, reptiles and mammals and insects and what not, that do not follow the laws laid down for the human world. The exceptions that these other creatures make to the laws governing human beings are actually the rules which their own little worlds are guided by. And because their rules are sometimes contrary to those of the human world, often there are clashes between and accidents or unpleasant incidents in the different life worlds.

The day-night law which determined when humans would sleep and when they would wake was one such rule that was contrary to the rule of the world of flying foxes. The flying fox would sleep during the day and fly around at night. All those things that humans did during the day, it would do at night— hunting or gathering food, for example. Just as human beings craved for food during their waking hours of the day, the flying fox would also go out looking for food during the night. And it so happened, one fateful night, that the flying fox felt extremely hungry just after midnight. So there was nothing to it but to go out in search of something to eat, and it had to do it before dawn, which it could sense was not very far away.

As it flew around looking for food, it came upon a walnut tree. 'Ah, walnuts,' it said to itself. 'I'll get some of those. Wonderful!'

But it was groggy from sleep and while plucking the fruit, one escaped its grip and fell down.

Now a crab was resting for the night below that walnut tree. When the walnut fell on it, it was rudely shaken awake. 'What is that?' the crab cried in alarm. 'Something must be attacking me. Help!' it said and ran helter-skelter. As it did so, it stepped on an ants' nest.

This nest housed some giant ants which were also sleeping in the night after a whole day of hard labour. When the crab scampered all over their colony, not only was their sleep disturbed, but their nest broken too. 'Who could it be? Who has trampled our house and disturbed our hard-earned rest?' they shouted in chagrin and looked around for the culprit.

The crab had meanwhile scuttled off in fear, unaware of what it had done to the ants. And as the ants scanned their vicinity, they saw that not too far away, slept a wild boar. 'Look,' some of them cried, ' it must be this boar. It is strong and mighty. It must have been its feet that crushed our nest.' And they all scurried up to it and stung it all over its body, profusely.

'Aghhhhhhhh!' cried the sleeping boar in pain. 'What is this sting?' it yelled, its sleep having now abandoned him. 'Oh, my skin smarts!' And it ran amok, looking for someplace to rub its back.

As it ran around thus, it came upon a clump of banana trees. 'This will have to do,' it decided in desperation, and started rubbing its back against the trunk of one banana tree and then the next, in order to take the sting away and soothe its skin.

But the boar was indeed very strong and mighty, as the ants had earlier determined, and the banana trees could not take the weight of its huge form. They started toppling over, one by one.

Now a tiny little bat used to live in that clump of banana trees. When the trees started falling one by one, its nest also was destroyed. 'Where do I live now, where do I live?' it despaired. 'I am only a small bat in this big world, and if I don't find any shelter, how will I feel safe?'

So saying, it started flying around wildly, looking for someplace safe to hide. Finally, it saw a small wet, dark cavity and in desperation, flew right into it. 'This must be the hollow of a rock,' the bat decided as it landed violently inside it. 'It certainly is warm and cosy.'

In reality, that warm and cosy cavity happened to be the inside of an elephant's trunk. When the little bat suddenly landed inside the hollow of its nose, the big animal got a rude shock. 'What on earth happened?' the elephant thought. 'There's something up my nose!'

'Help! Help!' trumpeted the big elephant, and started stomping around in great alarm. An elephant is not like a crab, nor even like a wild boar. It is bigger and stronger, and when it goes on a rampage, it can wipe out anything and everything in its way. That is what happened just then. The frightened elephant stepped on everything that was anywhere in its vicinity. Incidentally, it also stepped on a human being. Crushed by the immense weight, the human being died.

A great commotion now took place. Death had occurred for the first time in the universe created by Kasa Akhava.

So life was not endless?

What did it mean to die?

What was death anyway?

These and other questions started troubling the inhabitants of the earth now that they had witnessed a new phenomenon. Nobody had prepared them for it. There was great panic on earth. All living beings started feeling insecure.

When he saw how the incident had affected his creations adversely, the creator had little choice but to summon a meeting. When all living beings had gathered around him in his court,

Kasa Akhava started speaking, 'I know you are all troubled by this thing called death which you have never experienced nor seen before. Do not be alarmed! You can do nothing to prevent it. But know that you are not allowed to cause it either. This first death on earth therefore, needs to be investigated. We shall have to determine who is responsible for this human dying.'

He then turned towards the elephant and demanded, 'Tell me, elephant, why did you trample this fellow living being to death?'

The elephant was as much surprised by the turn of events as anybody else. It had never intended to kill anybody, and certainly not the human. So it replied humbly, 'O lord, I feel terrible about the whole incident. It is true that I did trample upon the human who died because of it, but it was not my fault that I went on a rampage thus. I woke up with this awful irritation up my nose and in trying to shake off whatever it was that was causing this unbearable sensation, I accidentally stepped on the human being who was sleeping under a tree. You see, as I got to know later, a little bat had lodged itself inside my trunk while I was sleeping.'

Kasa Akhava now turned to the little bat, 'Tell me, bat, why did you fly into this elephant's trunk?'

The bat was still shaken from the night's incidents. The boar had broken its tree house and it had had to fly around looking for shelter. How did it know it would scare the elephant so much that it would go and crush a human? In a shrill little voice, therefore, it answered, 'Dear lord, I did what I did from fright. I was fast asleep in my comfortable home in the clump of banana trees yonder, when an unruly wild boar came storming in, knocking down the banana tree where I live. It crashed down to the ground and I thought the world had come to an end. In utter fright and sheer confusion, I was flying around hither and thither looking for someplace safe to hide when I mistook the elephant's nostril for the hollow of a rock. I flew in blindly. How can I be blamed for this?'

So Kasa Akhava now asked the wild boar to step up. When it did, he asked, 'Tell me, boar, why did you enter the banana thicket and break down this bat's house?'

The wild boar was still smarting from the stings of the giant ants. It did not know what it had done to provoke them to hurl themselves upon him the way they did. On top of that, it was now being held responsible for breaking the bat's nest, causing it to frighten the elephant, leading to the death of the human being! Hurt and angry, it said now in a gruff voice, 'My lord, I was sleeping peacefully under a tree when those giant ants over there stung me for no rhyme or reason. In unbearable agony I ran towards the banana trees to rub my back against them. I had no intention of breaking them down or destroying the little bat's home. I do not see how I can be held responsible for the ultimate tragedy.'

It was now the giant ants' turn to explain their role in the chain of events. Kasa Akhava enquired, 'Tell me, ants, why did you sting this wild boar if he had done you no harm?'

The ants had been harried by the loss of their home and had no way of knowing that their stinging the boar would lead to a death in the end. Knowing now that the wild boar was not really responsible for their calamity, the ants said contritely, 'We were distraught and very angry that somebody had walked all over us while we were sleeping. We only got to know later that the boar had not destroyed our colony.'

Learning that it was the crab who had actually made the ants homeless, Kasa Akhava now turned to the crab, 'Tell me, crab, why did you scuttle over the ants' colony? What had they done to you?'

The crab was still suffering from a terrible back pain from the walnut that had fallen on it. It replied painfully now, 'O Lord, I did not mean to destroy anybody's home. If it was not for the greedy flying fox, I would still be sleeping under the tree. Instead, he dropped the walnut on my back and when I was leaping around in pain, I accidentally stepped on the ants' home. Surely, I can't be held responsible for the human's death because of that?'

Kasa Akhava had now reached the root of the problem. He turned to the flying fox and said, 'Tell me, flying fox, why did you drop the walnut on the crab?'

The flying fox did not have anything to say in its defence. It had, after all, disturbed the peace of the night and set in motion the series of events that had led to the final tragedy. 'I was hungry, lord,' was all it could say.

So everybody now realized that the flying fox was the one who was actually responsible. 'He should be punished!' they all said in unison.

But Kasa Akhava was not a cruel god. He had patiently heard each and every animal involved in the night's events, and given everybody a chance to defend themselves. Now he heard what all the other creatures had in mind for the flying fox— he also considered every form of punishment they suggested he should mete out to the guilty animal. Finally, he declared, 'There are many laws in the universe, and every law has a reason behind it. But mostly, the reason is maintenance of order and discipline in the created world. In this case, it is true that the discipline was broken and the flying fox is at the root of it. However, given the circumstances, I do not feel he deserves too severe a punishment. I will therefore decree that one of his legs be cut off. That is the penalty he will have to pay.'

Kasa Akhava's order was carried out immediately. After that, the assembly dissolved. Everybody returned to their own abodes.

In the course of time, however, the severed leg of the flying fox grew back again. Unfortunately though, it did not regain enough strength to perch. This is the reason why till today, the flying fox hangs upside down, dangling on one leg alone.

15. Zeliangrong

Termites and the human tongues

There was a time when all the people of the created world spoke only one language. This common tongue made communication between the people living in different places of the world quite smooth and simple. However, one man's misfortune changed this situation such that multiple languages came into being, and today, one human being cannot often understand what another human being is saying. This is the story of how that came to pass.

In a small village, there once lived a man named Aniuwang. This man was in love with a very beautiful woman. The beautiful woman also seemed to return his feelings and that made Aniuwang very happy. Whenever they passed each other, they would share stolen glances. Often, she would smile sweetly at him and he would feel like his heart was bursting with love. After this went on for quite some time, the lovers one day decided to meet somewhere outside the village and talk to each other, away from the intrusion of friends and family.

There was a big tree that stood majestically outside the village gate, as if standing guard over the village. The young couple decided to meet there.

On the predetermined day and at the appointed time, the girl reached the place where the big tree grew. But she could not see Aniuwang anywhere. 'Where could he be?' she decided. 'I hope he has not decided to back out now. Oh Aniuwang, love of my life, I shall wait under this tree for you till you come before me.'

So saying, she sat herself down in the shade of the tree.

In reality, Aniuwang had reached the place early, much before the appointed time. But instead of waiting for his lover in the shade of the tree, like the girl now did, he had climbed up the tree to look out for her. He waited patiently for the girl to arrive, and when she did, he found himself mesmerized by her beauty and unable to climb down. He also heard what she said about waiting for him but he found himself unable to speak, so tongue-tied was he at the sight of her. So there he was, perched on the tall branches and watching as the girl daintily sat herself down in the shade of the tree.

But what he saw next gave him the shock of his life!

After settling down in the shade, the girl began to grow restless as the time passed and Aniuwang did not show. 'Where could he be?' she said out loud. 'Ah well, I cannot just sit here and wait for him, doing nothing. I have to pass my time somehow!'

So saying, she calmly peeled off the skin of her head. Then, just as placidly, she placed her scalp upon her knees and started sifting through her hair. Even as Aniuwang watched, aghast, he saw her picking lice from between her hair strands. The horror was too much for him when he finally watched her put these lice in her mouth, chew them and swallow! In his shock and repulsion, he could not control himself. His bladder got inflated and he pissed—right on top of her from where he sat, up on the tree, looking down at her.

The girl was naturally startled out of her obnoxious indulgence when his urine fell on her head. She jumped up from where she sat and looked above her to see Aniuwang there. 'You pissed on me? You nasty man! Come down right now,' she demanded.

Aniuwang refused to descend. 'I know you now for what you really are, and I shall not come down to you,' he retorted.

'Well, if you don't come down, I'll have to climb up, won't I?' she said wickedly, but the frightened young man held on to his branch and wouldn't budge.

'You, big tree,' she commanded in the end, when even after much threatening and demanding, Aniuwang still refused to come stand before her, 'bend down before me then. If this man does not want to come to me, you can bring him down.'

To Aniuwang's sheer fright, the tree did as it was bid. Its branches lowered, bent before her, and with them, he was also lowered to the ground. No sooner was he at her level that the strange girl pulled him to her side and started bashing him up. Not until he was black and blue with her beating and had passed out from the pain did she leave the spot. When she finally left him for dead, she went back to the village and walked up to her brothers.

'Brothers,' she said to them. 'What a day I had in the forest outside our village gate today! A wild boar chased me, and I had to fight for my life. I managed to kill it in the end though, and have left it under that big tree near the gate. Go, fetch it and we shall have a feast.'

The girl's brothers eagerly rushed out of the village gate and towards the big tree. But to their surprise, they found the place empty. There was no wild boar there, which was to be expected. But strangely enough, Aniuwang's body also was not there. The girl's brothers did not find anything or anybody under the tree and they returned to the village empty handed.

Aniuwang, in the meantime, had crawled away from the tree's shade and into a ditch nearby. He had not, after all, died from the girl's beatings, although the girl had thought he had. In the ditch was a rat's burrow in which he hid himself. Unconscious, nearly half dead, he had lain there for a while when a wild cock had passed by, scratching around, scrounging for food. As it did so, it had accidentally covered the burrow's mouth with dried leaves and so, the girl's brothers had not seen Aniuwang in that condition.

Through his pain and despite his near-unconscious condition, Aniuwang had heard the voices of the girl's brothers as they had left disappointed at not finding the wild boar their sister had promised. When he was sure they were no longer around, he raised his head cautiously out of the ditch and looked around. What he saw now at first frightened him and then, he was amazed.

Not far away from where he lay, two snakes, a male and a female, were fighting each other. It was a deadly duel at the end of which, the female snake was killed. Although the male snake had been responsible for the death, it now seemed contrite at what it had done. Quietly then, it crawled its way towards a tree not far from where the female snake lay dead. Once there, it collected a twig and returned to its dead mate. Then, as Aniuwang watched in absolute wonder, it rubbed the twig against the body of the dead snake and—lo and behold!—it came back to life. Aniuwang could only watch mesmerized as the two snakes now slithered away from the scene.

He knew now that the tree had magical properties. Convinced that its healing effects could cure him as well of his injuries, Aniuwang gathered all the strength he had left and determinedly inched his way towards it. Somehow he eventually managed to reach there. Then, with another mighty effort, he tore at the bark of the tree. A piece of it came loose in his hands and very expectantly, he rubbed it against his entire body. Even as he watched, his bruises disappeared, his cuts healed, his pains left him. He was whole again, and hale.

He stood up and inspected himself for any more injuries. When he found none, he decided to return to his village. Before he left however, he cut out another piece of the bark of the magical tree and took it along with him. When he reached home, Aniuwang hid the bark in a *khuk* (a basket that stores treasured possessions). He did not however, tell anyone about what had transpired in the forest, or what lay hidden in the khuk.

It is amazing how momentous, life-changing incidents also have a way of fading from our memories, and how quickly, sometimes, we return to the ordinary, the everyday. For Aniuwang also, life quickly reverted to the usual daily grind. It was as if nothing had happened on that fateful day.

Every day, as he used to earlier, he would leave home in the morning, and every day, he would come back in the evening. His mother would look after him the same way as she had done earlier, being none the wiser. The only difference, though, was that Aniuwang would often steal up to his khuk and look in, as if to make sure that whatever was in it remained safe. His mother noticed that. Then again, every morning, before leaving home, he would caution his mother never to open the khuk and look inside. 'Never ever open it, Mother,' he would repeat every morning. 'Or I will not be responsible for what follows.'

Unfortunately, these constant warnings had the exact opposite effect on the one addressed. Aniuwang only managed to pique his mother's curiosity, if anything. Finally, one day, unable to resist herself anymore, the old woman waited for her son to leave home before creeping up to the khuk and peeking in. When she saw what lay inside, she was disappointed.

'A piece of bark? That's it?' she sulked. 'This is what he has been hiding from me?'

Then she looked closely at it, hoping to find something unusual about it. 'Nothing,' she finally concluded. 'There's nothing exceptional about this bark. If anything, it needs some air. Look how mouldy it is becoming. I know what I should do; I should put it out in the sun to dry. That way, my son can preserve the bark for much much longer!'

Quite pleased with herself for coming up with the idea and thinking that her son would only thank her for her intervention, the old woman did as she had decided. But no sooner had she placed the bark in the sun and stood up to go back inside the house when there was a loud sound of thunder and lightning from the skies. A sudden storm of enormous proportions broke out, and the bark was lifted up from the ground by a gust of wind. The old woman watched helplessly as it flew past her and up towards the skies.

She could not do anything to stop it from flying away but nonetheless, followed the piece of bark with her eyes as it reached the skies. There, she was amazed to see that the sun and the moon had both come out, and the two of them had started fighting over what she had thought was a worthless keepsake her son for some reason treasured. Even as she watched, the moon came out victorious, wresting the bark from the sun and departing.

The old woman stood transfixed as the skies cleared immediately thereafter, leaving no trace of what had just transpired. When Aniuwang came back and found her thus, he knew something terrible must have happened. People from the entire village had by now gathered at their house. They had also witnessed the strange occurrences and wanted to know the true story. Seeing her son, the old woman came to her senses and narrated the entire story from beginning to end. When she had finished, it was Aniuwang's turn to tell the villagers what that piece of bark was all about, why he had treasured it so and how it had come to be in his possession.

Needless to say, the villagers were astounded to hear the different pieces of the story come together. They marvelled at the turn of events and all agreed that the bark of that tree was too precious a thing to let go of.

'Our village needs the protection of that tree. We have to get the bark back from the moon,' the elders declared, and they started putting their heads together on how to go about it.

Many suggestions were made, discussed and discarded. But in the end, a decision was taken. The villagers who had assembled there decided to build a tower high enough to reach the moon. That way, they could climb up and retrieve what had been stolen from the courtyard of Aniuwang's house. But it was not an easy task.

'We humans alone cannot do this,' they agreed. 'This tree has curative properties for all animals and living creatures, as Aniuwang had witnessed in the case of the dead snake. And so, everybody on earth will benefit from it. We should therefore ask all the creatures of earth to help us build this tower.'

For a while thereafter, many rituals were performed to propitiate some of the creatures, favours were doled out and invitations were sent to some of them to come help. In other words, a lot of preparation was done before they could even lay the foundation for the tower. Once that was done, all the people and many of the creatures toiled hard from morning till night for days on end to build the tower to reach the moon.

It was a glorious day indeed when the tower was finally completed. Everybody was exhausted but exhilarated. They decided that they would all climb up to the moon and ask to have the elixir back. The first creature to climb up was the dog. It was Aniuwang's dog. It had also helped build the tower and when the tower was completed, it hastily jumped off from the top on to the moon's surface. Enthused by this, the people of the village all started climbing up the steep tower.

That was when tragedy struck. While propitiating the various creatures of the earth to help them build the tower, the people had forgotten to approach the white termites. These insects, though small, have the ability to overturn the strongest of structures.

While the tower was being built, they were left feeling offended that the humans had forgotten to ask their favour. As a result, they decided to start chewing at the foundation of the tower. Thus, while the tower was rising in height, its strength at the very bottom was being eroded by a colony of termites. Now, when the people of the entire village started climbing up the edifice, the foundation gave way. The tower collapsed and the people were all thrown hither and thither.

Some had made their way almost to the top, others were halfway up, some had just started their climb, and there were many more in the positions between. When the tower started shaking, they started falling off one by one. As they fell, they all screamed out and cried for help. There was utter confusion. And in the midst of this confusion, the common language that they spoke was lost somewhere. They started shouting different things, every person spoke in a tongue different from the next person's. And this is how the many languages of the world originated.

Meghalaya

A brief note:

This beautiful hill state, aptly named the 'abode of clouds' —albeit in a language not native to any of the indigenous communities inhabiting it—transitioned peacefully, through political dialogue, into a full-fledged state of the Indian Union in 1972. Formerly, it was the autonomous districts of United Khasi and Jaintia Hills and Garo Hills of Assam. In the early days, the three hill areas were independent kingdoms that were yoked to the administration of Assam by the British in 1835. Many of the traditional social and political customs and organizations—including the systems of kingship and chieftains—of the various communities and tribes of Meghalaya survive to this day. At the same time, despite (or maybe because of) the overwhelming influence of Christianity and the continued onslaught of the forces of globalization, there has also been a revival of some of the hitherto abandoned indigenous faith and belief systems in Meghalaya in recent times. The Khasis, Garos and Jaintias form the bulk of the population.

The Khasis, Jaintias, Bhois, Wars and Lyngngams of Meghalaya are collectively known as Ki Hynniew Trep. 'Hynniew Trep' or 'Seven Huts' refers to the seven families who were the first settlers on earth according to Khasi mythology. Many settler communities like the Axamiyas from the plains of Assam, Nepalis and Bengalis have also made their home in Meghalaya.

The Khasis are the largest group of people inhabiting Meghalaya. A small number of them are also found in neighbouring Assam and Bangladesh. They are Mon-Khmer in origin, with an Austro-Asiatic lineage. The family name and property of a Khasi household is passed on from one generation to the next through the youngest daughter (or Khun Khadduh) in the family. The Khun Khadduh is also therefore, expected to act as the primary caretaker of the parents and unmarried siblings. Among the men in the family, the maternal uncle wields a lot of power in the decision-making process. The continuation and frequent abuse of these traditional practices in contemporary times have led to many conflicts within the Khasi society.

The Jaintias are variously known as Pnars or Syntengs, the latter two names being exonyms. The historical Jaintia kingdom gave its people the name. The rulers of this kingdom were Syntengs, who had adopted Hinduism. But unlike the royals and the nobles, the common form of Hinduism was not widespread among the Jaintia people. Their traditional religion is known as Niamtre. Christianity has been widely adopted. The Jaintia people speak the Pnar language which is quite akin to the standard Khasi langauge. Like the Khasis, they also practise a matrilineal system of tracing lineage and determining inheritance. They are traditionally famous for weaving, wood-carving and cane and bamboo craft.

The Garos are a Tibeto-Burman community sharing close affinity with the Koch and Bodo languages. They call themselves A·chik Mande (literally 'hill people'). Like the Khasis and the Jaintias, the Garos are also matrilineal and the youngest daughter inherits the family property, unless the parents designate another daughter as the 'nokna' (or 'for the house or home'). In the absence of a daughter, a daughter-in-law or adopted child is accorded the same status. Unlike the Khasis and Jaintias of Meghalaya, the Garos did not traditionally have a well-organized council or durbar. A group of villages would be organized into the A·king, which would then be supervised by the Nokmas or chiefs. Christianity has greatly changed the traditional fabric of Garo life, just as it has transformed the customary life of so many other communities and tribes.

16. Khasi

On cutting the umbilical cord with heaven

After the earth had been created, three goddesses came to live here. They were the patron goddesses of fire, water and the sun. These three goddesses were accordingly named Ka Ding (Fire), Ka Um (Water) and Ka Sngi (Sun). Of them, Ka Sngi was the youngest and Ka Ding the eldest.

In those early days, the earth was just one flat, vast stretch of land. Everywhere around, there were the trees and the green grass that we see even today. The only difference was that they all grew and lived on a flat surface which was the face of the earth.

On this flat plane, a few rivers flowed along, crisscrossing the land, but there were no mountains, nor hills, no valleys, nor gorges that give our earth so much of its character today.

So what happened to change it all? How did the earth come to have these undulating hills that we call home today? How did the plain-faced abode of the three goddesses transform into this gorgeous earth that we inherited from them?

It all happened following the death of their mother. As with all change, the end of something old led to a new beginning.

The mother of the three goddesses lived in heaven. But she came down one day to visit her three daughters. The day she arrived, the loving and dutiful daughters were delighted. 'Oh Mother, how glad we are to see you. It has been such a long time!' they exclaimed and gathered around her and fussed over her.

The mother also was extremely happy to be with her daughters once again. Sadly however, this gaiety did not last long. The old woman, soon after descending to earth, fell ill.

The three goddesses nursed their mother with the utmost care and took exceedingly good care of her, but she just wouldn't get well again. 'She is getting worse every day,' the distraught daughters wailed.

After some time, in fact, she passed away. The daughters were inconsolable for a long time thereafter. They cried and cried and cried some more, but in the end, they knew they had to perform their rightful duties as the daughters of the dead woman. And one of the major responsibilities that now faced them was the disposal of their mother's body.

As the youngest daughter, Ka Sngi knew that this heavy responsibility now lay on her own shoulders. Being a matrilineal people, this is how the Khasis function. She decided that the best she could do, as the sun goddess, was to direct her mighty rays at her mother's dead body and hope to expend it. 'Sisters, step aside.

I shall have to use all the powers at my command now.' So saying, she burned with all her strength.

So fierce were the rays that now emanated from her that all the trees and the bushes, the grasses and the weeds were burnt to ashes. The water bodies of the earth—the rivers and small streams—all dried up. Everything that had covered the surface of the earth just disappeared. And yet, incredibly, their mother's body remained exactly as it was. The daughters were amazed!

'Little sister,' the second daughter now said. 'You have done your duty and tried your best. As the second youngest, let me try now. For unless we dispose of her body, our mother will not be at peace.'

So Ka Um now decided to bring all the waters at her command to help her in this task. She exercised all her powers to pour down incessant rain upon the earth, day in and day out, for many many days thereafter. So relentless was the downpour she caused that an immense flood now washed over the earth. Whatever had survived Ka Sngi's heat now perished under water.

Confident that she had done all that was in her power, Ka Um finally called off the rains. For a while thereafter, the three sisters waited and watched patiently as the deluge subsided, and the waters ebbed away. To their utter disappointment though, when the water was all gone, there still lay their mother's body, the same as it had been.

'Oh sisters, it is dreadful indeed that we have failed our mother so. But do let me try now. Maybe as the eldest daughter, I can perform the duty which you have both tried to perform but unsuccessfully,' the eldest sister, Ka Ding, said.

Anguished, but determined, Ka Ding thus stepped forward to perform the joyless task. She commanded a fire so fierce that its flames danced all over the earth for days. They swept over anything that remained on the surface of the earth, and blazed and smouldered with unyielding intensity. In the end, when the flames had died down, they found to their great relief, that their mother's body had been incinerated. Their duty was done. The three daughters then performed her last rites.

After they had said their final goodbyes to their deeply loved mother, they looked around them at the place that had borne the brunt of their powerful onslaught. They were amazed to find that the vast monotonous plain that had been their abode earlier had now vanished. In its place, was a new undulating surface that swelled up into the skies in some places and swooped down to the depths of the earth in others. There were deep ravines in some places, smooth plateaus in others. All in all, it was a new world.

As time passed, this new surface of the earth came to be dotted with the trees and weeds that had burnt down or drowned. Lovely flowers sprung up once again. Waters filled some of the ravines and in some other places, playful waterfalls started cutting down from high above the mountains. Blue mists floated up to the sky, while down below, all was green. It was a wondrous resplendent world, and into this world, human beings came to dwell eventually. But that is another tale entirely...

It is not a tale of love and devotion like that of the three goddesses and their mother. On the contrary, it is a tale of one man's greed and desire to rule over the world. And it happened not far from Shillong.

Just thirteen miles north of Shillong city, there is a dome-shaped hill. The locals call it Lum Sohpetbneng and the name literally means 'the hill that is the navel of heaven'. It is so called because the Khasis believe that the umbilical cord that tied the earth to heaven was attached to the dome of this hill. This cord was actually in the form of a golden ladder, or 'jingkieng ksiar', that descended from heaven at Lum Sohpetbneng.

In those days, human beings lived in heaven. But they were meant to be creatures of the earth, and so, every day, the humans in heaven would have to climb down the golden ladder to earth. Once on earth, they would labour all day—like they do now—and cultivate and reap the harvest from the land. At the end of the day, every evening, they would then have to climb back up the jingkieng ksiar. In all, there were sixteen families of human beings in heaven, and all of them followed this daily routine for generations on end.

Perhaps human beings would have continued to be inhabitants of heaven as well as denizens of earth forever afterwards, had it not been for one man among all the people of these sixteen families. He was a clever but sly man who resented being in heaven. It was after all, the realm of U Blei, who was God. And God ruled over everyone and everything, human and celestial, in heaven and on earth.

This man began to think that if he could just confine U Blei to heaven, he could perhaps rule over earth on his own. His ambition started growing inside him with each passing day, until it became an obsession. And then, he started scheming and plotting meticulously, taking no one else into confidence. He realized that the golden ladder was the only connection between heaven and earth. If he could sever that connection, would he not have confined U Blei to his heaven? Could he not then take over earth and establish his own rule there?

So he started hacking and hewing at the ladder every day on his way up and down. He did this when he was sure nobody was looking. This went on for many months, and with every chop at the ladder it became that much weaker.

Finally the day came when just one more blow would do the job, and the ladder would at last fall. After having waited so patiently all this time, he could barely wait to deal the ultimate blow. He had all but exhausted his power of endurance. So, at the first opportunity that showed itself, the greedy man ran to the ladder in a frenzy and dealt that final blow. It crashed down to earth. The separation of earth from heaven was complete.

In his great haste, however, the man had failed to notice that at the time of his last strike, only seven of the sixteen human families had descended to earth. He had seen them from afar, working in the fields, and had assumed that everybody had come down by then. He was wrong. So it came to pass that because of his folly, these seven families remained stranded on earth forever afterwards.

These are those seven families from which, the Khasis believe, all the other peoples of the world have sprung. With the passage of time, they spread out all over the world and populated other places and continents of the earth. They reproduced and multiplied over the generations and that is how different communities sprang up everywhere. In due course of time, they forgot their origins and adopted new ways of life.

The Khasis, however, remember. The people belonging to the indigenous Khasi faith, Niam Khasi, still pray to U Blei as the God Almighty. They still journey in thousands up to the summit of Lum Sohpebneng every year in the month of Rymphang (February). They feel close to U Blei there.

17. Jaintia

How to appease a malevolent goddess

There are supernatural beings everywhere in the Jaintia hills. They are benevolent or malevolent spirits but their munificence or ill-will is always only in response to the behaviour of human beings towards them. Such was the case with Ka Blai Pynsum Kule, who was a river goddess, and she was so called because she lived in the river named Pynsum Kule. The word pynsum comes from 'pynsumi', which means 'to bathe' and 'kule'

means 'horse'. The river had then been given this name because in ancient times, the chief of Mylliem and his people would bathe their horses in its waters. According to local belief, the river is as deep as twelve *rana*, that is to say, twelve staircases deep.

Now, this river was very intricately connected with the beliefs and practices of the day-to-day lives of the people of the village of Ummulong beside which it flows. This village falls under the Jaintia Hills district of Meghalaya. It is situated on the Shillong-Jowai road, about 51 kms away from Shillong, the capital of Meghalaya.

In Ummulong itself, about 2 kms away from the Pynsum Kule river, is a hill that is locally known as Lawania. Among the Jaintia people, there is a wondrous tale that is interwoven around these two places—the river Pynsum Kule and the hill Lawania, both of which are believed to be the abodes of many supernatural beings. It is a tale of love between two such beings, and of the fear and awe they have commanded from the Jaintia people for so long now for having the power to bring upon them the most horrible deaths and fearsome diseases. It is the story of the river goddess, Ka Blai Pynsum Kule, and U thlen, the serpent god who lived on the hill called Lawania.

Because U thlen always lived on Lawania, the people of the village used to refer to him as U thlen Lawania. But although he had a definite name, nobody ever knew what he actually looked like. It is said that U thlen was revered as the serpent god all right, but he did not really look like a serpent all the time. He could take on any shape at will. So one day, the local people of Ummulong village might see him as a snake—which is perfectly normal to expect of a serpent god—but the next day, he would have taken the form of a cock. On another day, for all they knew, he might appear before them in the shape of a ball. On some full moon nights, the people of the village also swore that they saw U thlen Lawania roaming about the hills and valleys, burning bright, as a big ball of fire. But no matter what shape he took, the people were extremely scared of him, because they all knew what a malevolent spirit he was.

But no matter how malevolent he was, he still had the capacity to love, and one day, he fell in love with Ka Blai Pynsum Kule. Maybe he had come to the river Pynsum Kule to drink its water one day, or maybe he had just been passing by, but from the day he set eyes on Ka Blai or the goddess of the river, he wanted nothing more than to be with her and marry her. He would climb down from Lawania every day and make his way to the river to catch a glimpse of her, or talk to her, and convince her to marry him.

U thlen's journey from Lawania to Pynsum Kule took him through a locality called Pohskur. This was the place where he would rest awhile every day on his journey back and forth. Usually, he rested on a big tree that grew in Pohskur. The first time the people of Ummulong village became aware of the fact was when one person from the village returned home in a stupor. Soon thereafter, he fell prey to an incurable illness. Finally, he died. When the people of the village tried to find the cause of his strange condition, they could find none. It was only after a few more instances like this occurred that they came to know about U thlen Lawania's resting place in Pohskur. Slowly, they realized that it was not safe to walk by that tree alone. But as with any other calamity that faces human beings, when the terror of U thlen Lawania struck, the people of Ummulong village also gradually learnt how to deal with the situation. They understood that U thlen could only stun the weak and defenseless. His gaze hardly ever affected those people who were firm and strong physically and mentally. And most importantly, he never showed himself to people unless they were alone. So everybody in Ummulong village knew not to go by Pohskur on their own; they only travelled in groups.

And, they prayed to Ka Blai Pynsum Kule. This river goddess was endowed with magical powers of her own *and* she was a benevolent spirit. The people of the village had been praying to her since time immemorial. They performed various rituals and offered many sacrifices to her to appease her. In return, she blessed the people and the village in many ways. She saved them from natural calamities such as earthquakes and cyclones, or helped them tide over difficulties like scarcity of water and food. She also had the powers to cure the sick and ailing. The people of Ummulong village thus loved and revered her.

Unfortunately, however, with the passage of time, and under U thlen Lawania's growing influence, Ka Blai Pynsum Kule's attitude towards the people of the village started changing. The serpent god was relentless in his wooing. Every day, he came to see her and to try and convince her to marry him. And every day, a little bit of his malevolence rubbed off on the river goddess. In the end, from her continued association with U thlen Lawania, she turned into a malevolent spirit herself.

She gave in one day, and married the serpent god. In due course of time, they had children. Now, as is the custom in the traditionally matrilineal Jaintia households, U thlen continued to live on Lawania hill. But he would visit his wife and children every now and then. Ka Blai Pynsum Kule, meanwhile, lived on in her former home, the river.

Even though they lived thus apart, the two supernatural beings, with their combined ill will now started plaguing the people of Ummulong village most frightfully. They would often cause harm to them and spare no one if they felt threatened or challenged in any way. Under the circumstances, diseases and death became common occurrences in the village and people started living in constant fear. Life became unpredictable and people would drown in the river all of a sudden, or they would be struck by deadly diseases.

For a long time thereafter, there was utter chaos in the village. The people felt helpless because the goddess who had been so kind to them earlier was now causing them so much grief. But human beings are resilient by nature, and they always find a way to face every calamity. The people of the village therefore, sat down one day to discuss the situation. After much deliberation, they came to the conclusion that no matter how malevolent she had now become, Ka Blai Pynsum Kule had the powers to protect them. Hadn't she done just that for so many generations now? So even if she had changed now, she would still have those powers within her. The need for them then, was to find a way to elicit once again her protective instincts.

Once the solution to their problem was thus found, it only remained for the villagers to find a way to make it work. Again, there was a lot of deliberation on the subject. And finally, there was a decision. A ritual would be devised and an appropriate sacrifice earmarked to appease the goddess. From past experience, they knew what the goddess was partial to. So they decided that in order to escape death or sickness, they would have to offer her a cock or a pig or a pair of yellow hens. They also charted out the rituals to accompany the sacrifice. That done, they invited people from all the nearby villages and beyond to come and take part in the ceremony.

It turned out that the villagers had been right about the goddess's likes and dislikes. Their offerings and prayers did indeed move the goddess, and she started protecting the people once again. The people, in turn, continued to revere her, though they also feared her, and they realized that they should steer clear of the abodes of these supernatural beings and leave them alone. The Jaintia people who practise Niamtre, the traditional religion, perform many rituals in front of the river Pynsum Kule till this day.

18. Garo

Healing with herbs

The Achiks of Achik Asong were peace-loving people, who lived fruitful lives. They cultivated their jhum kheti fields and lived off the bounty of nature. Indeed, they had a great reverence for nature, and nature too was therefore kind to them.

Among the Achiks, in the ancient days which this tale tells of, was a young man named Delong. His village was called Rongna and it was situated near a primitive forest that hid many secrets. But the people of Rongna felt that these secrets were best left unveiled. They would often, for instance, hear strange sounds like the beating of drums and gongs or the distant roar of thunder when there was no rain emanating from near the forest. Or sometimes, there could be heard the wailing and shouting of what sounded like human voices from the unexplored depths of this forest. It was said the forest was the abode of many supernatural beings, who did not appreciate any human interference. There were so many terrifying tales about the horrific ends met by the people who had dared to enter the forest in the days of yore that nobody from Rongna had even questioned these strange happenings in recent memory. But Delong shocked them all one fine day by declaring that he would enter the forest and seek some answers.

Now this young man was quiet and unassuming, loved by all. He was a good son, a good neighbour and a good soul, who helped all in need. He lived close to nature and had a shrewd mind. Being honest and upright, he was also fearless. Nobody knew how this sudden need for adventure and thrill had seized this young man who had so far been of a placid temperament. The villagers were all surprised to hear of his intent, and his parents, especially, tried all they could to prevent him from undertaking this dangerous journey into the heart of the unknown. Delong, however, remained resolute.

'There are many wild beasts in the forest, Son. Do not go,' his mother said to him.

'But I have a clear conscience, Mother. And don't our elders say that wild animals do not attack those who are fearless and honest?' he retorted. 'Weren't we all taught since childhood that beasts know instinctively if a human being is pure or not? That they only attack those who violate nature's laws and live sinful lives? Don't you think I have lived a good life, a truthful life so far? Why then are you scared?'

'But there will be other hurdles out there, Son,' said his father to him. 'What will you eat? Where will you sleep? How will you fend for yourself?'

'Father,' Delong replied. 'I shall not go unequipped. I have already prepared a deer-skin dress for myself, sharpened an axe and a dao, besides filling a leather bag with provisions and a pot, flint stones and other necessary things. Please do not worry for me.'

In the end, since nothing they said could deter their son, Delong's parents blessed him and sent him on his way. As his mother had said, there were indeed many wild animals that he encountered along the way. But he was not frightened. The animals also sensed his goodness and strength and let him pass.

The big tiger, the agile leopard, the fierce panther and the wolves, all looked at him as he passed, but let him pass.

The mighty elephant, the long-horned buffalo, the sturdy bison, the wild boar and the bear, all stopped a while as he went by, but let him pass.

The docile deer, the timid birds, the bees and wasps and ants and other insects, all watched him warily, but let him pass.

The python, the cobra and various other reptiles slithered around silently, sensing his presence, but let him pass.

Delong also felt a strange kinship with these animals and birds and reptiles of the forest and proceeded unafraid. He took his time to look around him, at the grandeur of the tall trees, the beauty of the wild flowers and the immeasurable bounty of nature. It was like he was rediscovering a whole new universe within the forest.

And unlike what his father had feared, Delong was fending quite well for himself inside the ancient forest. He felt safe under the green canopy of the majestic trees when he sat down to rest. The limpid streams gurgling their way through the small clearings under these trees proffered him the sweetest water he had ever tasted. He entertained himself by marvelling at the smoothness of the pebbles by these streams where he laid his bed of leaves every night to sleep.

In the morning, he would be awakened by the birds chirping, and the insects buzzing. He caught fish and crabs where he could, started a fire and boiled or roasted them to eat. There was also a bounty of edible roots and shoots, vegetables and fruits in the vast forest. In short, he never felt any want as he continued on his journey thus. Overwhelmed as he was with the way nature was now nurturing him, Delong wondered how anybody could ever think evil thoughts amidst such surroundings.

Fourteen days thus went by, with Delong wandering around, alone and contented. At the end of those days, he suddenly found himself in an open plain, covered in green grass and shrubs, resplendent with wild lilies and the most beautiful flowers Delong had ever seen. As he looked out at the expanse, he saw in the middle of the valley a small hillock, flat on top, clothed in the same bounty of nature that had been bestowed upon the ancient forest. From where he stood, Delong saw that the northern approach to the hillock was placidly guarded by a deep but small lake. It was fed by small rock-springs that slid down from the top of the hillock. On all the other sides, the face of the hillock was dotted with big rocks, seemingly impregnable. The entire scene was one of beauty and peace, and Delong stood for a long time soaking it all in.

But the sense of adventure that had propelled him thus far started goading him on again, and he decided to now unveil the secrets of this wondrous, seemingly impenetrable fortress of nature. Forging ahead through the tangle of creepers and flowers and shrubs and tall grass, Delong slowly reached the foot of the plateau. Then, he started diligently and cheerfully to climb up the sloping rock face.

Being a strong young man, it did not take him too long to scale the hillock. But what he saw when he reached the top nearly took his breath away. Protected as it was on all sides by the thick walls formed by the rocks, the flat land at the top was another whole new world for Delong. It looked like a wooded paradise built atop an overturned brass gong. At the centre were three huge rocks on three sides of a small meadow. From each of these rocks, three small rills flowed, sliding gently down to the placid lake below. The sight of the rocks fascinated Delong. He thought they looked like three sentinels standing guard over what lay beyond, or beneath. Having come this far in his quest, he proceeded even further now towards the rocks.

No sooner had he reached the foot of the rocks, though, that a big black dog appeared in front of him. It advanced towards him with a menacing snarl. Delong raised his hands in front of him to defend himself in case the dog decided to jump at him, but just as suddenly as the dog had appeared before him, its keeper also abruptly turned up, as if from nowhere. She was a dusky beauty, with a sweet voice than was also strangely commanding. The dog seemed to be under her spell, for no sooner had she uttered her command that it stopped snarling and slunk back until it disappeared from view altogether.

Then she turned towards Delong and asked, 'What brings you here, stranger? Don't you know this is the secret abode of the Queen of Herbs and Plants?'

Filled with awe at having discovered such an enchanted place, Delong answered humbly: 'I am just a simple man who loves adventure. I came here because my quest for knowledge kept egging me on, showing me the path that led to this beautiful plateau where we now stand.'

'Follow me,' said the young woman now, 'and I shall present you to our queen'.

Delong followed her obediently as they entered a cavern in the rocks. He did not have any fear in his heart as she led him through long corridors lined with rare and precious stones that glittered even in the dark. Delong calculated that they must have walked nearly seven hundred paces from the mouth of the cave before they reached a big hall. In the middle of the hall, he saw a fountain of crystal-clear water, surging out from the ground and making its way into a small trough along one side of the rock-lined corridor. As Delong would later come to know, this fountain was a thermal spring the waters of which were rich in many minerals hidden in the depths of the rocks below. Many subterranean herbs grew at the source of the fountain, bashful of the human touch. Of them all, the most precious were known as Ahning Samtha Gisim or Kalanggea, and Sulingji. Warm to the touch but refreshing to drink, the medicinal properties of the waters of this fountain could cure all human diseases.

Delong was made to sit on a flint chair which was also decked in various precious stones and metals. He did not have to wait long before the Queen of Herbs and Plants herself appeared before him. She was supremely beautiful and wore clothes made of the silken fibre of plants and decorated with lovely flowers. Delong was so charmed by her majesty and beauty that he was speechless. But the Queen of Herbs and Plants could divine what was in his heart. She was an enchanted creature and could therefore read Delong's heart and mind, his every thought and feeling, his desires and disgusts.

'You need not speak, Delong,' she assured him now. 'I have looked within you and seen everything there is to see. Be not afraid. You are perfectly safe here in my haven. I sense you are hungry and thirsty. Swallow this small morsel I'm giving you now and you shall not feel hunger and thirst for a long time after.'

Delong did as she bid him do, and he was surprised to see that indeed his hunger had been assuaged by the tiny morsel and his thirst quenched at the same time.

'It is late now,' she said when she saw that her guest was thus satisfied. 'Sleep now for you must be tired from your wanderings. I have assigned for you tonight a cozy nook of my cave home. Tomorrow, you shall see more wonders.'

Delong slept peacefully, and woke up refreshed. He felt ready to see whatever other amazing and wondrous sights and experiences awaited him next. When the queen appeared before him that morning, she once again offered him a small morsel of the same strange food that he had eaten for dinner the night before, and it was enough to satiate Delong's hunger and thirst. Then, she asked him to follow her out of the cave.

Out in the sunlight again, the queen pointed out to Delong her two gardens of priceless plants and herbs, one in the east and the other to the west. She promised to show him both very soon.

'Look to your east, Delong,' she said. 'Today, we shall be going into this eastern garden, where I grow all the rare herbs, plants, tubers and creepers that can cure every human ailment and perform innumerable miracles.'

Delong looked and saw that at the very entrance of the garden was a plant bearing exquisitely fine and small grains—an insignificant quantity of which he had been asked to eat by the queen the day before and in the morning. The queen explained to him now that it was a perennial plant named Dikge Mijanggi. It bore these seeds all year round, and only one tiny seed, if dipped in water and ingested, could dispel the most acute hunger and thirst. Then she led him into the garden and showed him her amazing plants.

There were plants that enabled the herbalist to control the actions and thoughts of human beings, animals and spirits. There were also those that gave her supernatural vision. Some of them were antidotes for the most deadly poisons, some that could heal any injury. Cures for leprosy, blood impurities, loss of strength and potency, the ailments of old age, and all other human sicknesses were also right there. There were those that acted as aphrodisiacs, some that could dispel other peoples' ill-will. A few herbs could give one the power to control wild animals, a few to control wild passions. One herb could make a person invisible, another could make her heavy or light, big or small. But alongside every herb that could cause any of these wonders, was another that could counter its effects. And only the Queen of Herbs and Plants knew the secrets of all the herbs, plants, creepers and trees that grew in her luxuriant garden.

That night Delong slept once again in his cosy nook, tired from his wanderings in the queen's eastern garden. He knew that the next day, they would be exploring the garden to the west, and he looked forward to the adventure.

When they climbed out to the top of the hillock once again the next morning, the queen said, 'In the west, Delong, I grow the most powerful poisonous herbs and plants. But they can do as much good as harm. It all depends on the person who is handling them, and his or her intent. Together, in my two gardens, I have all the rare herbs and plants of the entire world.'

Delong turned towards the western garden excitedly, but the queen stopped him. She handed him a dried root and said, 'Keep this in your hand. There are many plants in the west garden that let off poisonous vapours. They might suffocate you when in there. If you feel weird in any way, just sniff at this root, and you will be fine. Come now, let's go.'

The entrance to the west garden was kept blocked by a heavy flat stone. The queen naturally did not want anybody straying into it and falling prey to the noxious fumes so many of the plants there exuded. Once the stone had been removed, Delong and the queen entered. He came to know during his tour of the garden that the most potently poisonous of all the herbs and plants in this garden was called Mahadebni Sambisi or Mahanilokanto. To touch the plant meant death, to smell the plant meant death. No living being could be near the plant and breathe the same air as the plant and escape alive. Delong however, was unaffected thanks to the dried root the queen had earlier given him. There were many other herbs and plants besides and these could kill, maim, madden, or make malevolent all human beings, animals or spirits that came in contact with them.

Delong lived with the queen for a long time thereafter, acquiring her passion for herbs and plants. She knew that being a mere mortal, he would not be able to remember her entire repertoire of knowledge, but she made sure that he was imparted knowledge of the ones that would be the most useful in the human world.

Despite the amazing new world that had opened up in front of Delong, and despite all the satisfaction he felt from all the esoteric knowledge he was gathering, after a few months, he started feeling homesick. The queen, of course, divined his thoughts and did whatever she could to dispel them. This happened many times, but with the passage of time, the intervals between these episodes of homesickness started growing shorter. Finally, the rains came. One day, dark clouds gathered in the sky above Delong as he was taking yet another lesson from the queen. Suddenly, brilliant lightning and thunder roared in the sky. Then, the rains came pouring down.

'The rains are here, I have to leave,' Delong exclaimed. 'My parents are all alone and unable to work in the fields. I have to help them in the jhum kheti.'

There was a new determination in his voice and the queen realized the time had come to let Delong go back to the world of human beings. She gave him a leather bag filled with the roots and seeds of many herbs, plants, creepers and tubers, both poisonous and non-poisonous. Then she said to him, 'Go, Delong, I know your heart is no longer with us. But take these roots and seeds. Grow them in your very own garden, tend carefully to them and use their properties to serve other humans.'

Delong said goodbye with a heavy heart, but he was also at the same time yearning for his parents. But when he turned his back to leave, the queen again called out to him, 'Wait, Delong. I have seen into your heart and felt your yearning. Let me give you a little something to help you reach your parents sooner.' Handing him the root of a plant, she said, 'This is the root of the rarest kind of Dikge Kamal. It shall help you find your way back to your native village by the shortest possible route.'

Delong did indeed reach his parents' house sooner than he expected, but of course, it was much later than his parents had been expecting him back home. They had waited for him to come back to the village all these months and nearly given up hope. So when he did turn up now, they were overjoyed!

'Our son is back!' they announced to the whole village ecstatically and everybody came to see Delong and ask him questions about his adventures in the ancient forest. There was a big feast afterwards. Delong spoke to everybody and told them many tales of his various adventures. But the secret of the secret hillock, the abode of the Queen of Herbs and Plants, remained buried in his heart. He did not even tell his parents about his sojourn there.

The morning after he returned to his village, Delong woke up very early and disappeared into the forest again. He had with him the leather bag that the queen had given him, and a dao and a hoe. In the forest, he cleared a small site, divided it into two equal halves and planted the roots and seeds the bag contained. He arranged the plants exactly as the queen had arranged them in her garden of the east and her garden of the west. Finally, he cut down some bamboo from the forest and carved some wooden spikes and fenced his two gardens securely.

When he returned, his parents asked him where he had been. So did his relations and the other people of the village. But Delong was steadfast in his resolve to guard the secret of the queen's abode. He gave them some evasive replies. When he continued to do so every time he went to the forest and every time they asked him the same questions, they all finally gave up.

Meanwhile, Delong's garden was flourishing day by day. So he gradually started using his herbs and plants and the knowledge of their medicinal and miraculous properties to help the people of his village. He cured diseases of the body and the soul. He gave them antidotes for poisons and poisonous intents. In short, he became their most revered healer. Before long, his fame started spreading far and wide. People came to see him and seek his help from faraway villages and he never turned them back.

The realization had finally dawned on the people of his village that whatever he did inside the forest must be the cause for the good that he was spreading among them and among all the other people of the land. Therefore, they stopped pestering him with questions about his activities outside the bounds of the village. This made Delong happy for now he could concentrate on his assigned duty as healer of his people. He put his heart and soul, and all his concentration, into the job, so much so that he did not marry. All his time was dedicated to serving his people. He had no time for social relationships anymore, or for kinships of any kind.

But he had one friend, only one, named Neurot, who had been his confidant for long. To him alone Delong spoke about his days in the abode of the Queen of Herbs and Plants. And to him alone he imparted some of the knowledge he had gathered from the benevolent queen. He also took Neurot to see his twin gardens, where he would often speak about this herb or that, this plant or that, and their many wondrous qualities.

Unlike Delong, Neurot was a married man and worldly in his own ways. But he looked up to his friend and admired his selflessness and dedication. He soaked in all the scraps of knowledge that Delong passed on to him and wished he could learn more. Slowly, the desire started growing in him to see the source of all this knowledge that his friend possessed.

'Take me to the queen's cavern,' he started entreating Delong. Delong was hesitant at first, but Neurot was so persuasive that he finally caved in. It had been three years since Delong had come back to his village, and he was also secretly longing to meet the gracious queen once again. So he looked around inside his leather bag once again and located the rare root that the Queen of Herbs and Plants had given him to help him find his way back.

'Surely it will also lead me and Neurot back to the same place,' he hoped as the two friends prepared to embark on their journey. His hope was not misplaced and before long, Delong and Neurot found themselves at the foot of the queen's enchanted hillock.

When the queen saw the two men approach, she sent one of her companions to accost them before they tried ascending the rock face of the hillock. Neurot was surprised to see the girl suddenly appear in front of him and his friend. But what she said replaced his surprise with utter disappointment. 'The queen welcomes you back, Delong,' she said. 'You may continue to her abode. But she bids me tell you that your companion is a married man, a man encumbered with worldly concerns. And such men are not allowed to scale the heights to stand in her presence. You must therefore send him back home. Give him the rare root that brought you here, and it will lead him there.'

There was little either Delong or Neurot could do now, other than following the queen's instructions. With heavy hearts therefore, they said goodbye to each other. Delong climbed up the hill to be with the queen once again, and Neurot returned to the village, alone. The latter waited for his friend to return for many years thereafter. But Delong seemed to have disappeared yet again.

Finally, after many years, Neurot decided to go in search of his friend by himself. He tried to recall the route they had taken the last time and to follow it. In the end, just as Delong had stumbled upon the beautiful valley on his first journey into the ancient forest, Neurot also did manage to reach the valley where he had parted with his friend so many years ago. But the hillock that had stood at its heart, washed by the lake and guarded by the firm rocks, the hillock which he had last seen his friend ascending, was no longer there. Where did it go? Where was Delong, his mortal friend? And where were the magical queen and her enchanted abode?

Neurot had no way of knowing. His limited worldly vision did not allow him to know anything more than what he saw with his naked eyes. For all we know, perhaps the hillock was right there in front of him, and he could not see it because of his limited vision. Or perhaps the queen had indeed spirited Delong and her magical abode away to some other ancient forest in some other part of the created universe. Just like Neurot, we have no way of knowing.

What we do know however, is that Neurot returned to his village with great sadness at the loss of his friend. But he always respected his friend's memory. And he treasured the little knowledge that his friend had passed on to him—about the herbs and the seeds and the leaves and the roots that the Queen of Herbs and Plants had gifted human beings. It is from Neurot then that this knowledge has been passed down through the generations. The Achik people today know whatever little they do know about the many virtues of herbs and plants because Neurot had remembered a little.

Mizoram

Known as the Lushai Hills Autonomous District and included within the administrative bounds of Assam since 1952, Mizoram became a separate state of the Indian Union in 1987. Dotted by blue hills, undulating valleys and flowing rivers and placid lakes, it is literally the 'land of the hill people'. There are as many as 21 hill ranges and peaks in Mizoram, the highest among them being Phawngpui Tlang (7250 ft). Adjacent to Burma, it shares its biggest river, Chhimtuipui or Kaladan, with the neighbouring country. Mizoram also shares an international boundary with Bangladesh which was East Pakistan till 1971, and hostile towards India. Taking advantage of this proximity and disillusioned by the administrative apathy of the then Assam government, a section of the Mizos took up arms against the Indian State after forming the Mizo National Front (MNF). Following the MNF uprising of March 1966, the Indian State bombed several areas in Mizoram in response and killed many civilians. On the ground, the village regroupings and other measures that were taken to subdue the insurgency have quite changed the fabric of traditional Mizo life forever. The relative peace that Mizoram enjoys today was thus bought at a very high price.

The Mizos are a cluster of several tribal groups that claim ethnic kinship with each other. These include the Gangte, Lushei,

Paite, Lai, Mara and Ralte among others. The tribes are then sub-divided into sub-tribes, clans and sub-clans. The Hmars, for instance, are divided into Thiek, Biete, Faihriem, Lungtau, Darngawn, Khawbung, Zote and so on. Largely Christianized, a small section of the Mizos—the Bnei Menashe—however, claims Jewish descent. Over and above these many Mizo communities, there are also a few non-Mizo tribes—like the Bru (Reang), Chakma, Tanchangya—living in Mizoram.

The Chins are an ethnic group of Burma. In India, they are found in the states of Nagaland, Manipur, Assam and Mizoram. They share close ethnic ties with the Mizo and Kuki people and are largely Christianized. A small number among them claims to be part of the Bnei Menashe community—one of the lost tribes of Israel. The major tribes among the Chin include Asho, K'cho, Khumi, Zomi, Laizo, Laimi, Matu, Mara and others. They prefer to call themselves Zomi as the word Chin is alien to their language. The Chins in Mizoram live mostly in the Lai Autonomous District Council. A majority of them are political refugees who have been fleeing to the state over the years since 1988 in order to escape persecution and human rights violations by the Burmese military. With a numerical strength of about a lakh, they form a significant chunk of the population in Mizoram today. Though sometimes welcomed as the ethnic kin that they are, the Chins have also faced a lot of hostility over the decades.

One of the Kuki tribes of Northeast India, the Maras live largely in the southern tip of Mizoram. Some of them are also found in neighbouring Burma. Since 1972, they have been granted their own autonomous council in Mizoram: the Mara Autonomous District Council (earlier known as the Lakher Autonomous District Council). They were earlier called the Lakhers and have been known as Mara since 1978. There are various sub-clans among the Maras like the Sizo-Chapi, Hawthai, Hlaipao-Zyhno, Iana or Vytu, Lochei and Tlosai. They speak a language that is closely allied to the Mizo and

Chin lanaguages, and is Tibeto-Burman in origin. They are overwhelmingly Christian.

The Lusheis are a Mizo tribe. They are found spread over Mizoram, Burma and Bangladesh. In Mizoram, they are the most dominant community among the other Mizos tribes that include the Lai, Ralte, Hmar, Paite and Gangte. They are mostly Christian, with a few Bnei Menashe among them. They speak the Lushai language which is used as the lingua franca by most of the other, smaller Mizo tribes. As such, it was enlisted as the official Mizo language of the state of Mizoram. Traditionally, they are a patriarchal society. Each traditional Lushei village was governed by a hereditary chief known as a Lal.

In Northeast India, the Reangs are spread over much of Tripura, Assam, Manipur and Mizoram. They are also found in Bangladesh. Legend has it that they migrated to the Lushai hills along with a Tripuri prince who was exiled by the king and settled in the southern parts of Mizoram. The legend goes on to state that many of them eventually returned to the kingdom of Tripura. However, a sizeable portion stayed back in Mizoram. In recent times, the Reangs of Mizoram have again been forced to flee to neighbouring Tripura owing to ethnic violence and an inimical political climate prevailing in Mizoram since 1997. Largely Hinduized, some Reangs of Mizoram have also adopted Christianity. They are primarily an agrarian tribe.

19. Chin

White river gushing

All Chin tribes of the Northeast trace their origins back to Singlung or Chin-lung, an imagined homeland from which they spread out to the rest of the world. For some tribes, the name for Singlung is different in their respective dialects, but always, it means or refers to a cave or hole or crevice. They believe that it is this cave from which they emerged as humans. The reason there are more of some human communities and less of others in this world is because the members of some communities called out their names when they came out,

and when God thought there were enough of them, he stopped their way. Some other communities of people, however, walked out silently in huge numbers before God realized it. The Raltes say that before all the humans could come out of the cave, two Raltes who emerged together started talking to each other; and so loud was their chattering, and so incessant, that Pathian, the Supreme God, thought too many humans had already surfaced. So, he shut the mouth of the chasm with a stone.

This emergence of human beings from the bowels of the earth is often followed by the destruction of the original homeland. With the homeland lost, the people were forced to disperse to different places in the world. According to one version of this belief, it was a simple thirst for adventure that caused the abandonment of the original homeland of Singlung. But in most others, it is a (super)natural calamity. For instance, some Chin tribes believe their ancestors abandoned their home because a great darkness engulfed the world. Some of these tribes call this great darkness Thimzing, some call it Khazanghra, and yet others call it Chunmui. There are also those tribes which believe it was because of a great flood. The Zophei, for one, call this great flood Tuirang-aa-pia, which literally means 'white water (or river) pouring or gushing out'. This 'white river' is surmised to be the Chindwin, which originates in Burma. The river is known by many other names – Tuikhang, Tirang, Tuipui-ia and so on—the meanings of which are all the same. The claim, therefore, is often made that the original settlement of the Chins—indeed of all human beings—was the Chindwin Valley. The Zophei people have a fascinating tale to tell, of how this original settlement was lost to the Chin people.

In the valley of Singlung, was a village. The Zophei say that all human beings lived together in this village when the world was first created. At the very centre of the village was placed a large stone. The people of the valley knew that the stone had been placed there to cover a deep chasm. It was a long dark subterranean cave that ran beneath the entire length of the valley. At the end of its sinuous length, this cave connected with the endless sea. The people of the only village in the world called this vast sea Tipi-thuan-thum.

There are innumerable tales of sea monsters in almost every folk culture in the world. The Chins also have their own. The sea monster of Zophei lore lived in Tipi-thuan-thum. It was a large snake that lived in the dark underground cave, and it was known as Pari-bui or Limpi by the people of the village. Pari-bui was a much dreaded monster, for it caused much harm to the people. Every night, it would come out of its lair beneath the giant rock in the centre of the village and prowl for prey. And invariably, it would pick on the small children. The villagers were extremely sorrowed by the loss of their children to this monster every night, night after night, but were too scared to do anything.

'It is a monster,' they rationalized, 'and will eat us too if we try to prevent it from having its meal'.

Sometimes though, there would be a few brave individuals who would shout out, 'But its meal happens to be our children, our flesh and blood. How can we just stand aside and watch as it devours our offspring. If this were allowed to continue, we would soon be wiped out from the face of the earth. Is that what we want?'

It took a while, but finally, these brave individuals prevailed upon the rest of the villagers to take a stand. There were many deliberations and discussions about what could be done to prevent the snake from snacking on their children. Many strategies were proposed but soon discarded because of inherent flaws that were discovered by discerning members of the community.

In the end, a simple plan was hatched which would call for a lot of grit and gumption and in which all the villagers would have to participate. They called upon the finest craftsmen of the village, who then manufactured the strongest and biggest iron fish hook that could be made. The next step was the weaving together of the thickest and sturdiest rope they could weave together. The entire village then looked around for the biggest and fleshiest dog they could find. The plan was to use the dog as bait to draw the monster, Pari-bui, out of his lair.

On the appointed day, the villagers all gathered around the large rock that covered the mouth of Pari-bui's subterranean cave home. The dog that had been tethered and fed for this day was also carried to the spot and slain. The cadaver of the dog was then impaled to the fish hook which was in turn tied to the strong rope. As a body, the villagers then pushed the rock away from the mouth of the cave. Then, the slain dog was slowly lowered into the cave. All they could do now was wait for the monster to take their bait. So they waited.

Now Pari-bui, who only hunted at night, was doing what he did during the day, every day—he was sleeping. His sleep was first disturbed by the sound of the rock being removed from the mouth of his lair. He turned. When daylight started creeping into his dark cavern, he was slightly agitated. But still he did not wake up. Then the dog was lowered into the cave. He could smell blood and raw flesh, and felt his stomach turn with hunger. He could not resist opening his eyes and raising his head.

When he saw the cadaver, dripping with fresh blood, his jaws opened wide, as though of their own accord, and 'snap!'—they closed around the dog. It was a fat dog, and succulent, and Pari-bui enjoyed that first bite. But when he started biting in deeper, trying to tear the flesh out, the fish hook sank into his gullet and lodged itself there. The first part of the villagers' plan had succeeded!

Pari-bui started thrashing around in pain as the hook refused to dislodge. He did not, of course, realize that the more he struggled, the deeper it would sink into his flesh. And the deeper it sank, the more the villagers cheered for they thought they had finally succeeded in outwitting the monster. Unfortunately, however, outwitting the monster was only half the battle won. He was still alive and capable of doing harm. The thing to do now was to haul the snake monster out and kill it.

Feeling optimistic now that they could indeed slay the monster that had been eating their children and threatening their existence, the villagers started pulling at the rope, dragging Pari-bui out little by little through the mouth of the cave. Here is where they faced their greatest challenge, for the more they pulled, there seemed to be more of the snake inside the pit. They kept wrapping the portions of the snake's body that came out of the underground lair around the big rock they had dislodged and set aside near the mouth of the lair. Five times round the snake's body went, and five times round the villagers thought they had finally seen the last of Pari-bui's body being dragged out. But it was not to be.

The villagers were all tired, for Pari-bui was a fearsome monster with supernatural strength. He was outwitted and outnumbered, but not to be overwhelmed. In the end, somebody shouted out from among the villagers, 'There can't be much of him left inside. Let's just cut him off here and he'll perish.'

Tired and only too eager to give up, the villagers all agreed. A huge machete was fetched and Pari-bui was struck in two—the part of him that was above the ground stayed with the villagers, the rest slid down below, back into the darkness with a mighty thud. The earth shook and the villagers cheered.

The portion that remained above was pounded and prodded till everybody was sure the monster had been slain. The villagers felt very proud of themselves. That night, there was a big feast and everybody ate and drank to their heart's content. Later, they slept more peacefully than they had done in a long long time.

That night, something strange happened. In the belief that if one half of the snake could be destroyed, the other half would also perish, the villagers had left the mouth of Pari-bui's lair uncovered. The rock that had covered it had been left by the side, and it still had Pari-bui's upper portion tied around it five times over. Meanwhile, the villagers slept their deep sleep of contentment. But while they did so, water started seeping slowly out of the hole in the ground.

The slow seepage soon became a trickle, and then a torrent. Very soon, the village was inundated. The villagers were rudely woken up by the incoming deluge. They started running helter-skelter, but no matter where they ran, the water followed them. It was as if Pari-bui had turned into this torrential white water and was seeking revenge. Very soon, the original settlement of human beings, that village which Pari-bui had terrorized, was under water. Its inhabitants had fled in all different directions in search of high ground, and dry. And so it was that human beings scattered to the many corners of the world and took up habitation there. Some climbed the hills, some found distant valleys inaccessible to the white water gushing mightily. But everywhere, they started speaking new tongues now and practising different cultures, so that the world as we know it now took shape—diverse and dappled. We would do well to remember, though, that we all came from the same place, that same little village.

20. Mara

Before the final plunge

Laitha was a young man when he got married. His wife was a hard-working woman who helped him keep house. She also laboured alongside him in the fields. Life was beautiful for them after marriage. In due course of time, Laitha's wife became pregnant, and the young couple was very happy. The young woman, however, did not stop working in the field, for that was the mainstay of the family.

One day, when she was leaving for the fields as usual, the as yet unborn baby in her belly cried out, 'O Mother, I can sense that it is going to rain today. Do not get wet, carry a palm-leaf with you. It will shield you from the rain.'

'Bah,' said the would-be mother. 'You are only a foetus. What do you know about the outside world? How can you be so sure it will rain? The sun is shining bright, and I shall not heed your advice, little one!'

So saying, she left the house and was proved wrong when it did suddenly start raining in the middle of the day and she was soaked through. It continued to rain the whole day and throughout the night. The next morning, the sky was still overcast when Laitha's wife set out for the fields as usual. As on the previous day, the as yet unborn baby in her belly cried out again, 'O Mother, I can sense that it is going to be very hot and sunny today. Do not become dry of mouth, carry some water with you today. It will quench your thirst in the sun.'

'Bah,' said the would-be mother again. 'You are only a foetus. What do you know about the outside world? How can you be so sure it will be sunny? The sky is overcast, and I shall not heed your advice, little one!'

So saying, she left the house with a palm-leaf, but no water. Once again, she was proved wrong when the sky did suddenly become clear and the sun started burning down brightly. At the end of the day, she returned home very thirsty.

When the child was finally born, it turned out to be a boy. The young couple decided to call him Nara. It was time for the harvest when Nara was born. So, Laitha and his wife could not stay home. They decided to take Nara with them to the field. While they busied themselves harvesting their crops, they laid down their newborn son on the verandah of the *jhum* house.

The little baby lay there quite contented. Suddenly, he saw a kite hovering in the skies above him. It was crying piteously. Nara called out to it, 'O Kite, what does your crying mean? Is it going to be hot today? Or is it going to rain? Tell me!'

When Laitha heard the voice thus calling out, he thought it belonged to a grown man. Therefore, he called out, 'Hush, whoever you are. Do not speak so loudly. Our little baby boy is sleeping in the hut and he will wake up!'

A little later, Nara once again started speaking to the kite, and Laitha became very upset. 'Did you not hear me asking you to be quiet?' he called out. But when the same thing happened once again a little later, Laitha left his work and made his way to the jhum hut. When he reached there, however, he could not see anybody other than Nara. 'Whoever it was must have run away,' he concluded and returned to the field.

To his utter surprise, the same thing happened the next day, and Laitha was once again, very upset. With the intention of catching unawares whoever it was that was making so much noise near his sleeping son, he quietly made his way towards the jhum hut. What he saw there made him very afraid. It was his newborn son who was speaking to the kite, and saying, 'O Kite, what does your crying mean? Is it going to be hot today? Or is it going to rain? Tell me!'

'How can this be?' said Laitha to himself. 'Is my son a sorcerer, too, then?'

For Laitha was a skilled sorcerer himself, and he realized now that some of his powers must have been transferred to his son by birth. Most fathers would have been happy to find their sons had acquired their qualities, but the reason for Laitha's fear was that he did not wish to lose his magic. If Nara was so gifted as a child, he started wondering what he might grow up to be. 'What if he steals all my powers from me?' Laitha started dreading now.

He pondered over it for a long time, and in the end, devised a strategy to prevent it. Without anybody else's knowledge, he cut off a small portion of flesh from Nara's tongue and hid it in a tumour on his back. He created this tumour just below his shoulderblades, and for quite a few years thereafter, continued to live without any anxiety. For Nara had become an ordinary boy, his magical powers gone with that small portion of flesh his father had hidden away.

So Nara had a normal childhood. But one day, when he was twelve years old, he was walking down a street when he saw a young girl weaving. Seeing her at the loom, the young boy was tempted to create some mischief. He started teasing her, and to annoy her, he grabbed at her shuttle and threw it away. The girl tried to stop him from being so naughty, but when she saw she would not succeed by merely pleading with him, she baited him, 'If you stop teasing and taunting me, I will tell you a secret.'

That made Nara stop awhile. 'What secret?' he asked.

'I will tell you who you really are,' she said in return.

Nara was intrigued and he stopped bothering her. So the girl told him, 'You are a sorcerer by birth, but your father has deprived you of your magic powers.'

And she narrated the entire story of how that happened to Nara. The young boy was deeply disturbed and ran back home. When he reached, he pretended to fall ill, for on the way home, he had already thought of a plan to retrieve his magic from his scheming father. 'Oh, my stomach is aching. Mother, Father, help me!' he cried as he took to his bed.

The parents tried all ways and means to cure their son. They prayed to the gods, they performed all kinds of sacrifices, but their son refused to be 'cured'. One day, Laitha was sitting by his son's bed, deeply disturbed by the 'illness' that refused to go away, when Nara spoke up, 'Father, I have been ill for so long now. And there has been no cure. Maybe if you carried me on your back, I might find some relief for my pain.'

Laitha, however, remembered the tumour on his back, and although he did pick up his son, he sat him down upon his thighs instead.

'No, Father, hold me against you, carry me a bit higher,' Nara insisted. Laitha had no choice but to place Nara on his back. No sooner did he do this than Nara bit hard at the tumour on his father's back. He ripped it out and swallowed it whole. Immediately, he could feel his magical powers seeping back into him. But along with his own, both he and his father realized, he had also thus acquired Laitha's powers as well.

Laitha was distraught at having lost his powers. 'My son,' he pleaded, 'let me retain some of my powers at least! Do not take it all away.'

'O Father, I am sorry,' replied Nara, 'but I have swallowed it all'.

Nara grew up to be a wise man who used his magic judiciously, and for everybody's wellbeing. But it took a long time and all the years of Nara growing up for Laitha to finally admit that his son was indeed a great sorcerer. And he did this only when he was outwitted by his young son.

It so happened one day that Nara asked his father, 'Tell me Father, what do you think? Will selling pork fetch me more money or selling rice?'

'Why, pork of course, you silly boy,' his father laughed. 'Pork is dearer than rice.'

'Prove it,' challenged Nara and he carried some rice on his head, going door to door asking if anybody would buy it from him. Laitha meanwhile carried some pork in the same manner. But wherever he went, people would not dare enquire the price of the pork, for they knew it would be very expensive. However, they bought Nara's rice cheerfully, knowing it would not cost them a whole lot. Very soon, therefore, Nara's goods were all sold, while Laitha was left holding the pig in his hands, unsold.

'So, Father, am I right or are you?' Nara asked.

His father replied, 'My son, you are right. And I see now that you are a Tawsaw. You were full of wisdom and this wisdom was in you even before you left your mother's womb. I should never have doubted you.'

But just to make sure that his father would not doubt him again, Nara once again asked his father, 'Tell me, Father, what you think. If a deer and a rat come out into the streets, which one of the two would the people give chase to?'

'Why, the deer of course, you silly boy,' his father laughed.

So Nara let loose a rat in the streets and his father thereafter let loose a deer. But no sooner was the deer set free, it jumped, skipped and made its way quickly towards the wood. Nobody on the street even had time to notice it. But when Nara let loose the rat, people all saw it, and they chased it, and when they caught it, they killed it. Nara had once again proved his father wrong. And once again, his father said to him, 'My son, you are right. And I see now that you are a Tawsaw. You were full of wisdom and this wisdom was in you even before you left your mother's womb. I should never have doubted you.'

His father's recognition also strengthened Nara's own confidence in himself. He accepted now that he was indeed a very skilful sorcerer. 'I need not fear anybody in the universe anymore,' he realized.

Now, in a village some distance away, there lived another very skilled wizard. His name was Nasaipaw who was also the chief of his village. Laitha once decided to pay Chief Nasaipaw a visit. When he reached there, Nasaipaw asked Laitha, 'How did you reach this place? You came by the river of death, did you not?'

Not suspecting anything, Nara's father replied, 'Yes, Chief, I have indeed come to your village by the river of death.'

Nasaipaw said nothing, but started making beer. When the drink was brewed, he held a drinking party. Laitha was also offered his share. But no sooner had he tasted the beer than he fell down dead, so powerful was Nasaipaw's magic.

When the news of his father's death reached Nara, the young sorcerer was very angry. He decided to avenge the dark treachery, and accordingly, made his way towards Chief Nasaipaw's village. The powerful magician foresaw his coming, of course, and understood the reason why the dead man's son wanted to pay him a visit. He therefore summoned all the powers at his disposal and cast a spell on his own house. The door of his house would now prevent Nara's entry.

But Nara also was as shrewd as he was powerful. He did not try to enter the wizard's house through the door. Instead, he turned himself into a rat and dug a hole in the ground outside the house. Then he tunneled his way into the house to appear near Nasaipaw's hearth. Once inside, he changed back into a man.

Nasaipaw was stumped to see Nara inside his house when the latter made his presence known. But he decided not to make his surprise obvious.

Just as he had asked Laitha before, Nasaipaw now asked Nara, 'How have you reached this place? You have come by the river of death, have you not?'

Knowing not to trust this man, Nara replied, 'No, Chief, I have not come to your village by the river of death. I came instead by the river of life, to eat your rice and meat.'

Nasaipaw said nothing, but started making beer. When the drink was brewed, he held a drinking party. Nara was also offered his share. But Nara knew through his magic that the wizard had placed a large snake in the bamboo hollow from which he was supposed to drink. In the twinkling of an eye, when nobody was watching, he quickly changed himself into an eagle, and swooping down upon the snake, picked it out of the bamboo and threw it away. Then changing back his form, he drank the beer while Nasaipaw watched.

Then he himself cast a spell over the beer that his father's murderer would be drinking. So when Nasaipaw raised his bamboo hollow to his lips, it fastened itself to his mouth. Meanwhile, the pot which held the beer got stuck to his belly. Try as he did, Nasaipaw could not free himself. The enchanted drink also started functioning inside him and in the end, killed him. Nara then acquired all of the chief's property—his mithuns and his slaves—and returned home triumphantly.

So this was how Nara's life took shape and he grew from strength to strength. And because he was a good man, he used his powers for the good of everybody else. This also earned him many friends. One such friend was Kiatheu whom he first met while fishing in the river.

It had happened one day, when Nara had cast his net upstream. Kiatheu, meanwhile, had cast his net downstream. The two nets got entangled and the two men got into a fight. Now, Kiatheu was a tiger man, and so he was very fierce. He tried to eat Nara, but Nara fought back valiantly and tried to kill him instead. They fought for a long time and neither man could outdo the other. Finally, they gave up fighting and sat down on the ground, trying to catch their breath.

'What is your name, tiger man?' asked Nara.

'Kiatheu,' he said. 'What's yours?'

'Nara.'

And just like that, the tiger man and the wizard became friends. As a token of their friendship, they exchanged their fish. Kiatheu's fish, though, had no heads. Being a tiger man, he had eaten their heads as soon as he had caught them. Nara knew this, but being a good friend, he accepted them anyway and made his way home. Kiatheu, on the other hand, was still not wholly satisfied that Nara had truly accepted him as a friend. After all, it is not usual for human beings to be so friendly with tiger people. Therefore, he turned himself into a bee and followed Nara. He could do so because, like Nara, he was also a skilled sorcerer.

When Nara reached home, he handed over all his fish to his mother. His mother immediately sat down to wash and clean them. But when she saw that the fish had no heads, she enquired suspiciously, 'Why, Nara, the fish have no heads! Whatever happened to their heads?'

Now, Nara knew that the bee that had been hovering round him since he had left the riverside was none other than his newfound friend. He also knew why his new friend had followed him, and he had no intention of betraying him. So he replied, 'Mother, I was hungry and so I cut off the heads and cooked them. I ate them before leaving for home.'

Kiatheu was touched when he heard this, and he realized Nara was a true friend whom he could trust. So he gladly flew back home towards his village. His friendship with Nara now meant a lot to Kiatheu and he decided to invite his friend home one day. He sent word to Nara to come and stay in his village for a few days. Nara also treasured his friendship with Kiatheu and gladly accepted the invitation. A date was thus fixed for his arrival at Kiatheu's village.

As a rule, tiger people love eating humans. All of Kiatheu's neighbours and relatives who lived in his village were tiger people. It would be reasonable therefore, to deduce that they all eagerly awaited the arrival of Nara. But Kiatheu was loved and feared by all the villagers and his word hardly ever went unheeded. So when he cautioned all the villagers against trying to harm his friend in any way, they were not very happy, but they did agree to curb their appetites and leave Nara alone.

'And one more thing,' Kiatheu announced just before Nara was to reach their village, 'do not appear before my friend as tigers. Change yourselves into people, for otherwise, you might scare our guest.'

The villagers all did as they were instructed, but Kiatheu's parents were adamant. So Kiatheu put them in a basket and covered it with a lid. When Nara reached, he was given a rousing welcome into the village. Then he was taken to Kiatheu's house.

'Where are your parents?' Nara asked. 'I would like to pay my respects to them, my friend.'

'Oh, my parents are very poor people, and unworthy of being seen by you,' Kiatheu replied.

'Do not say that, Kiatheu,' Nara gently admonished him. 'Nobody should ever consider their parents unworthy of being seen. All parents deserve respect. Do take me to them.'

So Kiatheu was forced to lift the lid of the basket where his parents lay curled up. When they saw Nara, they jumped up and snarled at him, trying to bite him. But Nara was not afraid.

He only exclaimed, 'What beautiful parents you have, my friend! And you would not let me see them!'

This pleased Kiatheu's parents and they decided to be graceful to their visitor. They turned themselves into people immediately, and accepted the clothes and other gifts that Nara had brought for them. In return, they held a great feast. A big pig was slaughtered and the whole village was invited. They left no stone unturned to show their son's friend how pleased they were with his visit.

So Nara had a good time at Kiatheu's village. He stayed there for five days. When it was finally time to leave, Kiatheu took his friend to the orchard. He drew his attention to a tree which bore all kinds of heads instead of fruits. 'My friend,' he said, 'take as many of these as you wish'.

Nara thanked his friend for his generosity and plucked a whole lot of heads which he magically turned into beads. He put these beads away in his tobacco box and turned to take leave of his friend. But Kaitheu took hold of his hand and whispered, 'Listen, Nara, I brought you here to actually warn you. The tiger people are all lusting for your blood. I can see the hunger in their eyes. Beware! Do as I tell you and you shall live. But if you do not heed my advice, I will have to lose you to my villagers, my friend.'

'Tell me what you want me to do.'

'There is no need to say goodbye to anybody. Just leave quietly. I shall tell them you are still here. I can hold them off for the next five days, during which time you must travel full-speed back home. Do not halt on the way. And if you feel the urge to attend to the call of nature, always cover your excrement with yeast. That way, they cannot track you back to your village, and no one else in your village will be in danger.

'Meanwhile, I shall beat the drum for the next five days to make them believe you are still here. But after that, I cannot hold them back.'

'You are a true friend, Kiatheu,' said Nara. 'Thank you, I shall do exactly as you say.' And he left.

Unfortunately though, Nara could not journey continuously for five days and he stopped for a day on the way. Meanwhile, on the fifth day after he left, the tiger people at Kiatheu's village also came to know about his departure, and they immediately took off on his trail.

Now Kiatheu had his fears that Nara might not have been able to travel non-stop for five days, and so he accompanied the villagers in their quest. Tiger people move very fast and very soon, they all caught up with Nara. The clever man had, however, heard them coming and he immediately hid himself under a pile of leaves that had been gathered together by a wild boar.

While his people were sniffing around looking for Nara, Kiatheu saw the leaves heaped up and realized his friend must be hidden under the pile. So he sat himself down on it and asked the villagers also to rest for a while. Then he started talking to them.

'Brothers,' he said. 'Tell me what you fear the most.'

'We are like you, Kiatheu,' they replied. 'We think what you think, we fear what you fear.'

'Oh, but I would be really terrified if a cloud suddenly enveloped us and we were to hear a loud booming voice come out of this pile of leaves I am sitting on. Don't you think that would be awfully scary?'

'Oh, yes!' they said and they all stared at him wild-eyed.

Hidden under the leaves, Nara, of course, realized that his friend's conversation was for his benefit. He took the cue and using his magic powers, conjured up a huge cloud to appear. It enveloped the tiger people. Then, he started shouting wildly and loudly from under the leaves.

This scared the tiger men out of their wits, and they all ran away. Only Kaitheu stayed behind.

'Nara,' he admonished his friend. 'Why did you not listen to me? Why have you been so foolish?'

'I have indeed been very foolish, my friend,' Nara replied, shamefaced. 'Can you forgive me?'

Kiatheu, of course, could not be very angry with his friend for long. Seeing Nara away on his way to his village, he himself turned back towards his own village.

When Nara reached his village, he converted the beads back into heads and distributed them among his villagers. Everybody was very happy.

Now, Nara had a brother who was not as wise as Nara himself. Seeing Nara's popularity and the love and respect he commanded from the villagers, he also wanted to go to Kiatheu's village and get back some heads. He thought that would make him popular too. So he sent word to Kiatheu that he wanted to visit. Kiatheu could not say no.

As with Nara's visit, Kiatheu warned his villagers to be on their best behaviour and to act like people. His parents again refused to change their form. But when Kiatheu took Nara's brother to see them, and they snarled at him, the latter squirmed. 'Oh, they are so scary,' he shouted and stepped back. This made Kiatheu's parents very angry, but they had been told that Nara's brother was really stupid. So they left him alone.

When the time came for him to leave, Kiatheu again took him to the orchard and asked him to pick as many heads from the magical tree as he could carry. But Nara's brother was no magician and he could not turn the heads into beads, and so could only pluck and carry so many. Kiatheu gave him the same set of instructions as he had given to Nara and sent the young man off on his journey homeward.

Nara's brother, however, halted for two days at a stretch on the road. The heads he was carrying had become cumbersome and he wanted to find some twine to string them together so as to carry them more easily. He had to pay dearly for his foolishness. Kiatheu's villagers caught up with him easily and ate him up.

When Kiatheu reached the spot, he was very upset. 'Why did you all eat my friend's brother?' he demanded of them. 'Now Nara will be very angry with me. Ah, my brothers, you have put me in a very tight spot. There is only one way to salvage the situation now. Heed my word and throw up. Vomit out the flesh you have consumed. I will see what I can do.'

The tiger men had to obey Kiatheu's order and all of them vomited out the fragments of Nara's brother. The skilled sorcerer Kiatheu then went to work, piecing together the remains of Nara's brother's body. When the body was crafted again, he realized to his dismay that one piece of flesh was missing. It had stuck to the teeth of a very old tiger, who could not get it out. So the body that he refashioned had a gaping hole in the armpit. This hole Kiatheu filled with beeswax. Then he sent Nara's brother back home to his village.

When he reached home, Nara's brother cried out, 'Look, everybody, I have brought back some fine heads for you all. Am I not as brilliant as my brother?'

The brilliant brother, Nara, however, realized that something was amiss. He called out, 'You are not my brother. You are his corpse. The tigers have eaten my brother.'

'No, no, it's me. Why do you say I'm dead?'

'Look under your armpit. They've filled it with wax to cover up your cruel death,' Nara said to his brother. His brother looked and indeed, saw the wax. Curious, he pulled it out. But the moment he did so, he fell down dead.

This made Nara very angry. He sent a message to Kaitheu, asking, 'Why did you kill my brother? He was just a stupid fellow who meant no harm. Now I shall have to fight you to avenge his death.'

In return, Kaitheu sent another message, 'I gave him the heads he wanted and treated him well, my friend. Your brother died because of his own stupidity. I would not want to fight you, but if you must, then I will accept your challenge.'

So, a day was set for the duel, but before the actual battle, the two friends met for one last time and spoke. 'We have been good friends,' they decided. 'So if either of us dies in this duel, the victor will not hang the opponent's head up as a trophy. He may however, perform the *la* ceremony over his dead foe.'

Bound by this pact, the two friends fought each other mightily. They both used their magic to become invisible, so that for a long time each could not see the other. Then Nara crafted a waxen image of himself which he laid down on the platform of a jhum house. Meanwhile, he himself sat inside the jhum house with his bow and arrows, waiting for his friend-turned-foe to show up.

When Kiatheu saw the waxen image, he was fooled. He rushed towards the jhum house platform and transforming himself into a tiger, leapt at it with the intention of devouring it. Nara shot him twice with his arrows while he was still in the air, mid-leap. Kiatheu was wounded mortally. While his life blood flowed out of him, Kaitheu whispered to his friend, 'Nara, you are stronger than me, and better. I accept defeat at your hands.'

When Kiatheu breathed his last, Nara severed his head, killed a mithun, and performed the la ceremony over it. But since he had entered into a pact with his friend, he did not hang the head up on the verandah with his other trophies. It is because Nara valued his friendship and was true to his word that Lakhers never again did hang the heads of tigers or of men in their houses.

The death of Kiatheu, however, was not Nara's last brush with tiger people. The friendship that defined the tradition he left behind for the Lakher people was only the first encounter he had with them. More significantly, he ended up marrying a tiger woman. This tiger woman was called Vawri. When Nara married her, he had no clue about her true identity. He only got to know when the villagers started complaining.

Because of his powers and wisdom, combined with his desire to help people, Nara was in great demand, and as such, he had to be away from home quite often. Whenever he returned, he would hear that somebody in the village—his friend, or kin or neighbour—had been killed by a tiger person. One day, when he had arrived at his village from a long journey, the villagers surrounded him and declared, 'Nara, your wife Vawri is a tiger woman. We have discovered that it is she who devours our people whenever you are away. You must kill her, or she will kill us all.'

When Nara realized the truth of their accusation, he was heartbroken, for he loved his wife very much. At the same time, however, he could not allow the villagers to suffer because of his love. So he went with Vawri to the river bank one day when she left to fetch water. He had surreptitiously created a hole at the bottom of the bamboo pail in which she was to carry the water back. At the same time, he also bewitched her so that she could not see the hole at the bottom. He watched from the bank as Vawri stepped into the water to fill the pail. Every time she dipped it in the water, it came up empty and she could not understand why. Meanwhile, Nara sat on the bank and wept. He had summoned a huge flood with his sorcery and it was on its way. The skies had already opened up and it was raining heavily. The winds were lashing at the trees mercilessly and working up a whirlpool in the river.

His wife was perturbed when she saw Nara weeping thus. 'Something is strange today,' she declared. 'Why do you weep, my husband?'

'It's nothing,' he replied. 'It's raining hard. Just fill your pail and let's go.'

Before he could finish his sentence, however, the deluge set in and Vawri was swept away. Nara watched till she was out of sight. Then shedding some more tears, he went back home.

For days thereafter, he pined away for his wife. He did not eat for ten days, he did not sleep and he was always in tears. Nothing could make him happy again. The villagers, who loved him, were very concerned for his welfare. They realized why Nara was in this state. In the end, they walked up to him and said, 'Nara, you have done what you had to do for the sake of the village. We are grateful to you for that. But we cannot watch you wasting away like this. It is obvious that you cannot live without your wife. We have spoken about this and all of us think that you should find the place where your wife lies in eternal rest. Find it and go kill yourself there.'

Nara was thankful to the villagers for pointing out the way for him, and he immediately set out for the river with a gourd and a spindle. He threw them both in the water and said out loud, 'Spindle and gourd, float down the river. Find me the place where my wife rests.'

Then he followed the spindle and the gourd as they floated downstream on the river for a long distance. They came to rest after a long time in the ocean. Knowing that Vawri's body lay there, Nara too decided to jump in. Just as he was about to take the plunge, he saw a few soldiers making their way towards the shore. They did not seem to be from the neighbourhood. Nara called out to them, 'O you short-haired foreigners, here is my sword. You may have it.'

He flung his sword at them and they caught it deftly. 'O son of Laitha,' they bowed, 'you are strong as lightning'.

Then Nara once again called out to them, 'I am going below the water now and I have no need of the possessions that encumber me, for I go to join my wife. I am throwing them all away. If you wish, you may pick them up.'

So saying, Nara jumped into the ocean, but not before he had discarded his magic, his wisdom, his power, strength, and all the knowledge he possessed. The soldiers picked them up one by one, enfolding them in their turbans, and it is from them that we have inherited today the art of writing, the knowledge of the universe and everything else that makes human life fruitful. Nara gave them all to us.

21. Lushai/ Mizo

Over the waters, one world to the next

The closest thing to heaven, or paradise, that the Lushais have is Pialral. It is said that renowned hunters and great warriors can enter Pialral where they can live in great luxury, without any worries whatsoever. Women, however, were not allowed into this place, while small children of both sexes could enter if they died while still at their mothers' breasts.

Anybody who wishes to enter Pialral, though, has to cross the river Pial. It is the boundary between Pialral (literally, beyond the River Pial) and Mitthi Khua. This latter is the abode of the souls that have passed away from this world. This is where the souls rest before crossing Pial. On the border between this world and Mitthu Khua lies another water body. All the spirits of the dead have to pass through this water body, known as Rih Dil (or lake).

The Mizos share a close affinity with Rih Dil. It has spawned many oral narratives and traditional beliefs. It has also provided inspiration for many a literary creation in the Mizo oeuvre. However, due to the arbitrary political boundaries drawn by apathetic administrators, it now falls in Burma. The Mizos of the Northeast thus say now—no doubt with their tongues firmly lodged in the hollow of their cheeks—that Rih Dil is the largest lake in Mizoram, just that it falls in Burma.

The name of the lake, the Mizos believe, is derived from the name of a girl called Rihi. It was she who created the lake, they say.

Rihi lived with her younger sister in the ancient land of the Lushais. The two sisters shared a strong bond, not the least because it had been their fate to be subjected to the cruel treatment of their stepmother. Their father was also often instigated by the stepmother to mete out various atrocities to the two sisters. The father was so blinded by his devotion to his second wife that he never questioned her, no matter what she made him do to his own daughters. One day, she asked him to take the younger daughter into the forest and kill her. The pathetic man did as directed.

When Rihi found out about her sister's cruel fate, she cried and wailed, praying to have her sister back. She went into the forest and lay by her sister's dead body and refused to budge. Finally, a benign spirit, called Lasi by the Lushais, took pity on her.

'Young girl, do not cry. I am here to help you,' it said.

Rihi looked up from her sister's dead body on hearing the voice. On seeing the spirit, she asked, 'Oh, but what can you do? My sister is dead, killed by our own father, and I could not even protect her!'

'But you can save her yet, young girl,' the spirit insisted. 'Come with me and I shall lead you to a magical tree. It has the power to bring the dead back to life.'

Overjoyed, Rihi followed Lasi to the tree. When they reached it, she followed Lasi's instructions and plucked a few leaves. With the help of these leaves, she brought her sister back to life.

Now when the dead come back to life, they usually feel very thirsty. And Rihi's sister also woke up with a parched throat.

'Water, water,' she cried as she awoke from her deep dreamless sleep of death.

The lake did not exist at that time in the forest, and so Rihi could find no water anywhere nearby. As she looked around desperately, a sudden inspiration visited her. Instinctively, she used the leaves of the magical tree Lasi had given her to transform herself into a white mithun. It was not a form she could change back from, ever. She would never be human again, but she realized that if she did not make this sacrifice for the sake of her sister, the latter would not recover. For wherever the white mithun urinated, there formed a small pool of water. Rihi's sister drank from this water and was saved.

Rihi, however, was condemned to roam around the land in the form of the white mithun. She wandered around looking for a safe and permanent place to settle down in, but could find none for a long time. And wherever she went, she created many *rih note*, or small lakes, every time she urinated. These little lakes are still to be found in the Vawmlu Range, in Zur forest near the village of Natchhawng; at a place above Bochung village; and in the area around Khawthlir village. All these places are now in Burma.

After a long time, Rihi came upon Sanzawl village and thought she could make a permanent place for herself there. The river Run flowed not very far from the village and she lodged herself by the river.

'Go away,' she suddenly heard a loud booming voice speaking to her. It was the demon spirit of the river.

'Go away,' it threatened her. 'Or I will suck you dry. This is my abode and you are not welcome here.'

Poor Rihi was thus forced to move on again. She surveyed many other places thereafter, including the Champhai valley. And although she blessed every place she went to with many water bodies, none of these places were accommodating of her. In the end, she reached the place where the Rih Dil is situated, near the village of Rihkhawdar, at a distance of about two miles from Tiau, the river that separates Mizoram from Burma. It was here that Rihi finally found rest.

There are many elements of mystery attached to Rih Dil. Its situation in a swampy, unexplored area has given rise to many myths and legends surrounding the lake, not the least intriguing of which is that it is the bridge between this world and the next. Other fantastic tales woven around the lake is the belief that a large dragon or snake-like spirit lives in it. There are accounts of how Turkish or Portuguese traders, in the 18th century, dove into the lake in search of buried treasure—another widely held myth about the lake. They fled, some of them even died of fright, when faced with the fabulous dragon.

Stories of the existence of this fabulous dragon may have drawn inspiration from Buddhist traditions prevalent in Burma. Buddhist monks have claimed that snake-like dragons, or Naga, live in the lake, but make themselves manifest only to those they favour. Other oral and recorded narratives speak of the dragon making incursions into surrounding villages and pilfering livestock. All these legends and myths, in currency since time immemorial, have shed a supernatural light upon the very idea of Rih Dil. Demons and dragons, death and diseases, have all been attributed to the lake and its inhabitant(s), whether they exist in reality or only in oral lore. No wonder then, that the lake has also been traditionally associated with the afterlife. In fact, the reflections of the tree trunks growing on the edge of the waters of Rih Dil are often described as the inverted reflection of the fencing around the city of the dead, Mitthi Khua.

22. *Reang*

Rat to the rescue

When there was nothing, there was yet the darkness and the water. The darkness that enveloped the universe was immense and absolute; the water that covered the universe was deep and endless.

The Almighty god suddenly thought, 'There should be light.' And he created light. When the first rays of light fell upon the created universe, the darkness was halved. Thus, there came into being the light and the dark, the day and the night.

The Almighty god then thought, 'There should be land.' And he created the earth. When the solid ground came into being, the water found its way into the troughs and gorges that were formed across its face. Thus, the earth came into being, part land and part water.

The Almighty god's next thought was to create life forms to inhabit this earth. And he created the various kinds of plants and trees and shrubs and creepers. He also created the animals and the birds and the insects and the fishes. Thus, the world of flora and fauna came into being, making the earth full of life and beautiful.

The Almighty god was very happy with his creation and took great delight in watching life on earth go on. But eventually, he started feeling lonely. So, one day, he created an angel out of his own soul. He named this angel Achu Sibrai.

Achu Sibrai became the companion and confidant of the Almighty god. One day, the Almighty god handed over two stones to Achu Sibrai. As he did so, he said, 'It is from these two stones that my most special creation, the human being, will be born. Hold them dear and keep them safe.'

Achu Sibrai accepted the responsibility gracefully and gratefully. He placed the two pieces of stone under a chamthai plant. Not sure that this in itself would keep the stones safe, he then commanded the bird Bihangama to keep watch over them.

Achu Sibrai said, 'Bihangama, the Almighty god has entrusted me with the safekeeping of these two stones. I, in my turn, am relying on you to help me in this regard. Guard the stones with your life. Never let them out of your sight. These will one day give birth to the human species.'

Bihangama was overwhelmed by the faith that Achu Sibrai had placed upon her, and she decided to do all she could to keep the stones safe. She went to the foot of the chamthai plant and sat upon the two stones. 'They cannot be any safer than this,' she decided.

Bihangama sat on the two stones for a long time, till days turned into months and months turned into years. Years also eventually turned into centuries and then to ages, before anything of any significance took place. In the end, the two stones, like two eggs kept warm by the celestial bird, hatched simultaneously. She watched in surprise and delight as out of the two stones emerged two human babies, one male and the other female.

Bihangama was filled with love for the two small creatures. 'So this is what god's great creation looks like,' she thought to herself. 'Achu Sibrai asked me to look after them, and that is what I shall do now.' And she took great care of the human babies and brought them up like they were her own offspring and they started calling themselves Debatarani and Devalaxmi.

Bihangama stayed with the two young humans for a few years. After that, she left them to fend for themselves and flew away into the limitless sky.

Debatarani and Devalaxmi were now left all alone in the forest where Bihangama had watched over them. With their mother-figure now gone, they were at a loss. So the Almighty god descended to earth and created a large orchard for them. 'Eat of the fruits that grow in these trees that I have planted in your orchard,' he instructed them. Then, before going back to his abode, he pointed to one particular tree, and cautioned them, 'However, stay away from that tree over there. It bears a fruit, Thaioha. You are never to taste it.'

Debatarani and Devalaxmi did not see any reason to disobey the Almighty god and so, they lived happily in the orchard for a long time. Trouble started when the Almighty's throne was threatened by his once trusted companion.

Achu Sibrai, the angel created by the Almighty god, had been unhappy with his creator for a while before he decided to rise in revolt against the latter. He walked up to god one fine day and said, 'Get out of heaven. I do not consider you king anymore. From now on, I shall rule over the universe.'

Achu Sibrai, though, was not as powerful as the Almighty god. So when god decided to put up a fight to retain his throne,

Achu Sibrai was defeated. What is more, god threw him out of heaven, and told him to stay out.

Achu Sibrai felt humiliated, and his envy of god grew much stronger. Away from heaven, he started devising many plans to get back at his creator. But every plan seemed to have some flaw in it. In the end, he realized that one way to hurt god was to corrupt his favourite creation—the humans.

Achu Sibrai turned himself into a snake one day and paid Debatarani and Devalaxmi a visit. So that they should not get alarmed, he called out to them imitating god's voice, 'Come out you two, and talk to me!'

Debatarani and Devalaxmi did not suspect anything and appeared before Achu Sibrai thinking he was god. When they saw the snake instead, they were highly surprised. 'Who are you?' they asked and Achu Sibrai replied, 'I am here to help you.' Then he asked, 'How do you two live here? What do you do for food and drink?'

Debatarani and Devalaxmi had never had to worry about anything and so they said, 'We are very happy and comfortable here. We need not labour hard for god has given us everything. We drink from the streams and eat what we want from the trees in this orchard.'

Achu Sibrai however, continued to goad them, 'So you eat all the fruits of this orchard? Is there nothing forbidden by god?' The two human beings had to admit then that they were not allowed to eat the fruit called Thaioha.

Achu Sibrai had been waiting to hear just this, and he jumped at it. 'See how greedy god is!' he exclaimed. 'It is the most beautiful fruit here and god does not want you to eat it. The fruit can bring you knowledge, progeny and prosperity. Don't you want all that? And why is god so selfish that he is depriving you of it all? He is happy to keep you in ignorance, but are you?'

Achu Sibrai, to prove his point, started devouring the fruit with apparent relish while the two humans watched. They watched and the temptation grew to taste it themselves. In the end, Devalaxmi gave in and ate the fruit. Then she asked Debatarani also to try it. The snake went away happily when he saw that the humans had taken his bait and were eating the forbidden fruit.

Debatarani and Devalaxmi had never gone against god's wishes before this, and so they were a bit apprehensive after the deed was done. When god showed up in their orchard a few hours later and called out to them, they therefore did not appear before him. 'How dare you!' he growled when he saw that the humans had disobeyed him. 'Get out from my orchard right now.'

Debatarani and Devalaxmi therefore left the orchard and never again did they or their descendants see the face of the Almighty god. Out in the world, unprotected by god's grace, the humans were lost and lonely. They were living a very miserable life till Achu Sibrai decided that he should now try and establish his authority over the human world. To establish this authority, however, he would have to create a human world over which he could rule.

Achu Sibrai therefore sought the help of two other guardian spirits. One of them was the bird, Touchinchouma, and the other was a river, Taibuma. The three of them put their heads together and decided that the only way to do this was to get the two humans to procreate. To this end, they would have to cohabit sexually. So they got the two of them married.

Achu Sibrai however, soon realized that this was not the end of his task. After some time had passed, he went to see how the two were faring. Devtarani and Devalaxmi were not very happy. 'We are miserable,' they said. 'You said we would be free if we ate the fruit, but our freedom has brought us worries and troubles beyond our imagination. We have to toil day and night to gather our food, and find shelter. If we do not, we starve and are attacked by wild animals. O Achu Sibrai, help us, please.'

Achu Sibrai was pleased that the humans were submitting to his mercy. He decided to help them now. 'Do not worry,' he told them. 'If you cannot find food out in the world, you will need to grow your own. I shall teach you how.' He then proceeded to tell them about the kingdom of Narinaka where all the seeds for cultivating were kept. Narinaka, however, was the land of evil spirits, or rakhasas.

Achu Sibrai said he would help the humans procure the seeds from Narinaka if they agreed to pay obeisance to him and to remain obliged to him forever afterwards. He made this demand because, as he told them, the rakhasas were cruel creatures that killed and devoured at will. The creatures of earth were safe only because the kingdom of the rakhasas was separated from earth by a vast ocean. This ocean had ferocious waves and dangerous tides so that there was little movement between the two realms.

Achu Sibrai also told them where and how the seeds were stored and guarded in Narinaka. 'There are various species of paddy and cotton and vegetables and fruits and mustard seeds kept in Narinaka. They are stored in a vessel made of dried gourd and that vessel is hidden in a bamboo basket. The owners of these seeds are the rakhasas and they are very possessive of them. Even when they go hunting during the day, they carry the basket with them. At night, when they go to sleep, they keep the basket beside them. We could have tried carrying away their basket at night, but even in their soundest of sleep, they can smell the presence of intruders. If they wake up then and catch us, they will kill us surely.

'But despite all of this, I will help you. So do not worry. Just wait and see how I outwit the rakhasas.'

Achu Sibrai decided to take the help of the rat in his endeavour. The rat scuttled to his side when summoned and agreed to help. But he had a few requests of his own. He told Achu Sibrai, 'I shall be going to Narinaka to procure the seeds for the humans. But before I reach there, you must create heat from some source. It must be extreme and unbearable heat, the kind that will drive the rakhasas out of their huts and not allow them to sleep at all. Umaidong, the guardian deity of heat, will help you in this. Do this for at least a month before I leave for Narinaka.

Then, just as I reach there, you must invoke the aid of Nokba, the guardian deity of the cool air. This will soothe their nerves and make them fall asleep. My work will be quite easy after that.'

Achu Sibrai was highly pleased by the rat's intelligence and did as the rat had requested. He also arranged for a boat to carry the rat across the tumultuous ocean. When the rat reached his destination, he found the rakhasas in deep sleep, after the heat had died and the cool air had soothed their nerves. Having been deprived of sleep for nearly a month, they were now totally unconscious of the intruder.

The rat therefore had little difficulty in creeping up to the seed basket and cutting through the bamboo lid. When he reached the bitter gourd shell, he cut the lid on the gourd as well. Then once he managed to get hold of the seeds, he started his return journey to the land of the humans.

The rat had barely crossed the ocean and reached the humans when the rakhasas woke up. They smelled the rat and found their basket empty. Immediately, they set out to follow him. The huge ocean was not such a great obstruction for them, but when they reached the other shore, they could not proceed any further. Every step that they took was blocked by thick spider webs. The rakhasas got entangled in these webs and found themselves in a maze of confusion.

Achu Sibrai had woven these waves to deter the rakhasas and save the humans from their wrath. In fact, he had been waiting on the sea shore to accost them. When he saw them entangled thus, he said, 'You are not allowed to set foot on this land. Now go back to your own Narinaka.' The rakhasas had to comply.

Achu Sibrai then taught Devatarani and Devalaxmi how to cultivate the seeds procured from the rakhasas. He also taught them the different techniques of cultivation. Devatarani and Devalaxmi were grateful to Achu Sibrai and followed his instructions diligently. At the end of the crop cycle, they had a good harvest. The grains procured from this harvest were stored in a granary they learnt to construct. And Achu Sibrai was with them every step of the way, advising and instructing.

Devatarani and Devalaxmi now had plenty to eat. Achu Sibrai taught them how to husk the paddy and cook the rice that came from the paddy. Thus, they also came to know the secret of cooked food. Contented, they finally settled down to a happy married life. In due course of time, Devalaxmi gave birth to a male child. They called him Bruha. The Reangs trace their origin to this first child born to human beings. That is why they are also known as the Brus.

Nagaland

A brief note:

Since the 1940s, the land of the Nagas has been witness to a sustained struggle for political self-determination and realization of national pride. It is a struggle that is ongoing in some forms though contemporary political exigencies have diluted the initial fervour to a large extent. In post–colonial India, Nagaland was a part of Assam till 1963 when it was established as the sixteenth state of the Indian Union. It is bound on four sides by Assam, Manipur, Arunachal Pradesh and Burma. The Naga people are spread over these contiguous areas with which they historically share many socio-economic, political and ethnic ties.

Mostly mountainous, the state is home to sixteen major Naga tribes, and various other smaller tribes and sub-tribes. The major tribes include Angami, Ao, Chakhesang, Chang, Dimasa Kachari, Khiamniungan, Konyak, Lotha, Phom, Pochury, Rengma, Sangtam, Sumi (Sema), Yimchunger, Kuki and Zeliang, of which the most dominant are the Konyaks, Angamis, Aos, Lothas, and Sumis (Semas). Each of the Naga tribes has its distinct culture, tradition and dialect, and the individuals of every tribe are fiercely bound together by tribal and clan loyalties. Over and above the ideal of Naga nationalism, Christianity has also acted as a common bond between the different Naga tribes and sub-tribes. Almost all of them are Christianized. It is only the non-Naga populations of the state that practise Hinduism and Islam.

Among the dominant tribes of Nagaland and numbering around 200,000, the Angamis are the traditional inhabitants of Kohima district. The Eastern branch of the Angamis broke away from the parent tribe and is today known as the Chakesang tribe. The Angamis are known for the wet-rice terrace cultivation that they are experts in. Though family property is divided among both sons and daughters, the youngest male child inherits the parental home and is expected to look after the parents in old age and infirmity. Although fast dwindling in numbers, a small section of the Angamis still practises the indigenous religion of Pfutsana. By and large though, they are Christians.

The Aos are predominantly found in the north-eastern part of Nagaland, especially in the Mokokchung district. They number a little over two lakh. They were among the first Naga people to embrace Christianity, and today nearly the entire Christian population among the Aos are Baptists. They speak three languages: Chungli, Mongsen, and Changki, of which the last is spoken by very few. The Ao languages do not have much affinity with the languages of the other Naga peoples. Traditionally a headhunting warrior tribe, the Ao male had to earn the right to wear the tribe's shawl called Mangkotepsu through acts of bravery and proof of affluence. The Ao women who weave these shawls are expert weavers.

Lotha Nagas are a populous tribe in Nagaland numbering over five lakh. Their traditional territory is the Wokha district, which was the district headquarters of the Naga Hills under British-administered Assam. Wokha is famous for Mount Tiyi, where the Lothas believe the departed souls live. The Lotha villages situated on the hilltops of Wokha have many ancient stone monoliths called Longsu. Headhunters, till the advent of Christianity, a small section of the Lothas have embraced Catholicism while most of them are Baptists. Like most other Naga tribes, the shawls of the Lothas also indicate social status.

The woman's prestigious shawl is called Opvuram while men's shawls are known as Longpensu.

Found mostly around Zunheboto district of Nagaland, the Sema (or Sumi) Nagas were also a warrior tribe who practised headhunting. The influence of Christianity eroded many of the traditional practices among the Semas and put an end to headhunting. A very small proportion of them still practise their indigenous animist religion. Their total population stands at around 20,000, and they are also found in and around Dimapur, Kohima, Mokokchung and Tuensang districts of Nagaland, besides the Tinsukia district of Assam. Customarily, each Sema village has two clan heads who are known as Swu (Sumi) and Tuku (Tukumi). These heads are at the top of the democratic apparatus that regulates the collective life of the village.

23. Angami

Animals wild and tame

Rhiio was married to a beautiful woman who was also a good person. They were very happy and worked hard, side by side, in their jhum fields to grow crops to feed themselves throughout the year.

One day, Rhiio had just finished working in the field. His wife had already left to go home and prepare dinner. He decided to take a bath in the river nearby before returning home himself. As he was washing off his day's sweat and grime in the cool river water, he suddenly felt somebody behind him. Before he could turn around and see who it was, he felt a pair of hands close over his eyes. He tried to remove the hands and turn around, but whoever it was held him immobile. His movement restricted and vision thus impaired, Rhiio could do little but put on a brave front.

He shouted, 'Who is it?'

There was no reply. So he shouted again, 'Tell me who it is!'

Again, there was no reply. Now he started feeling a little afraid, and said, 'Whoever it is, let me go and I will do as you say.'

This got him the desired result and the owner of the hands replied, 'I will let you go surely. But you have to fulfil my wish if I am to heed yours.'

To this, a relieved Rhiio said, 'But of course, I promise!'

'Then let me marry your daughter,' his tormentor said.

'Hah!' Rhiio could not but laugh dryly. 'I do not have any children. No daughter, no son. How can I give you my daughter in marriage if I have none?'

'Oh, but you have a wife, no? She will give birth soon. When she does, you have to give me your daughter.'

Now Rhiio did not see any harm in playing along—for all he knew, his wife might have a son. So he said, 'I give you my word. If I have a daughter, she will marry you. If I have a son, he will be your lifelong friend. Now will you please let me go?'

As soon as he uttered the words, he felt the hands fall away from his eyes. He quickly turned around to see who it was he had made the promise to. To his deepest surprise though, he saw nobody behind him. He realized it must have been a spirit that had extracted such a grave promise from him. Disturbed, he returned home and narrated the entire episode to his wife. His wife reassured him that he had done the right thing, 'You did what you had to do to get away. If and when we have children, we shall see what we can do. Till then, there is no point worrying about it.'

Years passed, and when the spirit did not reappear, Rhiio and his wife all but forgot about the incident. Meanwhile, they had had a beautiful daughter who, as the years went by, grew up to be an attractive young woman. Rhiio and his wife doted on her and allowed her all the freedom and independence she wanted. She would roam around the village and the fields nearby with her friends. She would go into the forest and play there for long hours.

That was why, when she did not come home till late in the evening one day, the parents did not immediately get alarmed. But when evening turned into night and she had not come back, they started worrying. They went looking for her at her friends' houses and all her friends said the same thing—they had been playing near the jhum fields at the edge of the forest. She had been with them till they reached the village entrance. After that, they could not see her and took for granted that she had gone back home.

A sudden realization now dawned on Rhiio—he remembered the incident with the spirit so many years back. And he knew with dead certainty now that the same spirit had come back to extract its price for letting him go. He had pushed the incident to the back of his mind and lived all these years in the false hope that his daughter would never go away, but the past has a strange way of catching up with people. The past had now caught up with Rhiio.

There was nothing Rhiio or his wife could do to change fate, and so they were forced to give in to it and get on with their lives. They missed their daughter, but in time, her absence also became a fact of everyday life for them.

Then suddenly one day, after many more years had passed, the young girl, now a young married woman, came knocking on her parents' door. She called out to her mother who came running to see who it was. All she saw was a young woman at the threshold, and she could not at first imagine who it could be. Then her eyes fell on the basket the woman held in her hand, and she recognized it as the one that her daughter had been carrying with her the day she got lost. She looked closely at the woman again, and was overwhelmed with joy to realize it was none other than her own daughter standing there. She cried many happy tears and called out to her husband, 'Come, Rhiio, come and see who has come to pay us a visit.'

Rhiio heard the excitement in his wife's voice and came running out. Oh, what a joyous reunion it was, of father, mother and long-lost daughter!

'O Daughter, we have missed you so,' they said. 'How many tears have we shed and how many sighs have we shared between us at your loss! Where have you been all these years? Tell us, do. You were only a girl when you left us, now you are a woman!'

'Father,' she said turning to Rhiio, 'on the day I failed to return home, I was carried away by a spirit. I was very scared at first, but he told me that you had pledged my hand in marriage to him even before I was born. He would not let me come back to you, and I also accepted my fate, and your decision.'

Then turning to her mother, she said, 'Mother, do not worry. As time went by, he turned out to be a loving and gentle husband. I have been very happy with him.'

Rhiio however, was not convinced. He wanted to see for himself how his daughter was living. 'Tell me where the spirit lives, Daughter. I shall pay you a visit.'

'Oh, but Father, you cannot. It is far far away, and not a place that humans can visit so easily.'

But Rhiio was adamant. In the end, his daughter relented. 'Very well, Father,' she said. 'If you want to go, then go after I have left. I cannot be seen accompanying you or leading you there. But what I can do is to drop husk from my basket here all along the way, from here to my husband's house. Follow the trail and you shall find me at his house at the end of your journey.'

Rhiio was fine with that and agreed to follow his daughter's instructions. The daughter left. A little later, he followed her trail and reached his son-in-law's house. When he called out to his daughter, the spirit came out. Seeing Rhiio there, he was surprised but not hostile. He welcomed his father-in-law warmly and pressed upon him to spend a few days at his house. Rhiio agreed.

Looked after by his daughter and son-in-law, Rhiio had a good time there. He also observed how the spirit was treating his daughter, and was convinced that his daughter had been right in calling him a good husband. The guilt that he had been feeling, the same guilt that had led him here, started dissipating. 'I have not ruined her life, after all,' he decided, satisfied.

He could not, however, stay there forever. Soon, it was time for him to return. The day before he was scheduled to go back to his wife, his daughter spoke to him confidentially. The spirit was away from home at the time, and she told her father, 'My husband will offer you a gift when the time comes for your departure. He will ask you to choose one, and Father, you must choose the bamboo container there. Trust me, it will do you good.'

Rhiio had no reason to distrust his daughter and he agreed once again to follow her instructions.

When the spirit came back home, they had dinner and went to bed. The next morning, when he was taking his leave, the spirit said, 'Dear Father-in-law, do not worry about your daughter— we are very happy together. I thank you for your visit, and as a token of my gratitude, I would like to offer you a gift. Tell me, what is it you want?'

Rhiio had known this was coming, of course. Without hesitation therefore, he pointed to the sealed bamboo container his daughter had told him about. 'I want that,' he said.

Even if the spirit was a little taken aback by his father-in-law's request, he did not show it. Instead, he said, 'Then it is yours.'

As he handed over the container to Rhiio, however, he warned him, 'A great treasure lies within. But be careful not to break open the seal before you reach home, or else, all will be lost. And even when you reach home, you must close all the doors and windows of your house before opening it.'

Rhiio agreed to do as instructed and left. He slung the container over his shoulder and walked his way home. The burden was very light when he left his daughter's house, but as time passed and he trudged on, it started to grow heavier and heavier.

This started to arouse his curiosity. He also started feeling some movement inside and his curiosity doubled. He wanted very badly to open the container and take a peek inside. 'What harm can that do?' he wondered. 'I will only take a quick look and close it again.' So saying, he broke the seal.

Out jumped a horde of animals and scampered away from him. Rhiio was stunned, and quickly shut the lid again. He promised to himself not to open it again till he was safely home. The container continued to grow heavier and heavier, but he did not give in to temptation again.

After a long trek, when he finally reached home, he called out to his wife and told her about his experiences of the past few days. She chided him for having mistrusted their son-in-law's words. 'Let us go in and see what else is in there,' she said to him.

So husband and wife went into the house and shut all the doors and windows. Then, Rhiio opened the lid again and out poured many more animals—pigs and goats and all other animals which have since stayed with humans in their homes and been called domestic animals. The ones that Rhiio had lost along the way remained wild and untamed, out there in the jungle. And this is how human society came to distinguish between the wild and domestic animals.

The Angamis to this day believe that wild animals belong to men, while the domesticated ones belong to women.

24. Ao

Load put down

An Ao man had a lovely wife. The two of them had a very happy married life, and spent their days in easy companionship. After some time, there came into their lives a little baby girl who made their lives so much more beautiful. Both husband and wife doted on their daughter.

Life could have continued in this seemingly idyllic manner, had not jealous fate intervened. The wife suddenly fell sick one day, and just as suddenly, passed away. The husband and little girl were left to fend for themselves, without an anchor in life.

For a little while thereafter, the bereaved father tried his best to look after his daughter on his own. He showered all his love and affection on her, but to his great sorrow, he found that no matter what he did for her, it never seemed to be enough. The girl always had some need that he could not foresee. He realized that what the little girl really needed was a mother. But he had been so in love with his dead wife that he would not even consider remarrying.

Slowly, however, he found that he could not be both father and mother to the child. If he wanted to play the role of her mother to perfection, he would have to forego his role as bread-earner. His work had often forced him to stay away from home for long durations while his wife was alive. After her death, he found himself confined to the house. As a result, his work and earnings suffered. He slowly started accepting the fact that if his work suffered, he would not make much of a good father and bread-earner for his daughter. The need to remarry started weighing down on him despite his reluctance.

The people of the village and his friends and relatives also started pressuring him to marry again. 'You are young,' they said. 'And the girl is still a child. You both need a woman to look after you. We will find you a good woman. Get married.'

In the end, he relented. The woman he married this time tried her best to please her new husband. The man was pleased. But he was still cautious when it came to his little daughter. 'She means more to me than anything. Take good care of her, Wife.'

'I will,' said the woman, and the man was happy.

Life returned to normal again for the little girl's father now that he was free of his constant anxiety for her wellbeing. In due course, he decided that he could now return to his regular work, maybe even travel for work like he used to earlier. So when the next opportunity came, he seized it. 'Wife, I am leaving on business tomorrow,' he informed his new wife one fine day. 'While I am away, take good care of my little girl. I am leaving her in your care.'

'Go, Husband,' she replied cheerily. 'Do not be troubled with worries. I am here to look after the little one.'

And the husband left.

But it so happened that the new wife had been less than honest with her husband all this while. She had pretended to love the little girl like her own whenever her husband was around. In his absence, however, she would often ill-treat her. So badly did she behave with the little one that the girl could not even complain to her father about the ill-treatment meted out to her, for fear she might have to pay for it later on.

Meanwhile, all the woman secretly wanted was for the little girl to get out of her way, so that she could enjoy her husband's company on her own. She did not like all the attention her husband showered on his daughter by another wife. The day he announced his departure now, the stepmother was overjoyed. Finally, she had the opportunity she had been looking for to get rid of the girl.

'With her father gone, who is going to save her from my wrath?' she said to herself and smiled inwardly. 'This is my chance to finish her once and for all.'

The day after her husband left, therefore, the stepmother decided to execute her intention. She cooked a very tasty dish for the little girl, one that she liked best. But she added an extra ingredient—a lot of extra chillies. She added so much of the chilli that it was bound to affect the little girl quite adversely.

When she had finished cooking the dish, she called her stepdaughter to her and said, 'Listen, Daughter, I have cooked this dish with a lot of care. But it is not for you. I know you like eating it, but you can't. I am telling you this because I am going to the granary now to get some rice to cook and eat with it. Till I get back, do not under any circumstance eat this dish. Am I clear?'

'Yes, Mother,' said the little girl.

But then, she was only a little girl, and like all children, very curious. When they are told not to do something, children will anyway go and do it—that is how they learn the facts of life;

but that is also how they often fall into trouble. The stepmother knew her words of caution would not be heeded, and the more she insisted that the little girl should stay away from the food, the more tempted she would be to taste it. And that is precisely what happened.

No sooner had she stepped out of the house, the poor child picked up the dish to taste it. The cruel stepmother meanwhile stood just outside the house and peeked in through the holes in the bamboo walls. She waited for the right moment to pounce on the little girl. When the girl had put the first morsel into her mouth, the stepmother jumped right into the house and shouted, 'Aha! There you are, ignoring my instructions. And for that, you shall suffer.'

The chillies, meanwhile, were having their effect upon the girl and her mouth was burning.

'Mother, Mother!' she cried. 'It is hot, Mother. I need some water. Give me some water! My mouth is on fire.'

'And so it should be,' laughed the stepmother. 'I told you not to touch it, and here you are eating out of it with your left hand. Who is going to eat the food now that your left hand has touched it? I don't care if your mouth burns. You shall get no water, and no respite. Eat now! Eat up the whole dish. That will be your punishment.'

The terrified little girl had no choice but to continue gobbling up the hot dish. The chillies used by the stepmother were so strong and pungent that they immediately acted upon her delicate stomach, churning it and burning her insides. She could not survive the chillies, and just as the stepmother had desired, she died.

The heartless woman was overjoyed but, of course, she could not show her joy for fear her husband would discover her role in the little girl's death. She wailed and cried in mock sorrow and invited all the people of the village to come and share in her bereavement. She had a big pig slaughtered and made arrangements for a lavish funeral feast.

Now, the feast was supposed to be on the same day that the husband was to return from his trip. The husband, of course, had no idea about his loss. He was coming back home filled with joy, expecting to see his lovely wife and little daughter again. But as he made his way back, he saw a basket and a dish by the side of the road leading to his house. He recognized them immediately as belonging to his daughter. He was perplexed. As he moved further on, he saw a big dead pig with a white mark on its neck. Once again, he recognized it, this time as belonging to himself. He realized that these were omens, trying to tell him something. So he rushed the rest of the way home.

When he reached there, he was shocked to see the dead body of his beloved daughter. He realized then that the basket, dish and pig that he had seen on the way back home had been left on the roadside by his daughter's soul on its way to Wokha hill. He rushed towards his wife and asked her, 'What is the meaning of all this? How did my daughter die?'

'Oh, Husband, our daughter fell ill immediately after you left home. She just wouldn't recover although I nursed her and tried to get her to recover her health. Forgive me, but I couldn't save her!'

But the husband saw through her false show of grief and contrition, and realized that his daughter had not died of any illness. If she had, her soul would not have tried to reach out to him the way it did. By now, he had rightly read the signs and realized that it was the stepmother who had killed his daughter. In grief and anger, his heart now started filling up with thoughts of revenge. 'This woman will have to pay,' he said to himself. But out loud, he only said, 'Wife, thank you for looking after my daughter and trying your best. It is destiny that she had to die so young.'

This convinced the wife that she had fooled her husband successfully, and she performed all the duties of a gracious hostess during the funeral feast with a light heart.

When the funeral rites and feast were over, the guests left. The husband then said to his wife, 'I am going into the forest.

There is something there that I need to attend to. But I want you to meet me halfway when I am returning. Come into the forest and look for me. Bring along some madhu (rice beer).'

The wife did not suspect anything. She only thought that her husband was really pleased with her tale of devotion to his little daughter. Otherwise, why would he ask her to accompany him on his way back from the forest? So she did as she was told. She carried some madhu with her and made her way into the forest at the time specified by her husband before he had left.

She was very happy and was looking forward to the rest of her life with her husband, without a stepdaughter to come between them. When she entered the forest, therefore, there was nothing in it that could frighten her. She walked ahead with light steps and a song on her lips. And then, she saw her husband walking towards her. Her pace quickened. She reached the spot where he waited and her heart started beating very fast as she stood facing her husband.

'Husband,' she said, 'here is the madhu you had asked for'.

But before she could hold her arm up to offer him the beer, her husband suddenly turned into a huge snake. Instead of the man she loved, she now found herself facing a beast preparing to devour her.

'You killed my beloved daughter, you vile woman!' the snake hissed. 'And for that, I shall eat you now!'

So saying, the snake opened its mouth wide and gulped down the murderous woman. Then it changed back its form to that of the man who had lost his only daughter and returned to the village. The village forever afterwards came to be known as Khuyu village. The word 'Khuyu' means 'load put down'. Since the small girl's soul had put down her heavy load of basket, dish and pig in that village on her way to Wokha hill—that place where all souls go to after death—the Ao people continue to call it by that name.

25. Lotha

Born of bloodshed

The people around us have descended from a brother and a sister who survived the worst carnage our ancestors ever saw or participated in. Surprisingly though, this brother-sister duo had nothing to do with the turn of events that led to this catastrophe. At the centre of it all was a woman named Lankongrhoni who lived in a village with her handsome son Arilao.

Arilao was all Lankongrhoni ever had and treasured. She doted on him and thought he was the handsomest son any mother could hope for. Indeed, Arilao was so handsome that every young girl and woman in the village wanted to marry him and every young boy and man envied him. This envy often turned into anger, for young men of marriageable age were always spurned by the women they liked. 'Oh, but you are not Arilao!' the women would all say. 'We dream only of being with Arilao.'

Eventually, this anger brought them all together and they started talking among themselves. 'Something has to be done,' they would often say. 'This Arilao is getting in our way.'

Finally one day, they devised a plot. They decided to organize a fishing trip and invited Arilao to join them. 'We will poison the river fish and catch them,' they all said. 'And whoever does not come fishing will be fined a big pig.'

Arilao was anyway eager to go, and the fine was an added incentive. His mother, Lankongrhoni, was reluctant to let him go. She did not trust the young men of the village, although they were all friends and family. 'Do not go, Son,' she pleaded. 'I have a bad feeling about this.'

'But Mother,' Arilao reasoned, 'If I don't go, we will lose our pig. Is that what you want?'

So there was nothing Lankongrhoni could do about it but bid him goodbye when, a couple of days later, all the young men of the village went on the trip. It was a merry trip to the river bank and they laughed and joked all the way there. The evil intentions of the rest of his companions remained well hidden from Arilao.

When they reached the river bank, the men got together and felled a large tree. Then, from its trunk, they hewed a trough big enough to hold a grown man. When that was done, one of the young men said, 'Now let us lie down in this trough in turns and see who looks best inside it.'

They all took it as a funny game and took turns trying to fit into the trough. But every time somebody lay down, the other men would shout out, 'No, no, you do not look nice lying there!'

In the end, it fell upon Arilao to lie down inside the hollow. As soon as he did that, the other men started chanting, 'Arilao looks best, Arilao looks best. We will now pound him, we will now pound him.'

So saying, they pounded Arilao repeatedly with the bag of fish poison and killed him. Finally, they dumped his body in the river. Then they turned to return to their village, satisfied that their competition was now no more.

Among these young men, however, there was one—and only one—who loved Arilao deeply and was his true friend. He had been forced to come along on this murderous trip fearing the fine, but his heart was not in it. He did not see Arilao as a rival, but loved him like a brother. So while Arilao was being killed and his body dumped in the river, he walked downstream a little distance away from the other young men. There he sat, by the river's stream, and shed many tears. 'Arilao, my friend, how vile an end you have come to, and for no fault of yours!'

As he sat thus weeping, a fingernail came floating down the river and rested near him. He realized it belonged to Arilao, and so he picked it up gently, wailing, 'Is this all that's left of you, my friend?'

He then wrapped it up in a leaf and slipped it into his belt before rejoining the others. There was a huge haul of fish that day and all the young men of the village went back very happy.

Lankongrhoni saw them as they were nearing the village and came out to meet her son. But she could not see him. She kept asking the young men by turns, 'Where is your friend?' or 'Where is your elder brother?' or 'Where is your younger brother?'

And all of them just said, 'He is right behind us, laughing and talking to the girls—as usual.'

At the end of the line was Arilao's friend, who walked alone, weeping. When Lankongrhoni saw him, she knew something was amiss. 'What is it, son, tell me!' she demanded.

'No, mother, do not ask me,' the friend urged. 'I cannot tell you. The news will only bring you sorrow.'

'You make me sad by not telling me, son. Don't do this to me.'

So he told her and handed her the fingernail he had hidden.

'Is this all that's left of you, my son?' she wailed, but soon enough, regained her composure. She decided to hide her grief from the treacherous villagers and said nothing more.

Instead, a few days later, she made an announcement in front of them, 'I shall hold a feast for all the children of the village. Tomorrow, I shall slaughter my biggest pig and feed your children. Do send them to my house in the morning.'

The villagers therefore brought their children to Lankongrhoni's house the next morning and left them there. Then they went to their fields to work.

Lankongrhoni had meanwhile slaughtered her biggest pig, as promised, and she made the little children eat the food that she cooked. When the feast was over, she left them inside her house and went outisde. She stood against the wall and called out to them, 'Children, are there any holes in the walls of my house?'

The children looked around and cried out, 'There is one here, granny.' And she stoppered it.

Then she asked the same question again, 'Children, are there any holes in the walls of my house?'

The children again looked around and cried out, 'There is one here, granny.' And she stoppered that too.

And so it went on till all the holes in the house were blocked.

Then she cried out, 'Children, are there any holes left in the walls of my house?'

The children looked around and cried out, 'There are none, granny.'

And she was satisfied. Then she called out, 'I am going to light my pipe for a smoke, children. Give me a brand.'

They handed her one. With this, she set the house on fire and burnt all the children alive. Then she turned around, found a thread that hung from the sky, climbed up the thread and disappeared.

Meanwhile, the villagers were totally unaware of what had been happening down at their village to their children. They were busy working in their fields. Suddenly, a crow appeared, dressed as a little girl, and cawed, 'Arilao's mother has wiped out the children of the village.'

The cawing carried from field to field,and parent to parent. The villagers were taken by surprise and said to each other, 'What does it mean for a crow to be cawing like this? Has something really happened to our children?'

They rushed back to the village to see for themselves, and what they saw horrified them. Their children had all been burnt to ashes! Oh, how they wept and wailed to see this! But very soon, their grief turned to anger and they turned on each other. 'It is all your fault!' they said to the person next to them. 'You should have known better!' they cried. Finally, they all fell on each other and killed one another. In this way, the entire village of our ancestors was wiped out that day.

Only two children, orphans who had had no parents to take them to Lankongrhoni's fatal feast, had stood watching it all from a distance. When they saw the villagers slaughtering each other, they grew very frightened and hid themselves in a fowl-house. In this way, they escaped the bloodbath. When everybody else was dead, they came down from the fowl-house and started a new life.

The people around us are all descended from this brother and sister duo who survived the worst carnage our ancestors ever saw or participated in. They had nothing to do with the turn of events that led to this catastrophe. At the centre of it all was Lankongrhoni and her handsome son Arilao. But they all died or disappeared. The siblings procreated the human race—many of us humans even emerged from their fingers and toes.

26. Sema

Death is not the end

Our ancestors tell us through their tales that death may not be the end, that beyond death there might still be redemption, there might yet be punishment. Sometimes, beyond death, there may still be alive the malevolent influence of one who was evil in life.

Muchüpile was in love with a young man. But this young man married a pretty girl he loved. They were very happy together. This was not something that Muchüpile could digest easily. So she came to the couple's house one day when the husband was away and killed the young wife. Then, she threw the young woman's mangled body away in the heart of the forest. When the young husband returned, he was distraught at not finding his wife. To give him support in his grief, Muchüpile came to live in his house. She consoled him and looked after him, and gradually, she insinuated herself into his life.

With his wife gone, the young man needed somebody to look after his house and Muchüpile seemed like the best option. So he married her and made her a part of his life. Her objective achieved, Muchüpile happily cooked and cleaned for her husband.

One day, she went to the forest to pick bamboo shoots for the evening meal. She was happy to find some very luscious ones growing in the forest not far off from the house. She picked them and cleaned them and started cooking them in the pot. As the water boiled, the bamboo shoots boiled with it, singing, 'Muchüpile *pfo pfo*', 'Muchüpile *pfo pfo*'.

'It is only the water boiling, the bamboo shoots with it,' she said to herself, but the song continued. It irritated her very much, and finally, she walked up to the pot to do something about it. As she did, she realized that the bamboo shoots she had picked for cooking had been growing in the exact same spot where she had dumped her husband's first wife's body. Only, she had forgotten. But now, she had no doubt in her mind that the singing bamboo shoots were none other than her co-wife come back to taunt her. So she picked up the entire pot of cooked bamboo shoots and threw it out in the backyard. Then she cooked something else for dinner that night. When her husband came back, both of them had their evening meal and went to bed. Life went back to normal soon.

A few days later, her husband was in the backyard when she heard him cry out, 'Wife, come here, quick!'

Muchüpile ran out immediately, but stopped short when she saw what her husband was pointing to. It was a big mishiti (lime) tree that she had never seen growing in their backyard before. On top of the tree was a succulent lime that her husband was reaching for to pluck.

'Look, Muchüpile,' he said as he plucked it. 'It is so beautiful. Somehow, it reminds me of my former wife.'

Muchüpile was angry but of course, she could do nothing to prevent him from remembering his dead wife. She watched silently, therefore, as her husband brought the fruit into the house and placed it in a basket. Then both she and her husband forgot about it. The next morning they went to the fields as usual.

When they got back home, both husband and wife were surprised to see that the housework had all been done and the food cooked and ready to eat. It astonished them no end, but since they had no clue about who their benefactor was, they could do nothing about it.

The next morning, they went to the fields again. Once again, when they got back home, both husband and wife were surprised to see that the housework had all been done and the food cooked and ready to eat. 'Who is it?' the husband cried out aloud. 'If you are anywhere around, show yourself.'

But nobody responded. So once again, there was nothing to do but eat the food and go to bed. The same thing happened the next day. In the morning, they went to the fields as usual. When they got back home, they once again found the housework done and the food prepared. 'Who is it?' the husband called out again. 'If you are anywhere around, listen to what I have to say. I shall give you food even if there were nothing left for myself. Just show yourself to me.'

Again, nobody responded, and the same thing happened the next day and the next. In the end, the husband decided to do something about it. One morning, he pretended to go to the fields with his wife as usual. But in reality, he hid himself in a corner of the house and waited for the mysterious person to show up. What he saw gave him the biggest shock of his life! Out of the lime fruit he had plucked from the tree in the backyard and placed in the basket, stepped his dead wife. Unaware that she was being watched, she started doing all the household chores the way she used to when she was alive. The husband could not believe his own eyes!

Overjoyed, he jumped out of his hiding place and embraced his wife from behind. 'Where have you been? Where have you come from now?' he demanded.

'Husband, you have found me! I am so glad,' cried the dead wife. And she went on to tell him the entire story of how Muchüpile had killed her in his absence and thrown her body into the woods. 'I grew back as a bamboo shoot, which she picked and cooked. When she realized it was me, she threw me away in the backyard. There I grew into the lime tree you saw. When you plucked me from the tree, you gave me back my human shape. All that was left was for you to rediscover me, and here I am,' she concluded.

Hearing her tale, the husband was filled with anger against his treacherous second wife. 'She shall be taught a lesson,' he declared.

So when Muchüpile came home that evening, his mind was made up. She called out to him from the threshold, 'Husband, come to me. Help me with my load!'

The husband ran at her, and instead of helping her unload the basket from her back, he struck her down and cut her into pieces. Then, he threw her body, flesh and bones, all away some distance from his house. His former wife having now regained her human form, they started living together again.

But as they say, evil never dies. As the days passed by, and they walked past the spot every day where the dead Muchüpile lay, they were touched by the same evil. Muchüpile's flesh had rotted away, and her bones had turned to dust. But her evil lived on. This infected the happy couple. Soon, their limbs started swelling and they died as well. The husband had also, after all, committed an act of murder.

Tripura

A brief note:

One of the smallest states of the Indian Union, Tripura is bound in the east by Assam and Mizoram. To the north, south and west, it is surrounded by the land mass of Bangladesh, a country with which it shares close historical, socio-economic and ethnic ties. Tripura has a glorious history of monarchy on the one hand and ethnic variety and unity on the other. Since the coming of the British to this part of the world, however, the monarchs of Tripura started losing their power and glory. At the same time, the groundwork was also laid for the subsequent escalation of ethnic strife. In post-colonial times, Tripura witnessed some of the worst incidents of ethnic violence. Due mainly to the huge influx of refugee populations and other migrants into Tripura, the state is the second-most populous in the Northeast, after Assam. The phenomenal rise in Bengali population and influence, especially, was seen as a huge threat to the ethnic fabric of the state. Nativist sentiments gave rise to insurgent armies which continue to operate although their strengths have been depleted to a large extent.

The Indian Constitution recognizes nineteen ethnic groups and some sub-groups, of which the Tripuri people are the most numerous. Other major indigenous groups of Tripura include the Reang, Jamatia, Chakma, Halam, Mog, Munda, Kuki and Garo.

All of them taken together, however, are significantly fewer in number than the Bengali population of the state. The Bengali language also predominates. Among the indigenous languages, Kokborok is the most prominent. Other indigenous languages spoken commonly are Mog, Bishnupriya Manipuri, Manipuri, Halam, Garo and Chakma.

Chakmas are found in large numbers in the Chittagong Hill Tracts of Bangladesh and the Rakhine state of Burma. They migrated to Tripura and other parts of Northeast India following various kinds of political and social persecutions. Developmental policies adverse to their habitation in Bangladesh also displaced and forced a large number of them to migrate to Northeast India, especially to Arunachal Pradesh, Tripura and Mizoram. Originally surmised to be speakers of a Tibeto-Burman language, the Chakmas gradually developed their current language, Changma Vaj, following centuries of close proximity to the eastern Indo-Aryan linguistic groups of Bangladesh and India. They write this language in a script called Ojhopath which is similar to some of the scripts found in Thailand, Cambodia, Laos and parts of Burma. The Chakmas are divided into forty-six clans, or gozas, and are primarily practitioners of Buddhism.

The Kolois are a Tripuri tribe found mostly in west Tripura. At various times in history, they have been aligned with the Halams, Reangs and Kukis as well. They speak Kokborok, which is akin to the Bodo language of Tibeto-Burman origin. The Koloi society is organized into various clans that are patrilineal by practice. Among these clans are the Waptom, Wakbur, Rujgui, Bukang, Abel, Kuchhu and Chorai. Traditionally jhum cultivators, the Kolois used to grow their own cotton to make thread, and weave their own clothes. Christianity has brought many changes into Koloi life, tradition and society over the years.

The Noatias are another major Tripuri tribe. Noatia refers to the 'New Tripuri' indicating that this community of people entered the Tripuri fold much later than the others. There are eleven sub-clans among the Noatias, namely, the Aslong,

Murasing, Keowa, Gorjon, Khalicha, Tongbai, Laitong, Deildak, Anaokia, Khaklo and Totaram. These clans are spread over Bangladesh and Northeast India. In Bangladesh, they live mostly in the Chittagong Hill Tracts and in Northeast India, they live mostly in south and west Tripura. *Huk*, or jhum cultivation, was the mainstay of the Noatia people in the early days, though they have since moved to more settled forms of agriculture.

The Tipras, or Tripuris, claim to be the original inhabitants of Tripura. They are actually a conglomerate of five communities, together known as the Pancha Tripura since the days of the Manikya monarchy. These five communities include Old Tipra, Noatia, Jamatia, Reang and Halam. Initially, the Debbarmas or Tipras, from whom the royal lineage was drawn, could alone lay claim to this identity. Subsequently, however, in an effort to foster ethnic kinship and harmony, the Manikya kings allowed the other communities to amalgamate and enter the fold. Each of these communities is further divided into various sub-tribes, clans and sub-clans. Most of the Tripuri people are Hinduized, but a small section of them also practise Christianity.

27. Chakma

Crab, spider, pig and plenty

Till the universe came into being, there was nothing but water everywhere. A vast, endless stretch of water that just *was*, and flowed nowhere, never rippled, never stirred. The wind, you see, had not yet been created. And how would this vast sea experience any animation without the wind to disturb its ever-placid surface?

Nobody knew how deep this water was, because nobody ever wondered about its depth, because there *was* nobody to ask such questions. But perhaps the gods knew, because the gods were there, and the gods knew all. And one of the gods was Gozen. He was the one who brought the universe into being just by willing it to do so.

First, there appeared a gigantic tree that grew in the middle of the vast expanse of water. It was so big that a bird—like the best birds of flight that we know today—would tire flying around its main trunk, and settle down midway to catch its breath. From this main trunk emanated several branches, each almost as huge, and so heavy that they bent down with their own weight and submerged into the water. There, they grew additional roots and looked like separate trees. Ah, yes, the roots too were humungous and they nearly tore at the heart of the endless sea.

From the many many massive branches of this tree, Gozen plucked one leaf—and what a big leaf it was, too!—and he sat himself down upon it, and said, 'Now I shall meditate.' He did not plan how long he would sit and meditate, and we do not have the knowledge of how long he actually did sit thus, motionless and mulling over the act of creation. For there was nothing to mark the passing of time—no sun or moon, no seasons or seasonal flowers, indeed, no concept of time at all.

But after what could have been an eternity, or a few moments thereof, Gozen opened his eyes. He opened his eyes, and before him stretched a vast expanse of land, with the tree at its centre. The earth had been created!

Gozen, of course, was aware that while he had been meditating, Kangara, the crab, had been at work, clawing at the soil in the bed of the endless sea, digging it up, turning the water's surface upside down. It had piled up the soil at the root of the tree, creating, finally, the earth.

'There is more to do,' said Gozen, and he set aside his meditation and busied himself, creating a new sea. This new sea he placed upside down, high above the earth, so that it could not be reached by anybody on land, and he called it Agaz, or the sky. Then, upon this sea that was actually the sky, he placed a boat, which floated upon it, gracefully.

'This sea-sky shall be the source of light for the earth below,' decided Gozen and from the heat of his celestial body, he created a great ball of light. He called this ball of light Bel. As a brother and companion to Bel, Gozen next created Chan from the calm light of his eyes. Both Bel and Chan were to act as the custodians of light, and he instructed them to journey across the sky and dispel the darkness from the earth.

'I shall travel from east to west every day,' said Bel to Chan. 'When I am tired, you step in.'

So, every evening, when Bel got tired from his long journey across the upside-down sea-sky, Chan would continue illuminating the earth. The two brothers thus gave birth to the phenomena of day and night. Gozen then decreed that the days would be warm and the nights cool.

Having set the affairs of the sky to order in this manner, Gozen now turned his attention to the earth. 'It will not do to have this vast stretch of land just lying there. I shall have to give it some character,' he decided. And he created mountains and rivers, hills and forests, plains and deep gorges. This varied and undulating land is the earth as we know it, and Gozen called it Pitthimi. He also peopled it with all kinds of creatures and gave them each a name. To some of these creatures he gave the gift of flight, to some the muscles to walk and run, to others the apparatus to swim underwater. 'They should all be distinct from each other,' he said, feeling quite pleased.

But then, Gozen had been indulging in all his creative endeavours from afar. He had never visited the earth in person, or taken a close look at all the hills and valleys, birds and creatures that he had brought into being. Slowly, he started to feel the urge to see his handiwork from close quarters. As the feeling grew, he descended one day from heaven and alighting on Pitthimi, started looking around, delighting in all that he saw around him. It gave him immense pleasure that he had brought all the things he saw into being.

He couldn't stop marvelling at all the abundance he saw around him as he walked all over earth from one corner to another. And he couldn't stop walking and walking around. But suddenly, as he walked, he felt as though he was being followed. 'Who is it?' he called out. '*Keduga?*' he said. But nobody answered. He tried to brush off the feeling that he was not alone and continued inspecting his creations. But after a while, he once again felt that somebody was there, close at his heels, following him. '*Keduga?*' he cried out again but he got no answer. This happened a few more times till Gozen became quite annoyed.

'Whoever it is, why don't you answer me?' he finally demanded, and thinking that he could take them by surprise, turned around quite suddenly to confront whoever was behind him. To his utter embarrassment, he saw that he had been followed all this while by his own shadow! 'How silly of me,' he said and was about to dismiss the entire episode when a sudden thought occurred to him.

'I was so sure somebody was following me because my shadow was indeed behind me all this while. It is insubstantial right now, but what if I did give it a body and made it truly "somebody"? I could mould it in clay and breathe life into it,' he contemplated. And so out of his misadventure on earth was born a creature moulded in Gozen's own form. He called it Keduga, or man, for he had mistaken his shadow for a man-like form in the first place.

Keduga lived alone on earth for a while, but soon thereafter, he started feeling lonely. There was nobody to keep him company, speak to him in his own tongue, or share his feelings. Gozen understood his predicament and decided to create a woman. He scraped the dirt from his own body and moulded it between his palms, and finally gave shape to the first woman. He called her Kedugi.

Humankind was now born, and Gozen summoned the first of its specimens to him and spoke to them. 'I shall keep you in Pitthimi, and make you its masters. All the rest of my creation shall be of use to you. The trees I created will bear you fruits, the animals I shaped will yield their flesh. Partake of these judiciously and be healthy and strong. Sleep on the grassy carpets I have planted for you and beget children and multiply your kind,' he instructed and left for heaven.

Left to their own devices now, Keduga and Kedugi strived to make the best of what they had been provided with. They did not of course know how to make fire, or grow crops, build houses or weave clothes. So they lived where they liked, ate what they came across and wandered about in the skin they were born in. In due course of time, they also bore children, who then grew up to bear more children, and so on and on, till the earth was populated by human beings in a multitude. And all of them lived in peace and plenitude, for the earth gave them all that they needed for their survival.

Calamity struck, however, in the form of a severe *khabat* that set in one day caused by a deadly frost. Keduga and Kedugi's children, who had been provided for by Gozen's abundance so far, suddenly found themselves facing a barren earth which could provide them with no sustenance whatsoever. The trees died, their fruits and flowers destroyed by the khabat. The birds, animals and fish also froze in the face of the icy cold, and perished.

'It will not be long now before we all perish as well,' cried the children of Keduga and Kedugi. Without food, they could not muster up the energy to face the cold. Surely the khabat would be the end of the human race as well?

When he heard their cries, Gozen was deeply disturbed to see the plight of the human beings. 'I created them from my own shadow, they are all a reflection of me. Now I must do something to save them,' he decided. Kalayya, one of the gods, he thought, would be able to avert the imminent catastrophe, the annihilation of the human race.

So he summoned him and instructed, 'O Kalayya, can you see the deadly khabat that is threatening to destroy the race of Keduga and Kedugi? Can you see what the icy frost has done to the rest of my creation already? Come, Kalayya, come to my aid. Go down to Pitthimi and avert the crisis.'

So Kalayya descended to earth as instructed. He put an end to the khabat and gave new life to the trees and animals, birds and fish, and all other forms of life that had perished or become endangered in the frost. But he knew that this could not be the end of his task on earth. He would have to make sure that such a calamity would not occur again.

'All my hard work will come to naught if something like this should recur, or if there is not enough food to go around for the children of Keduga and Kedugi,' he realized. 'I cannot leave without ensuring that they are well provided for.' And so he summoned all the trees on earth to stand before him and he asked each one of them in turn, 'Can you provide enough food for the children of Keduga and Kedugi?'

After what had just passed, not all the trees were very confident. And they could say with no conviction that they would be able to provide enough food for the human race forever and ever to come. Slowly, one by one, they slunk away from the presence of Kalayya. In the end, only one tree was left—it was the *jagana* tree. Kalayya could see that the tree was bent from the weight of all the fruits that had sprouted on its many branches. He was not surprised therefore when it proclaimed very confidently, 'O Kalayya, as you can see, I have fruits in abundance. My limbs are aching with the weight of the many sweet fruits that hang from me. Surely you can see that I alone am capable of sustaining the entire human race? Surely you do not doubt my ability to grow more and more fruits for as long as humanity would need them?'

Kalayya was convinced and he left for heaven, pleased that he had provided for the children of Keduga and Kedugi for all time to come. The jagana tree also made good its promise for a long time thereafter. Human beings were well fed and they proliferated immensely. But then, nothing lasts forever. The tree could not bear as many fruits as the rapidly multiplying human race needed for its consumption. It started falling short. One day, a few humans went hungry, because the number of fruits was less than the number of human beings on earth. They approached Kalayya about it, and asked him to ensure that this did not happen again.

So Kalayya came down to see the tree. He asked, 'What happened, jagana tree? You said you will never fall short!'

'It happened only once,' replied the tree. 'It will not happen again, I'll make sure of that. The animals came and ate some of the fruits, which is why I fell short.'

Somewhat convinced, Kalayya returned to heaven. But the same thing happened the next day, and the humans complained to Kalayya. Once again, Kalayya came down to earth and asked the tree, 'What happened, jagana tree? You said you will never fall short again!'

The tree once again replied, 'It will not happen again, I'll make sure of that. The animals came and ate some of the fruits, which is why I fell short.'

This continued for the next few days, the next few weeks, the next few months and finally, for a whole year. The jagana tree continued to blame the animals, instead of accepting its shortcoming. Finally, after a year, Kalayya lost his temper. 'That tree is a braggart. It must be taught a lesson!'

So he came down to earth, where the tree stood, and kicked it with all his might. So violent was his rage, and so strongly did he strike the jagana, that the tree writhed in pain and its trunk became all knotted and twisted. Then, Kalayya cursed it, saying, 'No human being will ever eat your fruits from this day forward.' This is why Chakma people do not eat the fruit of the jagana tree even today.

The arrogant tree was suitably punished all right, but this did not put an end to human misery. In fact, hunger continued to haunt them all the more, now that even the few fruits of the jagana tree were no longer edible. The crisis had reached such a point that Kalayya now found himself compelled to seek Gozen's intervention. 'There is no other way to save the children of Keduga and Kedugi,' he realized, and made his way to Gozen's abode.

Gozen patiently listened as Kalayya narrated all that had transpired on earth. Then, after he had assessed the situation, he decided that the only course of action left now was to somehow get Mah-Lakkhi-ma to visit Pitthimi. And once again, he placed the responsibility upon Kalayya. 'Listen, Kalayya, this is the only way the food shortage will ever end. Go then, and get Mah-Lakkhi-ma to come with you,' he said.

Kalayya did as he was asked to and made his way to where Mah-Lakkhi-ma lived. When he reached there, he paid his respects to her and once again, as he had done before Gozen, narrated the entire tale of human suffering before her. 'Mother', he prayed, 'only you can teach the humans how to grow their own food and fend for themselves so that they would never have to go hungry again. Please come with me to Pitthimi and put the human race out of its misery.'

Mah-Lakkhi-ma, of course, is not so easy to please, and she decided that she would test Kalayya before making up her mind about going to earth at his request. But she did not want Kalayya to know that he was being put to test, and with infinite sweetness she told him, 'O Kalayya, you have come from afar, and must be tired from your journey. Therefore, rest tonight, and tomorrow we shall embark on another long journey.'

Kalayya was then entertained with food and drinks and Mah-Lakkhi-ma asked her attendants to take good care of him. Little did the god know that this was his test, and he was very pleased to be showered with all the bounty at Mah-Lakkhi-ma's abode. He ate to his heart's content, and when he was served with wine, he drank that too—in gulps at first and then, emptying tumbler after tumbler—till he became quite inebriated indeed.

Drunk and all out of control now, Kalayya started shouting at the top of his voice, showing off and bragging about all that he had done, and breaking the pots and pans at Mah-Lakkhi-ma's abode as he did so. But he did not stop at that and went on to show utter disrespect to Mah-Lakkhi-ma herself. When the goddess heard all the commotion and came to see what the matter was, he started bragging in front of her as well, sometimes addressing her as *jedai*, sometimes *kakki*, and sometimes *bhuji*.

Mah-Lakkhi-ma was disgusted at Kalayya's behaviour and disappointed that he had failed her test so miserably. She told him in no uncertain terms that she would not go with him to earth, and would have nothing to do with preventing the extinction of the human race, which was certainly imminent.

When Kalayya returned and shamefacedly reported his failure to Gozen, the latter was despondent. 'Yet, I have to do something. I cannot let this one setback be the end of my creation,' thought Gozen as he mulled over how to appease the goddess now that such damage had been done and she had been angered by Kalayya's behaviour.

This time, he decided, he would have to send somebody who would not get seduced by the distractions planned by Mah-Lakkhi-ma. And he realized his son, Biyetra, would be up to the task. So he got Biyetra ready and instructed him, 'You have to succeed where Kalayya failed. You must resist all temptations that wily goddess lays in your path. You must be strong, and you must bring Mah-Lakkhi-ma to Pitthimi. Be respectful to her, and she will oblige.' So saying, he blessed his son and directed him to go forth.

Biyetra, however, was a clever god. He would never undertake any task in haste without understanding what it involved. That way, he could be aware of the pitfalls and avoid failure. So he bowed before his father and said, 'Father, I will fulfil the task you ask of me. But by all accounts, it is not going to be so easy to appease the goddess. So let me understand the entire problem for myself, first-hand. When I am more knowledgeable, I will preempt failure. I will also be ready for any surprises the goddess springs at me.'

Gozen was pleased at his son's sagacity, and gave him permission to go down to earth and live among humankind for a while. So Biyetra came to live among the children of Keduga and

Kedugi, and to learn their ways. He saw how they lived and what they ate and how they could never grow anything for themselves and lived on only those things that had been provided to them by his father.

'You have to learn to fend for yourselves. My father's bounty will not last forever,' he warned them. And he taught them how to build the *mazaghar* with bamboo and *sunn* grass. They now had a roof over their heads to shelter them from the vagaries of the weather. Next, he also fetched some fire from heaven and taught them to cook food, so that they would not need to eat nature's produce the way nature produced it. But of course, nature had its limitations and unless humans learnt how to grow their own food, they would soon be facing another crisis. Biyetra understood this very well and he also knew that his own limitation was that he could not teach humans to create food. This was something only Mah-Lakkhi-ma could do. 'It is time now,' he realized, 'for me to fulfil my father's wishes and to go to Mah-Lakkhi-ma's abode. If these humans are to be self-sufficient, she has to take them under her wing.'

But Biyetra also remembered what had happened when his father had last sent an emissary on the same task. He also recalled how his father had warned him that the goddess was very wily and would resist coming to earth as much as she could. So he made certain preparations. He decided to take along with him three companions: Kangara, the crab, Sugar, the boar, and Magarak, the spider. Together they set forth till they reached the shores of a huge sea of milk. It was a wondrous sight to see this vast white expanse stretching before their eyes and they knew this was the place where earth ended and heaven began.

Crossing this vast sea was, of course, not a problem for Biyetra as he was a god, and he leapt across the sea to the other shore, taking his three companions along with him. Once on firm ground again, he took leave of his companions. Do wait for me here, my friends, and I shall return shortly,' he said before departing for the abode of Mah-Lakkhi-ma.

When he reached there, Biyetra was overwhelmed by the sumptuousness he saw all around him, and the warmth of the welcome that the goddess accorded him made him feel wonderful. He paid obeisance to Mah-Lakkhi-ma as was wont, and just as Kalayya was before him, was asked to stay back the night. He knew this was the night of his test, but he had come prepared. He knew, of course, that he could not afford to insult his hostess by refusing the bountiful food and drink she laid before him. So he let her attendants pile his plate with all kind of delicious food and fill his glass with the best of wine. However, when he saw his chance, he spilled all the wine served to him while nobody was looking. In this way, he managed to stay sober without insulting the goddess.

Being omniscient, Mah-Lakkhi-ma naturally saw through Biyetra's cunning, but she was very pleased with him for being able to resist temptation while at the same time knowing how to be respectful where respect was due. So she summoned him to her and said, 'I will come with you to Pitthimi, Biyetra, and not allow your visit to be in vain. Let humankind benefit from your wisdom.'

Then she filled her bag with all kinds of grains and vegetables that would be palatable to human beings. She took with her seeds of paddy, sesame, millet and cotton. She also packed into her bag some yam, green leafy vegetables, marmah, chindira, brinjal and other edible plants. When she was ready, she summoned her mount, the bird, Me-Me-Chagli. Sitting on her back, she then set out on the descent to Pitthimi along with Biyetra.

Before they could reach the earth, though, they would have to cross the sea of milk yet again. And when they alighted on its shore, Mah-Lakkhi-ma looked out at its vastness and said despairingly, 'O Biyetra, you have brought me this far, but I doubt we will be able to go any further. This milk-sea is huge and Me-Mc-Chagli is not strong enough to fly across it with me on her back.'

Biyetra understood that the goddess was still trying to find some excuse not to go to earth with him. But he had come prepared, hadn't he? Why, after all, had he brought with him his three companions who had been waiting all along on this very shore of the milky sea, awaiting his signal to come forward and help him in his endeavour?

Biyetra respectfully smiled and said to the goddess, 'O Mother, let us not lose heart since we have come this far. I have made arrangements for us all to be safely transported across this seemingly endless sea.'

And he called out to his companions and they presented themselves before the goddess. Biyetra turned to Magarak, the spider, and instructed, 'O Magarak, weave us a thread so long and so strong that it may connect this shore of the milky sea with the other from whence begins our Pitthimi.'

Now the spider was not loth to help, but it appeared to be hesitant about something. Mah-Lakkhi-ma, the omniscient, understood what was in its mind. So she said kindly, 'Fear not, Magarak. Do as Biyetra asks. Your thread will never end, not if you weave this thread across the milky sea, nor ever again.'

Delighted with this boon, the spider set to work, connecting the two shores of the sea. And thanks to the goddess's boon, it continues to weave its threads even today.

After its work was done, Biyetra summoned Sugar, the boar and Kangara, the crab. He requested Mah-Lakkhi-ma to mount Me-Me-Chagli, who then sat on the back of Sugar. The boar then stood on the back of Kangara, and the crab swam slowly across the thick foam of milk and cream. All this, while Mah-Lakkhi-ma held on firmly to the spider's thread and kept her balance, managing not to fall into the perilous sea. Finally, they all reached the other end—where the earth began and human beings lived.

Happy with Biyetra's respectful demeanour and sharp intelligence, Mah-Lakkhi-ma then turned to him and blessed him. 'Biyetra,' she said, 'you have done a great service to human beings by bringing me here, and you have done it without compromising yourself or others in any way. Therefore, I grant you this boon, that forever after, humans will worship you before they worship any other god.'

And since the pig and the crab had aided the benign god, she also blessed them—the boar with the possession of bodily fat, which would make it the most excellent of all animals, and the crab with the ability to move with equal agility in both land and water.

Then, she settled down on earth to live among the children of Keduga and Kedugi. She gave them all the seeds that she had brought with her and taught them how to sow those seeds, how to tend to the plants that grew out of them, and how to harvest and, finally, cook them. She gave them the knowledge of jhum cultivation so that they would always be able to cultivate their own food and never ever go hungry again. Thus, all human plenitude came from Mah-Lakkhi-ma.

28. Koloi

Seven kingdoms for seven siblings

Sardeng had two dutiful daughters who helped him out in the jhum fields every day. But Sardeng was a poor man and he could not afford to build a good enough *tong* (jhum hut) for his two daughters. The tong was in a very sad state, dilapidated, with almost no roof on it. And yet, Sardeng could not afford to repair it, such was his miserable state. When it rained, therefore, the two sisters would sit huddled inside the tong, getting wet, nevertheless, for the roof leaked relentlessly.

One rainy season, when the rains were particularly merciless, the two sisters were drenched nearly every day, and would cry on each other's shoulders seeing their own pathetic condition. 'If only somebody would repair our tong roof for us,' the elder sister cried out one day. 'I would marry anybody who could build us a strong tong.'

The next day, however, the sun came out and neither of the two girls thought anything about what the elder sister had said the day before. A few days later, though, they came back from their jhum field to see that the broken-down tong had been repaired by somebody. 'How is this possible?' they exclaimed in utter surprise, and rushed inside to see that their things had been placed inside the tong in an orderly manner and the whole hut was as good as new.

'Did somebody hear what you said that day, Sister?' the younger one ventured, scared.

'I don't know. But if they did, I would be honour-bound to marry them,' the elder sister replied.

As it turned out, a python had been passing by their tong that day, and it was he who had repaired the hut in hopes of marrying the impetuous girl. Now, when he heard her say this, he suddenly appeared before the two girls and proclaimed, 'It was me, young girl. I repaired your tong for you. Will you marry me now?'

The elder sister could not very well say no, and so they were secretly married.

Once the marriage ceremony was over, she asked her younger sister to invite the python to a meal. The younger sister was reluctant at first. 'He is a python, after all, and I am scared of him. O Sister, do I really have to invite him to eat?' she wailed.

But when she saw that her sister had accepted the snake for her husband without any inhibition, she decided not to create a fuss. She called out, *'Kumui, Kumui, Kumui, maichana faidi ba'* (brother-in-law, come for food). The python slithered out of the field and ate the rice they had cooked, along with them.

Every day thereafter, the two sisters would go to the jhum field as usual and when it was time for their midday meal, the younger sister would call out, 'Kumui, Kumui, Kumui, maichana faidi ba'. And every day, the python would crawl from the field and share the rice they had cooked.

One day, the elder sister was away from home and Sardeng came to the jhum field to see what state the crops were in. What he saw amazed him. He could hardly believe his eyes when he saw the huge python sliding up to his younger daughter when she called out to him. He demanded to know the whole story and, when his younger daughter had narrated it to him, he was beside himself with rage. 'My daughter marrying a snake? How is that possible? I can never allow it!' he roared. Then he asked his younger daughter to call out to the snake again while he waited with her at the tong, a sharp dao in hand.

'Kumui, Kumui, Kumui, maichana faidi ba', sang out the young girl, and the python began to slither towards her. But when he raised his head to have the food, Sardeng raised his dao and severed the python's head in one clean stroke. He threw the head into a *lunga* (gorge), and then carried the rest of the python's carcass back to the village. There he had the meat cooked and everybody ate their fill. Sardeng also set aside some of the meat for his elder daughter.

Now the elder daughter had had a very bad day, all day. Her heart had been heavy and filled with foreboding for some reason, and as she walked along, her ornaments had started falling off her body of their own accord. 'There go my earrings,' she said, as they dropped at her feet, and then, 'How falls my nose ring?' as it slipped off.

Suspecting something was wrong with her husband, as soon as she got back home, she took her younger sister with her to the field. There she asked her to call out to the python as she usually did. The younger sister did not dare say anything of what had transpired that day, and instead, called out to her brother-in-law as usual, 'Kumui, Kumui, Kumui, maichana faidi ba.'

But although she called many a time, the snake did not appear. So, scared and apprehensive, the elder sister now cried out in desperation, '*Bhang ai, bhang ai, bhang, aimi chana faidi ba.*' (Husband, husband, husband, come and eat).

But of course, there was no snake yet again. 'Maybe something terrible has happened to him, Sister. Come, let us go look for him,' she urged.

So the two young girls set out in quest of the python. As they walked around looking for him, calling out every now and then, they suddenly chanced upon some lovely khumpui flowers, blooming abundantly in a gorge by the river. This was the same lunga where their father had thrown the severed head of the snake.

'Oh look, how beautiful these flowers are,' exclaimed the younger sister when she saw them. And she joyfully stretched her hands towards the flowers, plucked one and tucked it behind an ear. But the moment she did so, it withered and died.

'How strange,' thought the elder sister. 'Here, let me try doing that,' she said to her sister and plucked one of the flowers for herself and tucked it behind her own ear. It remained as fresh as ever and did not wither.

'Now I know my husband is here!' she exclaimed. And when she looked into the river, she felt sure that that was where she would find him. So she made her way towards the river, and gradually started immersing herself in it. The younger sister watched in trepidation, and started crying as first the elder sister's feet sank under water, then her waist, then her breasts, and only her head was visible above the surface. 'Don't leave me, Sister,' cried the younger one. 'It wasn't my fault our father killed your husband. Yes, he did it, after making me call out to your husband. I am sorry, but please do not leave me. Who will I live with, who will keep me company if you go away?'

'You are innocent, little Sister. Of that I am convinced. But I have to go find my husband. However, I will make sure that you will not be alone,' said the elder sister. 'Do as I say and you will soon find yourself a good husband,' she continued. 'Go on ahead, walk alone, till you come upon a banyan tree at a crossroad. It shall have six branches. Climb to its top, and when you have done that, say these words out loud, 'There is no one more beautiful than me. I am fit to be a queen.' Say these words and see what happens.'

No sooner were these words out of her mouth, the elder sister disappeared below the surface of the water and was gone.

The younger sister cried for a while, feeling sorry for herself, but soon she decided she would do what her sister had asked her to do. So she walked ahead till she came to the crossroad where grew the banyan tree that had six branches. She climbed to the top of the tree and said out loud, 'There is no one more beautiful than me. I am fit to be a queen.'

As chance would have it, a king was just passing at the crossroad at that very moment, and he was standing directly below the banyan tree. When he heard the younger sister utter those words, he was intrigued. So he called out, 'Who is it who claims to be fit to be a queen? I am a king and if you are truly as beautiful as you say you are, I shall marry you. Come down and show yourself to me.'

Thus coaxed, the younger sister climbed down from the tree. The king saw that she was indeed very beautiful and he was immediately smitten. 'I shall surely make you my queen, though I have many wives. Come with me and we shall be married and live in my palace,' he said as he led her away.

The elder sister's prophecy had come true and the younger sister was very happy for some time. The king loved her more than his other wives and pampered her a lot. Life at the king's palace should have been idyllic then, but it was not so for long. The king was away for long stretches of time, and the other wives made no secret of the fact that they were jealous of the younger sister. They left no stone unturned to make her unhappy in the king's absence. However, the king's love was compensation enough for her and after she had lived with him for a few months, she found herself with child.

It was a joyful time indeed, and the younger sister was eagerly waiting for the arrival of her child when the king suddenly announced one day that he was going away on a hunt. 'Oh, please don't leave me now, in this state,' she pleaded. 'I might have the child any time now.'

'But my dear,' the king tried to cajole her. 'I am only going hunting so that I can bring you back the meat that you like so much. It is for you that I am leaving and I will be back soon, do not worry.'

And he left.

No sooner had he turned his back, though, than the young queen started having labour pains. She called her servants to her side and told them to run after the king and call him back. The servants, however, demurred. They had been warned by the king's other wives not to listen to the new queen's orders. So instead of running after the king, they went and informed the other queens about the young queen's condition.

The other queens saw their chance now to get rid of the newcomer once and for all. They came running to her side now with seven blindfolds. These they tied around her eyes and refused to give her any place inside the palace to settle down to deliver her baby. They kept shifting her around here and there, making up excuses and citing different problems with each place the young queen wanted to settle down in for childbirth. Finally, they took her to the riverside where they lay her down.

Here the queen delivered not one, not two, but seven children, six boys and a girl. But since she was blindfolded, she could not make out anything. The other queens dropped each of the seven babies into the water and told the new mother she had only given birth to pieces of wood and stones. The new mother was overwhelmed with sorrow, but there was little she could do.

She waited in fear and trepidation for her husband, the king, to return. When he did, the other queens rushed to his side and told him that his favourite queen had given birth to wood and stones. 'She is evil, that one,' they said. 'She should not be living in the palace.'

The king was convinced that there was something evil about his youngest wife, and egged on by the other wives, he gave orders for the youngest one's ears and nose to be cut off. Then he banished her to the forest where she was made to live by the river and rear goats.

Now, our story would have ended on a very sad note indeed, if the elder sister had not come to the rescue yet again. When she had immersed herself in the waters of the river in search of her husband, she had actually found what she was looking for. Beneath the waters of the river, she had found a beautiful palace. There, her husband, the python, lived. When she reached the palace, husband and wife were united after their tragic separation and they had been living together happily ever since.

Ever since the cruel co-wives had drowned the children of her younger sister in the waters of the river, the elder sister had brought them to live with her. The seven siblings now lived in the underwater palace with their aunt who showered on them a lot of love and care. They lacked nothing and grew up to be strong, healthy and beautiful children.

They would often go up to the surface of the water, though, and play around on the riverbank. One day, when they were thus playing among themselves, it so happened that some girls from the village nearby had placed their earthen pots on the river bank and gone down to the river to bathe. When they came back, they found that their pots were broken. The children had accidentally broken them, of course, but the village girls had no way of knowing that. They never saw the children playing, because they never before played while there were other people around.

After the same thing happened a few times, the people of the village got alarmed and went to the king. 'There is something in the river,' they said to the king. 'Something that breaks our women's pots when they place them on the bank.'

Neither the king nor anybody in his court could unravel the mystery, for it had become a very mysterious and inexplicable thing for the people of the village. Finally, the king decided, 'If there is indeed something strange happening down there, the only way to warn off the miscreants would be to gather as many people as possible on the bank of the river.'

So he proclaimed, 'We shall have a boat race on the river. Bring everybody you know to the river bank on the assigned date.'

Now this was a great occasion. Everybody was excited about the boat race for it promised to be a gala event, something nobody in those parts of the kingdom had ever witnessed before. As the excitement peaked, the news even travelled to the seven siblings' aunt in the water palace. She decided that this was the right time for the king to be made aware of his folly. And she sent her six nephews and niece to watch the boat race, telling them about the events of their birth, the unfairness of their father, the king, the sorry plight of their mother, and everything else that had any bearing upon their lives. Then she taught them exactly what to do and how to behave in front of the king.

The children had grown up to be very beautiful and they stood out in their majestic demeanour among all the people of the kingdom who had come to that place on the river bank on the day of the boat race to watch the water sport. Indeed, such was their presence, that even the king noticed them. And not only did he notice them, he also eventually approached them, unable to resist himself.

'Who are you?' he asked as he stood before them. 'I don't think I have seen you children ever before in my kingdom.'

So saying he extended his hand to touch them, but the children, tutored by their aunt, started screaming and shouting, calling the king a monster.

'I am not a monster, children,' the king protested. 'I am the king of your country. Tell me who you are and where you come from.'

'If you must know, then listen. We are your children, you are our father,' the children at last said to him. Then they told him they were actually six princes and a princess. 'Our mother is your wife,' they said. 'Only, you don't know it.'

So the king took them back with him to his palace and summoned all his wives before him. 'Are these your mothers?' he asked.

'No, none of them,' they said. 'These women are not our mothers. Our real mother is living by the river, grazing goats because you chased her away.' And they narrated the whole story of how they were born of the king's youngest wife, and how they had been drowned by their stepmothers and who brought them up, and everything else that had any bearing upon their lives and the king's and their mother's.

When he had heard the entire tale, the king realized that he had been very gullible and foolish. He had caused his wife great distress and done her and his children a great injustice. 'I shall have to make amends,' he resolved, as he sent his men out in search of his banished wife. When they brought her back to the palace, he found to his utter surprise that her ears and nose, which he had ordered to be cut off, had been restored to their original form. The king understood then that his queen had been really innocent.

'It is the other evil wives of mine who shall be punished,' he proclaimed and he handed out befitting punishments to each of them.

The seven siblings, along with their mother, came to live with their father, the king, in his palace. When they came of age, the king divided his kingdom into seven equal parts. Each part was then entrusted to the rule of each of his seven children. And that is how ancient Tripura came to be known as the land of six brothers and a sister.

29. Noatia

From dispelling darkness to diseases

The creation of the universe, according to the Noatia people of Tripura, started with the creation of the earth, the sun, the moon, and man. Their creation myth, therefore, is known as Ha-Chal-Tal-Barak, which literally means Earth-Sun-Moon-Man.

Like most creation myths, this particular one also states that in the beginning, there was nothing but a vast expanse of water, still and placid. There was no sign of life anywhere around.

But suddenly, nobody knows when or how, life manifested itself in the form of a flower that floated on this placid water. Seated on this flower was Prabhu or Matai, who is the Supreme Being. For some time thereafter, nobody knows when or for how long, Matai sat upon this flower and was lost in meditation. When he finally opened his eyes, nobody knows when, he could not see anything around him. For everything around him was enveloped in utter darkness. There was no light.

'I have four eyes,' said Matai to himself, 'and yet, I cannot see'.

He wondered for a while how to dispel the darkness, and in the end, plucked out one of his own eyes and flung it out across the water's expanse. 'This eye shall be known as the moon,' he decided, and ever since, this fourth eye of the Supreme Being has been floating in heaven, twinkling at night, driving away the darkness, and has been called the moon.

However, the moon could not work alone at removing the excessive darkness that had cloaked the universe for so long. Its light was weak and it needed a companion. So Matai plucked out another one of his eyes and flung it out in a similar fashion across the water's expanse. 'This eye shall be known as the sun,' he decided, and ever since, this third eye of the Supreme Being has been floating in heaven, shining brightly, driving away the darkness, and has been called the sun.

Having thus removed his two eyes, Matai went into deep contemplation yet again. He closed his two remaining eyes and contemplated thus for a long time, nobody knows for how long a time. Finally, when he opened his eyes, he saw that the all-encompassing darkness had retreated forever, with the sun and moon there to counter it. And with the creation of the sun and the moon, day and night also thus came into being.

Matai was very pleased to see this new development, but his sense of contentment did not last long. Very soon he began to feel lonely. 'The moon has a companion, but I don't,' he sighed.

'Maybe I should do something about it,' he thought. And so he decided to create for himself a consort.

However, he had no idea what his consort should look like. As he glanced around the vast watery stretch, looking for inspiration, he spotted his reflection upon the water's calm surface. 'My companion should look like me, of course,' he decided. And so, out of his own shadow, he created his consort.

With her creation, another flower came into being and floated alongside Matai and she took her place upon it.

Now there were two of them—Matai and his consort—to discuss the process of creation that the Supreme Being had started. They engaged in long conversations, planning the creation of land in the water that they saw all around them. They also debated the conception of other forms of life. While they did so, they also conjoined, as a result of which Matai's consort came to be with child. In due course, she gave birth to three children. Brahma was the eldest of these three children of Matai and his consort.

Time passed, again nobody knows how much time, but the children of Matai and his consort eventually attained maturity. The Supreme Being decided that now was the time to set about completing the long-intended task of creating land on the still waters around. So he summoned Brahma to his side and said, 'Son, it has been a long-standing desire of your mother and myself that we create land and have some solid ground around us. But as you can see, there is nothing but water where we now are. Therefore, Son, I entrust you now with the task of fetching me some soil from Gairang country. With that mud, we can lay the foundation of our world.'

Brahma was only too eager to comply with his father's request, and immediately set off for Gairang. He picked up some mud from that country and brought it back to their own watery world as directed.

There, he set about creating land from the mud. He started by placing some reeds across the water. Over these reeds, he placed a few stones. Over these stones, he cut off pieces of his nails and placed them there. Over his nails, he put down the clump of mud he had brought back with him. And when he did so, the mud started multiplying and land started forming. Thus did our earth come into being.

They all watched with joy as the earth took shape. But sadly, when they wanted to step down from their floating flowers, they found that the earth had not solidified yet. It was muddy and soggy and there was still a lot of water underneath. In fact, the land mass created by Brahma was only just floating on the surface of the water that had hitherto covered their world from end to end.

'This land needs solidifying,' Brahma then realized. 'I cannot allow it to remain wet and afloat forever. This is not the kind of earth we need.'

He pondered over his problem for a while, nobody knows how long a while, and finally summoned a little bird to his side.

'Listen, little bird,' he began. 'Do me a service and dance upon this earth that I have created.'

The little bird complied. It danced and it danced upon the soft, soggy earth. And as it did so, it kneaded and kneaded the soft earth and hammered and hammered it down. When it had finished dancing, the earth had solidified and become hard—the way we know it today.

Then Brahma and his siblings all set about procuring the seeds of various life forms from Gairang country. Every kind of flora from bamboo to paddy to different vegetable and various kinds of trees, bushes, shrubs and plants were obtained. They were all planted on the new earth and that is how the idea of cultivation took root. Later, human beings also acquired the knowledge of cultivation, but that happened a long time down the line. After all, at the time when the plants and trees and vegetables were being put in the earth, there were no human beings in existence. They were yet to be created.

Yet, humans were supposed to be the most beloved creatures of the Supreme Being to roam the earth. This he had determined even before he had started the process of their creation.

To begin, therefore, he summoned his eldest son yet again and said, 'Brahma, my son, I wish now that humans be created, but for that you shall need more of the mud that you got from Gairang country. It is with that mud that you shall give shape to the human being.'

The dutiful son, Brahma, did as he was bid. He travelled to Gairang country yet again and brought back some more mud. Delighted, Matai now asked him to start creating human forms out of it.

The process of creating human beings, however, turned out to be very challenging for Brahma, the creator. For every time he built a human form, the rakhasas or evil spirits would swoop in and devour them. The son of Matai was deeply perturbed at the way the rakhasas were creating hurdles in his path. Unable to think of any way out of his dilemma, he went up to his father.

'Father,' he pleaded, 'show me some way to outwit these evil spirits. They are posing a great threat to the creation of the human race.'

When Matai had heard the story, he pondered over the problem. Finally, he said, 'My son, first create a *chui* (dog). This chui shall act as the guardian of the human form while you construct it. It will chase the rakhasas away.'

Convinced that his father had at last found the solution to his problem, Brahma hurried back to his task. He created the chui as instructed and directed it to stand guard over the human forms while he shaped them. The chui had a loud bark, and every time the rakhasas would swoop down to devour the human forms, it would raise a hue and cry. Afraid, the rakhasas would run away.

Thus it was that with the help of the dog, the creator brought human beings into existence. He breathed life into them and gave them speech. He made them male and female and he bade male and female for cohabit.

Before allowing them to go out into the world on their own, he asked them to come before him. Then he said to them, 'I have made you distinct from each other, but each of you should live with the other. I shall teach you how to cultivate and work in the fields side by side. You shall also be given the knowledge to build your own shelters to protect yourselves from inclement weather. My father has created the sun and moon, and both day and night. Work hard during the daylight hours, and rest at night. Use your leisure hours fruitfully. Procreate and proliferate.'

Thus edified, human beings went out into the world and began to live as instructed by their creator. Jhum farming was their means of producing food and sustaining themselves. They made houses in which they lived together as husbands and wives and families. As the families grew, so did the community. They learnt more trade; their activities increased. There was prosperity all around. Matai and his son, the creator, were happy with the way things had shaped up in their world.

This state of bliss was, however, not to last forever. With an increase in the number of people on earth, and the simultaneous proliferation of their activities, ills and anxieties also started manifesting themselves, nobody knows exactly how. Sicknesses and troubles of the body and of the mind also grew exponentially, nobody knows exactly when. Maladies like fever and diarrhoea started plaguing humankind. Various other diseases also started attacking the human form. In great suffering and unable to tolerate the pricks and pains of these illnesses, human beings finally decided to go to the Supreme Being with a prayer for deliverance.

'O Matai,' they supplicated, 'see what has become of us, your favourite creatures. We suffer, we cringe, but there is no relief. Your son bade us work and then rest, live fruitfully and proliferate. How do we do any of it if we are thus in pain? Our physical forms are buffeted by so many maladies and our mental peace is robbed by growing tensions and worries. Show us a way out, O Supreme Being!'

Matai heard the distress in their voices and was deeply moved. He realized that if he did not give them something to alleviate their pain, they would never be at peace. So he contemplated on their condition for a while, nobody knows how long a while. In the end, he handed them the juice of an unknown root. As he did so, he said, 'You shall have no way of knowing what root this juice is derived from. But whenever you feel physically unwell, or your bodies are in pain, drink this juice, and it shall cure your condition.'

The human race was thus given their first medicine, and having thanked Matai, the supplicants returned to their respective homes. They found that the juice did indeed bring them relief whenever they were suffering from any disease. Thanks to it, they could now return to their day-to-day routines of cultivating in their jhum fields, hunting in the jungles, spending time with their families and working for their communities.

30. Tripuri

Love that lit up the skies

There used to be, in the days of old, a beautiful village, situated on a sloping hill. A noisy and boisterous stream ran past the village, creating a nearly idyllic setting. Life itself was nearly perfect here, at least on the face of it.

But even in the most amazing of all idylls, even in the most perfect of all situations, there is always that little slice of imperfection, that small shadow of hell that dogs the human individual.

Often, this individual hell, these little complications that introduce a sliver of darkness that cuts through some of the most brilliant colours of life, are created by the norms of human society. These norms are often binding obligations one has to one's community and obedience to its edicts. And it is these that often expose the fact that idylls are just an illusion, a mirage.

Love is also an idyllic state of the human heart—or mind, or soul, whatever you may prefer to call it. Societal sanctions are often required to bring love between two human individuals to fruition, to give the idyll a chance to take root and flourish, at least for a while. But when these sanctions, and the authority that the society or community exercises over the individual, turn out to be inimical to love, tragedy strikes. Like thunder and lightning.

The Tripuri people, in fact, believe that thunder and lightning themselves were created as a result of a love lost. They say that the death of two young lovers, who preferred to end their lives than let society end their love, gave birth to the twin phenomena of thunder and lightning. This is the story of these unfortunate young lovers, and it began in this idyllic village situated on a sloping hill, beside a noisy and boisterous stream.

A man named Champarai lived in this beautiful village. He had a small family with a wife named Khulumati and a son, who was called Nugurai. Champarai's son Nugurai was a good-looking young man, the heartthrob of all the young girls of the village. He was indeed unequalled by all the men of the village, not just in looks but also in bravery of spirit and physical strength.

This family of three led a quiet life, with Nugurai helping out his father every day in the fields, and his mother taking care of all the other affairs of the family. They did not want anything, for their needs were few and they were at peace with the world, sustaining themselves with honest and hard work.

Life would perhaps have continued in this untroubled manner had not one day something remarkable happened. It was an incident that changed the courses of their lives altogether. Khulumati was in the stream, bathing that day, and Nugurai was in the jhum fields nearby, tilling the soil as usual. Suddenly he heard his mother cry out from the water, 'Nugurai, my son, come running. Come, come, for I need your help!'

Nugurai was a dutiful son and loved his mother intensely. He never disobeyed her orders and that day also, therefore, he did not waste a minute after hearing his mother's summons. He dropped everything he was doing and rushed to the stream's edge to see what the matter was with his mother.

When he reached there, he was amazed at what he saw. His mother was in the middle of the water, pointing towards something and asking him to hurry. He looked in the direction in which she was pointing and saw that it was a young girl, floating on the water. Khulumati had seen the body thus floating by and known that if anybody could save the young woman from the fast-flowing waters of the stream, it would have to be her son.

'Jump in, son, before she gets washed away further down the stream. Hurry!' she exclaimed.

Without wasting another minute, Nugurai jumped in and made his way towards the young woman. Finally, when he had his hands wrapped around her frame, he started swimming against the strong surge of the stream towards the edge where his mother stood.

'Ah, what a lovely young girl! Why would she be floating in the stream?' Khulumati wondered. And she said to her son, 'Nugurai, let us take her home in a hurry and see if there is any life left in her.'

Though there was barely any sign of life in her, Nugurai did as his mother asked him to. He carried the girl with infinite tenderness and took her to their house. Now the village *oju* (doctor), Chadrai Sardar, happened to be Nugurai's uncle. When they reached home, he was immediately sent for.

The oja examined the girl for a long time. In the end, he proclaimed, 'Nephew, this girl still has some life left in her.' But, he cautioned, 'we shall have to drain out the water that she has swallowed. Then she will need constant care and attention for the next few days. I shall also make her some medicines. Make sure that she is administered the medicine at regular intervals. I have hopes that she will recover quite soon.'

So after the water was flushed out of her body and the medicines given to her, the girl regained consciousness. Over the next few days, under the tender care of Khulumati, she also started recovering her strength. She said her name was Nakhapili, but try as they would, Khulumati and Champarai could not get her to divulge the names or whereabouts of her parents, nor why she had been afloat on the river. After a while, they gave up trying.

The girl was very sweet-tempered and had a lovely demeanour, and since they did not have any girl of their own, Khulumati and Champarai as good as adopted her as their own child. Khulumati, especially, showered all her love on Nakhapili and treated her like a long-lost daughter.

Nakhapili also took to her adoptive family very well and became part of the village community. Her friends, the other village girls, would often tease her about Nugurai and how he had tenderly carried her up from the stream to his house. They would talk about the handsome young man incessantly, pining for one look from him, wishing they could be his bride. All this talk had its effect on Nakhapili and she slowly found herself falling in love with Nugurai.

In the few months that followed her rescue, Nakhapili fell even more hopelessly in love with Nugurai. The young man also, in the meantime, was not immune to her charms and beauty. Gradually, Khulumati started observing that during the day, Nugurai would often run back home from the jhum field under this pretext or that. It did not take too long for her to realize that her son was being drawn home by Nakhapili's charms. A quick look exchanged surreptitiously, a hand brushing against another while the girl served the boy home-brewed beer in a bamboo funnel, all idioms of the unspoken language of love. Yes, the two of them were falling madly in love with each other. And the village girls were all growing immensely jealous of the mysterious girl.

Khulumati and Champarai, on the other hand, were in two minds. They liked Nakhapili, no doubt. But they had no idea about her parentage, or where she had come from. One day, Champarai called his son to his side and said, 'My son, your mother and I have noticed that you are quite smitten by Nakhapili. You have seen how we took her into our house, made her a part of our family and gave her a new life. You know too that we love her as if she were our own daughter. However, without knowing anything about her family background, how can we allow you to marry her? For that is what you want, is it not?'

'Yes, Father,' Nugurai answered. 'I do want to marry her and make her my wife. That way, she can be a permanent member of this family. But tell me, Father, have you not yourself often said what a well-mannered and gentle girl she is? Has Mother not frequently remarked on how dutiful she is, and what good care she takes of the two of you? Does all of this not prove that she must have definitely come from good stock? What more do you need from a daughter-in-law? As for me,' he continued emotionally, 'I love her, Father. And I do not think I can ever love another. She is the one for me. Allow me, therefore, to marry her.'

His son's reasoning seemed sound enough to Champarai. So he discussed the issue with his wife some more and in the end, they decided to allow the two lovers to unite in matrimony. They had in any case, been looking for a suitable bride for Nugurai and who better to fit into that role than Nakhapili whom they had observed and known from such close quarters?

This particular idyllic love, then, seemed to be set to last and find fruition in matrimony. But we have already remarked how idylls are often proved to be illusory and ephemeral. Nugurai's and Nakhapili's love story also, was thus set to have a tragic ending.

Khulumati and Champarai made elaborate arrangements for their son's wedding. The whole village pitched in to make their marriage celebrations an occasion to remember and even the young girls of the village eschewed their jealousy for the joyous event that was to happen. People from the nearby villages and the family's relatives—both near and distant—were invited, and it was to be a great day.

The day of the wedding arrived only too soon, or so it seemed to all who were engaged in the preparations, but at least, everything had been arranged perfectly. The *haya* (wedding platform) was decked out with beautiful flowers and everybody remarked how spectacular it looked. The bride and the groom were seated on it, looking perfect, while the *achai* (priest) conducted the ceremony that was to make them man and wife. But then, tragedy struck.

Among the invitees to the wedding was a cousin of Champarai who reached the wedding venue with his wife and daughter just a few minutes before the wedding ceremony was to conclude. When they reached the haya to take a closer look at the bride and the groom, the cousin's wife suddenly cried out, 'Why if it isn't Nakhapili, my half-sister!'

Suddenly, there was a great commotion and the wedding ceremony had to be stopped for all those who were present wanted to know the entire story about the mysterious girl, whose secret was about to be revealed. Khulumati and Champarai, of course, were the most interested and they questioned the woman, 'What do you mean your half-sister? We found her floating on the stream. How did she reach there?'

Oh, there were many many other questions which were asked and answered. In the end though, what transpired was that Nakhapili's family had been thinking all this while that she had committed suicide by jumping into the raging waters of the hilly stream.

Many of the people present wanted to know the whys and wherefores and the excitement would have continued unabated had not somebody suddenly exclaimed, 'Chaparai, if she is your cousin's wife's half-sister, it means she is related to you, no? You would share the same gotra. And you know you cannot marry your son to somebody from your own gotra. That is practically incest!'

Now this was just what fate needed to drive a wedge between the two lovers. Everybody started talking at once and the entire community demanded that the wedding be cancelled immediately. The achai was consulted and he also said the same thing. Khulumati and Champarai bowed down to the wishes of the village people and made Nugurai and Nakhapili descend from the haya. The sandalwood paste from the foreheads of the bride and the groom was wiped off and the guests were all asked to leave. Everybody left, satisfied that they had done the right thing and upheld the traditions of their forefathers. They also praised Khulumati and Champarai for being able to take the tough decision.

Nobody, however, thought to find out what the two young lovers were going through just then, how their dreams of a future together had just been shattered, how they felt like there was no meaning left to life. And they talked about it after the excitement had all died down. And they decided they had to take their fates into their own hands.

'Let us run away,' they said, and in the middle of the night, they quietly made their way out of their house. They ran for some distance till they were clear of their own village and finally chanced upon a quiet village not very far off. They rested the night there, and when the next morning dawned, they saw that it was a beautiful village, much like the one they had left behind. It stood on the edge of a deep ravine, below which ran a fast-flowing stream.

'We could live here as husband and wife,' they agreed. 'After all, we were as good as married. What good are the norms of society to us if they do not allow us to stay happy?'

So they settled down in this new village, and started living together as man and wife. So despite the fact that there were forces that had tried to pull them asunder, the two young lovers finally started enjoying the bliss of married life. And yet, the strictures of a society governed by tradition and inflexibility were hell-bent on destroying every little happiness they had built for themselves despite all odds. It was not too many months later that Nugurai's parents appeared at their doorstep.

'We heard you were living here, Son,' Chaparai said. 'And we have come to bring you back home.'

Nugurai was overjoyed at first, but then he realized that his father meant only him, and he started to feel a deep anger building up inside him.

In the meantime, his mother had turned towards Nakhapili and started shouting at her, 'I took you into my house and gave you all the love due to one's own daughter. But I did not know that I was only feeding milk to a serpent. The same serpent has now bitten me, and destroyed my family. You are an ungrateful girl and I wish I had left you in the stream to die that first day when I saw you. Oh, I curse the day when I saved you from death's jaws!'

Khulumati's tirade shocked Nakhapili no end! This was the woman who had saved her, whom she had called Mother, whom she had actually felt like a daughter to. Where had she failed? Had she not performed her duties as a daughter? Had she ever been ungrateful to her in any way? What was her fault? That she had fallen in love?

'Mother!' she cried out in great sorrow, 'Mother, you gave me everything a daughter would ever want from her own mother. And I have always been grateful to you for that. But now you say I should have died, that you should not have let me live. If that is your wish, Mother, then as a dutiful daughter, I shall fulfil that wish.'

And with tears streaming down her cheeks, she turned around and ran out the door of their hut. But she turned around one last time and nearly choking on her tears, said, 'Mother, just give me this one blessing that in my next birth at least, I get your son as my husband.'

Then she was gone before anybody could stop her. She ran straight to the ravine by the village, below which the turbulent stream ran. Nugurai, now overwrought with grief and anger, also followed her. But before he could stop her, Nakhapili had jumped into the ravine below. He joined her.

And this would have been the end of our story—in the death of two young lovers, with the end of love in life. But strangely enough, the lovers did not die. Nakhapili, who had jumped first, did not fall into the stream below. Instead, she ascended to the skies above. The skies had been overcast with black looming clouds all day, and the moment Nakhapili ascended to the heavens, there was a flash of lightning that lit up the dark skies.

Then Nugurai jumped and he too was lifted up into the skies above. The moment he reached the skies, the clouds thundered and then, the two lovers were lost to human sight forever after.

AND OUR
CLOTHES GOT
DIRTY AND
WE ALL WENT
HOME

www.ingramcontent.com/pod-product-compliance
Lightning Source LLC
LaVergne TN
LVHW050857200726
843508LV00011B/2043